The Orphaned World

The Chronicles of Datch

By David Hallam

ISBN: 978-1-917238-19-9

DEDICATION

For Emma.

ACKNOWLEDGMENTS

I want to say thank you to all the staff in my local public house for putting up with me sitting in bar and asking for more beer to keep the creative juices flowing. They were very happy to supply me with it.

I would also like to thank Mick the Hat for all his help with proof reading. I did ask Microsoft to improve my spell checker. They did a lot of checking and concluded that it wasn't the spell checker that was the problem, it was the speller. Googles Bard has also checked my story and has told me to take English lessons.

Enjoy the book!!!

Road Trip

The Pack was taking a few months off from gigging. They had been doing gigs for nine Bellatrixian years which was equivalent to twenty Earth years. These had been pretty much none stop except for a few weeks here and there. The bikers had decided to go to Traxsent for a few weeks at the hotel where Datch and Carina had been joined a couple of years before and that was to be followed by a very long beach holiday.

The younger members of The Pack had decided to have an adventure. They had heard about a newly discovered orphaned world that had been pulled into orbit by another star. It was at the right distance to thaw out and appeared to have had an ancient race on it. However, all that was left were a few ruined cities and what appeared to be launching sites for the populations escape from their world before whatever disaster caused the world to leave its parent star.

The scientists studying the world had asked for would be explorers to come and help. However, they could not fund the transport as they only had a small budget and limited resources. The Pack thought it was a great idea. That is the younger members anyway. Fred had said that as it was a dead world there was no chance of them getting into trouble while they were there and the bikers were going to sit this one out in a bar somewhere.

The Raven had been refuelled and its systems checked. The star system with the planet in was a little over two thousand light years away and at interspace seventeen it was going to take over a week to get there. The trip included seven stops to refuel due to the Raven only having a four hundred light year range. The last stop was also for the briefing given by the scientists about the planet and any safety protocols that they needed to know. They all had been doing research and training for the trip. Datch had also acquired a vehicle for use on the planet which would just fit in the cargo bay. Therefore, they only were taking two of the bikes with them.

Datch was sitting in the Raven's cockpit waiting for his new co-pilot. Dapo had been learning to fly and for this trip was going to be acting as co-pilot. He came walking up the cockpit towards the pilot and co-pilot seats.

"Hi Dapo." Said Datch turning around.

"Hi Datch. This seems strange sitting here." He said sitting down in the seat next to Datch.

"What?"

"Me being at the front."

"Oh, don't worry about that you'll soon be wishing you're sitting in your normal seat. Do you want to take her up?"

"Err, no. I think I'll let you do that. I don't want to put a dent in anything."

"Ok." said Datch laughing.

"Yes, my take off and landings need some work. I parked my ship in the concourse of the space port last time I was in the sym."

"Well, on my first attempt I parked it in one of the skyscrapers."

They were both laughing when a head came up the stairs.

"What are you two laughing at?" came a voice from the back of the cockpit.

Datch turned to see Carina and Krissy coming up the steps.

"We were just discussing our first attempts at landing in the simulator and laughing about how bad they were. Has Hagger and Rosey turned up yet?"

"Yes. They are just stowing their gear." Said Carina.

At that point Tish came up the stairs followed by the others and everyone started to sit down.

As there was only seven of them everyone was sitting at the front of the cockpit, Carina and Krissy behind Datch and Tish and Rosey behind Dapo. Hagger had got the short straw and was sitting behind Rosey.

"Everyone got everything?" Asked Datch when everyone had taken their seats.

"Yep." said Tish.

"OK, Let's get this show on the road."

Datch turned to the front.

"What do I need to do?" asked Dapo.

"Just watch and learn." Said Datch.

Datch put his headset on and Dapo followed suit.

"Yuland Control, this is the Raven ready to depart heading for the Tucanea star system."

"Thank You Raven, Traffic is currently heavy. Lock on to Beacon 234323 for orbital interface. Lift off and wait for beacon. Three minutes."

Datch pressed some virtual buttons that Dapo was now able to see.

"Copy that Yuland Control. Lifting off and waiting for beacon."

Datch pulled back on the power controls and the Raven started to move. It reached twenty metres and hung there waiting.

Dapo was looking all around the cockpit. His headset was letting him see all the sensor data, virtual instruments and enhanced visual displays.

"Wow, I didn't see all this in the sym." Said Dapo

"No, you wouldn't. The simulator only gives you the things you need to fly with. The Raven has a lot of extra systems that are all filtered into the heads up displays."

The beacon turned green and Datch pulled back on the engines power control. The Raven shot into the sky falling in behind a freighter. Datch matched the speed and followed it to orbit.

"Raven, this Yuland Control we're handing you over the Bellatrix control. Have a safe trip."

"Thanks, Yuland control."

Datch pressed a virtual button.

"Bellatrix control this is the Raven requesting free space exit to the Tucanea star system."

"Raven, please follow beacon 117239 for orbital vector to free space exit."

"Copy, that Control switching to beacon 117239."

Datch press a few more buttons on the virtual keypad and then changed the Ravens course onto the new heading.

The Raven past one of the orbiting space stations and then headed for clear space.

"Raven, beacon will drop in thirty seconds."

"Thanks Bellatrix control."

Moments later the beacon vanished from the heads-up display.

"Bellatrix control, beacon has terminated."

"Have a safe trip, Raven."

"Thanks control, Raven out."

"Raven set course for the Tucanea star system, interspace seventeen. Standard alarm please."

"Course laid in. Journey time will be twenty-one point seven hours."

"Engage."

The Raven turned in space and then stars winked out before flicking dimly.

They got up and headed to the rec room.

"So, I have sorted out the vehicle and we pick it up at our last stop. It has eight bunks, a living area and an operations centre. It's not that big and the storage area is going to be used for supplies. So only take your essentials as there is not much space." Said Datch.

"What about food?" asked Tish.

"We are having survival packs that give us all the energy and minerals we need for our bodies. We are limited for space, but I have a supply of chocolate."

"So, we don't have a replicator?" asked Rosey.

"No, sorry."

"Oh. Basic rations it is then." Said Krissy who had lived in the jungle and had to eat anything she could get hold of.

"OK, we have twenty-one hours to the first stop so let's put a movie on."

They sat down to watch a movie or two.

The next few days were busy one's with landing on space stations to refuel and stretch their legs. Sometimes it would be early morning and sometimes the middle of the night. Dapo landed the Raven a couple of times and launched once. Even though it was just under two thousand light years away from Bellatrix, the actual distance was in fact two thousand two hundred light years due to where the space stations were.

The first six stops were a case of land, refuel and launch. If they were during the day, they would have a walk about, if not, Datch and Dapo would oversee the refuelling and then they would be under way again.

Totalination

Seven days later the ships alarm went off. Datch got up and got dressed. Carina had stopped in Krissy's room last night as Datch had been getting up at odd times for docking and refuelling so he needed his sleep. It was about 5am and they were scheduled to arrive at the space station at 6am ship time. This was the last stop before the system with the planet in. They were going to get a briefing on the planet by a science team and pick up their vehicle.

Datch met Dapo coming out of rec room with two cups of coffee in his hands.

"Morning Datch."

"Morning."

"Here you go. Thought you may need one. I know I do."

"Thanks, I do."

Datch took one of the cups and had a sip.

"Ah, That's better. OK let's go and get ready."

Datch led the way to the cockpit and sat down.

"Raven, Current status?"

"We are currently eight light years from destination and all systems are operating withing normal parameters."

Datch took another drink of coffee.

"Do you want to take her in?"

"Err, it's a bit early for me and didn't you say this one is a busy station?"

"Yes, it's the main staging post for the new planet and also is on one of the main routes to the galactic centre."

"If you don't mind, I'll let you do it. I don't feel confident enough yet."

"Ok, no probs."

They sat and finished their coffees looking out at the stars.

"Are we calling the others?"

"No. We'll let them sleep. I need to sort the vehicle out first anyway."

"When do we get it?"

"As soon as we're ready for it. I've had a message on my vid com saying it's ready and waiting for us. I think we'll load it when we land and get it over and done with."

"Sounds good. I can't wait to see it."

"Me neither. OK, looks like we're getting close. I'll contact the system."

Datch put on his headset and pressed a couple of virtual buttons.

"Totalination control, this is the starship Raven on route to Artemis station for refuelling and supplies."

"Good morning, Raven. This is Totalination control. Do you have any cargo?"

"No cargo, we are enroute to Omega-Theta. We do have a vehicle waiting for us at the station."

"Are you part of the expeditionary force?"

"Yes sir, we are due to be briefed by the scientists around lunch time."

"Copy that Raven, please inform the station about the vehicle before landing so you can be directed to the correct bay. Please follow beacon 453TLT395ATM for the space station and welcome to Totalination space."

"Locking on to beacon, control."

Datch adjusted the ships course and the beacon turned green in the heads-up display.

"How come you didn't ask for automated approach?" Asked Dapo.

"If we had auto enabled, I would spend a lot of time switching beacons, we had to do it six times for the last one. Also, I like the whole landing on the space station thing. It's more fun than on a planet."

"Don't you worry about hitting things?"

"No, not anymore. When you get use to flying the Raven you find she becomes an extension of your body. You want to go that way and she just does it." said Datch waving his arm to left.

"Wow and I'm still worried about the power controls."

Datch laughed.

"You'll soon get the hang of it."

The star that was in the centre of the cockpit view was now getting bright and starting to move to the right-hand side.

"Interspace drive will disengage in three minutes." Said the computer.

"Looks like show time."

"Raven, this is control. We're handing you over to Artemis station."

"Copy The control. Thanks."

"You're welcome, Raven. Control out."

Datch pressed some more virtual buttons.

"Good morning, Artemis station. This is Raven on approach. Please be advised that we are enroute to Omega-Theta and we are picking up a vehicle from your station."

"Good morning, Raven, do you have a shipping code?"

Datch picked up has vid com and pressed a few buttons.

"Artemis, the shipping code is DTYULBEL172ATV99716."

"Thank you, Raven. On exit from interspace lock on to Beacon ATM1175 for auto navigation."

"Copy that Artemis. Ready to lock on."

"Looks like we have to have auto navigation after all." Said Dapo.

"Yes. ok, get ready!"

The star light suddenly flooded into the cockpit as they dropped out of interspace. In front of them sat a huge space station with four cylinders spinning around a central column, two massive arms spread out from the centre with hundreds of docking ports running up their sides and the bottom cylinder had a large hole at its base. There were hundreds of ships coming and going from it and Datch counted at least twenty star liners docked on one of the arms. There was no planet here, just the station. The systems planets were nearer the star. This was a deep space station.

"Artemis Station, this is the Raven. We're locked on to beacon."

"Copy that Raven, you are thirty fourth in the que."

"Thanks Artemis station."

The Raven came to a stop three quarters of the way down the station.

There were three very large ships hanging in space near the station. They looked about the same size as the Carpaycus. They had the markings of IPSF ships.

"Wow, look at that." Said Datch.

Dapo followed where he was pointing.

"What are they here for?" Dapo asked.

"I suspect they are science ships here to study the planet. This is the main holding area for the star system. It's just the first time I've ever seen grouped together apart from at Arcaneus and Olympus. This must be an important discovery if they have sent three ships to study it."

"Yes, and we're part of it. How cool is that."

"Well, it will be a claim to fame in a thousand years or so."

"You mean we're not famous enough already?"

They both laughed.

Just then the Raven started to move. It headed down towards the bottom of the station taking a wide curved path lining itself up for entry to the internal landing bays. The Raven came into position in front of the stations main entrance. Then it started to move forward towards the station. As they got closer the entrance was massive. It was nearly half the size of the Carpaycus.

The Raven entered the inside of the station. There were hundreds of landing pads laid out all around the inside of the cylinder, some were small while others were very large. The Raven headed for one at the back of the cylinder.

"Raven, you will have landing control in thirty seconds. Pad number is 352." Came a voice from the comms.

"Copy that Artemis. Standing by." Said Datch placing his hands on the controls."

The beacon turned red.

"You have control Raven."

Datch careful dropped the Raven down on to the landing pad for a very gentle touch down. There was a clunk as the pad clamps engaged. Datch shut down the engines.

"Artemis, Raven has landed."

"Thanks Raven. Enjoy your stay. Control out."

The pad started to move down inside the hull. It took a couple of minutes before it came to a stop. The whole pad then turned through one hundred and eighty degrees before moving backwards down another shaft into a brightly lit bay where it came to a stop.

Datch shutdown the rest of the systems and got up. They headed down to the cargo bay and dropped the ramp. The pair of them walked down the ramp into the bay. Two crewmen were waiting for them.

"Good morning, sir. We are here to help with the cargo handling and also carry out any services your ship needs."

"Good morning. Can we please have the ship refuelled and we also have a vehicle to load. We were thinking about loading the vehicle first if that's ok?"

"No problem, sir. We have the vehicle here and if you can just verify owner ship, we'll transfer it to your cargo bay for you."

The man got out a vid com. Datch looked at it and an inventory list dropped down listing the vehicle and the extras that Datch had asked for. Datch accepted the items and then sent his ID to verify the delivery of it.

The man looked at his vid com.

"Thank you, sir. If you would like to fully open your cargo bay doors, we will get it loaded for you."

"Sure, I'll go and do it." said Datch and walked back up the ramp.

Inside the cargo bay near the space suits was a touch screen panel on the wall. Datch looked at it. They had only ever used the smaller door as the bikes could fit through it easily.

He studied the panel and after a few moments found the button he was looking for and pressed it. The rear wall of the cargo bay slid to the side disappearing into the wall. The opening was now the full width of the ramp.

Outside came the sound of turbines starting up. Then one of the stations crew came walking backwards around the corner talking into his headset. Slowly a large black pointed nose appeared which was followed by a large back cab with a row of tinted windows. Above the windows were a row of large flood lights and a scanning array, then the bit by bit the rest of the vehicle slowly appeared. It had six large wheels on each side which all turned independently allowing it to turn on the spot. There were also six jet thrusters that were mounted at the front, centre and the rear along with a transceiver array sitting on the roof.

The vehicle was slowly driven up the ramp. It was a tight squeeze as it slowly edged it way into the cargo bay. It finally came to a stop with only half a metre of space around it. The turbines shutdown and the door at the side opened. The other crewman climbed out of the door and got down.

"Quite a vehicle you have here, sir." he said.

"Thank you." Said Datch.

"If you don't mind me asking. Are you going to the new planet?"

"Yes, we're heading there later today after a briefing in the conference suite."

"Well, you have picked the right vehicle for it, sir. It's a superb piece of machinery. Also, You can find the conference suite in zone 274."

"How do we err, get there?"

"If you go through the security point to the lifts, they will take you to the transit hub. You'll be able to take a low gravity transport from there, that will take you almost all the way to zone 274. When you get off the transport follow the signs for the business area and you're there."

"Thank you again. Please add a ten-credit tip for you and your co-worker."

"Thank you, Sir. We'll get on with your refuelling now sir."

"OK. Thanks."

With that the crewmen left and Dapo came walking up the ramp.

"It's not as big as a thought it was going to be." Said Dapo looking at it."

"It is bigger, but it is in storage mode at the moment."

"Storage mode?"

"Yes, the sections slide inside of each other. It's about three times the length when it's normal size. Come inside and I'll show you."

The two of them climbed up the steps and into the door at the side.

Inside was a large cockpit with eight seats. Two of them had steering consoles and the rest had various science stations and vid screens in front of them. At the back of them was an area that opened out to a small room of sorts that was the width of the vehicle. A very small circular table was in the centre with what looked like cupboards on either side. Then behind that was another small room at the rear that had eight short what looked like selves and another door in the centre with a sign on it saying 'Bathroom'.

"It's err, very compact. How are we all going to fit?"

"These sections here move back as does that bit over there and them bits there opening out into two large rooms and the sleeping area."

"Cool, What powers it all?"

"It's got a fusion reactor under the floor over there and an emergency backup supply for one hundred hours. Also, each of the wheels has its own drive motor so we can keep moving no matter what. If we get stuck, we can also fly for short distances."

"Wow, does it have a Solar Ball suite to?"

"No. sorry."

Just at that moment a head appeared at the hatch.

"Morning." It said.

Datch turned to look.

"Hi Krissy." He said.

"Wow. This is cool." She said coming inside.

"Yes, but there is no Solar Ball." Said Dapo.

"This is a camping trip Dapo, not a trip to the video arcade." She said looking at him.

Dapo looked at Krissy for a moment trying to think if she had mentioned Video arcades before.

"Video Arcade?"

Krissy smiled.

"Yes, it's place to go and play video games like solar ball but on vid screens."

"Oh."

Dapo was sure she sometimes used the Earth names for things just the confuse them. After all, as Earth had not made contact the things she came out with were not in the galactic database and therefore the implant would just say 'unknown'.

"So, where is my bed?"

"The bunks are still folded away over there so you can't see them yet." Said Datch.

"Oh. OK. so, which is my seat?"

"Which system have you been learning to use again?"

"I'm on the Environmental detectors."

Datch pressed a button on one of the vid screens and a cockpit layout appeared. He looked at it closely for a moment.

"Err, that one there, I think." He said pointing to one of the seats on the left.

"Cool." She said and went over to it and sat down.

"Err. the console doesn't work."

"No, it won't. The systems are all in storage mode at the moment. You'll have to till we get to the planet."

"Oh. I've been learning all about the systems and wanted to make sure I'm familiar with them. I want to do my best when we're out exploring on the planet."

"Don't worry, you'll have plenty of time to use it later."

"Ok."

"Right, let's go and have some breakfast before someone comes and presses the wrong button and its rear ends up in the landing bay." Said Datch.

They got up and headed back into the cargo bay closing the door behind them. There wasn't a lot of space to get around the vehicle and they had to squeeze their way past it to the exit into the rest of the ship. On the way Datch shut the main cargo bay doors. This meant that they not only had to squeeze past the side of it but also the rear to get out. The front of the bay had a bit of space because the bikes were there. They made their way past them and headed to the rec room.

One by one, the rest of them came to breakfast. After a few minutes, they would go to the cargo bay, then come back and say things like, "It's big, isn't it?" Finally, after they had all had a good look, Datch would have to point out that he was not turning it on until they reached the planet. When they finished breakfast, they headed off into the station for a bit of sightseeing and shopping on their way to the conference suite in zone 274.

The station was as big as a city, with large transport tubes traversing the central hub that ran the full length of the station. Buildings reached up to the artificial sky, where the hub was located. A warm, golden glow shone down on the buildings below, giving the effect of being outside on a sunny day. The station was a self-contained city, complete with recreation areas and even a swimming pool all rapped into a steel tube.

They found a shopping mall and bought some fresh food for when they reached the new planet and also a few more adventuring supplies namely food packs in case they had an emergency of some kind and got suck for a while. After that, they found a café and had a bite of lunch.

"So, what do you think we will be doing?" said Krissy who was getting very excited.

"I'm not sure. I'm hoping they will let us explore one of the ruined cities." Said Datch.

"That would be so cool." Said Carina.

"I want to find out what they looked like." Said Rosey.

"We know they were humanoid and around our height. That was in the information we were sent when we applied." added Tish.

"Yes, but that's all we know." Said Rosey.

"Well, we'll find out soon what we will be doing." Said Datch.

They finished their food and headed off towards the conference suites.

They arrived at zone 274. The conference suite they needed was easy to find as there were a number of IPSF officers checking ID's on the way in and it was a hive of activity.

They joined a que of waiting to get checked in. Slowly they made their way to the front.

"Hello sir. Are you from the exploration force?" Said the security officer.

"Yes sir, I am Datch Thome and this is my party, Carina, Krissy, Tish, Rosey, Dapo and Hagger."

The officer looked at his vid comm and found the entry.

"Can you confirm that you have an all-terrain vehicle?"

"Yes sir, it is in the cargo bay of our ship."

"Do you also have all of the required supplies?"

"Yes sir."

"Excellent. If you could all step forward one at a time so I can scan your ID's please."

They did and had the ID's scanned.

"Thank you for that. Please note that during the length of the expedition you wlll be under the command of the IPSF xenobiology section."

"Yes, we understand sir." Said Datch.

"Excellent. If you would head down the corridor over there to suite seven for your briefing, it will be starting in about fifty minutes."

"Thank you, sir." Said Datch.

They headed down towards the suite.

"Fifty minutes, that's nearly an hour." Said Krissy.

"No, half an hour, we're on ship time. Twenty hours from now on until we go home." Said Dapo.

"Oh, Ok."

They reached the suite and went in.

The suite was a large semi-circle, with a large holographic display on the stage at the far side, along with a podium at the front. Around the room were a number of tables, each with seats and packages on them. There were already a number of groups sitting at the tables.

At the door was another officer.

"Good morning, sir. Are you here for the briefing?"

"Yes sir."

"Can I have you name sir?"

"Yes, It Datch Thome and this is my party."

"Thank you. One second."

He looked at his Vid comm.

"Ah, yes. You are on table nine, over there. If you could take a look at the package on your table. It contains details about the procedures that you will be using on the surface of Omega Theta." The officer said pointing at a table.

"Thank you, sir." Said Datch

They headed over to the table and sat down. Datch picked up the pack and opened it.

It had a number of maps of the terrain, some of which had large black areas with unknow on them. They spread them out over the table looking at them.

"I don't see a city anywhere." Said Rosey sounding a little disappointed.

"Nor me." Said Krissy.

They scoured the maps looking for any sign of buildings, but they couldn't find any.

"Err, we're not in the cities." Said Datch after looking through all the documents.

"So, where are we going?"

"I don't know. But none of these maps have a city scape on them. Let's look at the other bits."

They fetched out a number of other sheets and started reading them. They were mostly procedures about what to do if they found alien artifacts.

The fifty minutes soon went by and the room filled up with groups of people. Then a group of five people in uniform came in and walked up onto the stage.

The leader of the group walked up to the podium.

"Good afternoon, everyone, I am Dr Geeson. Welcome to the Omega Theta expeditionary force. Before we get started on the details, I would just like to thank you all for volunteering for this trip. Without your help it would take years to explore this new world and revel its secrets."

He paused and pressed a button on the podium. The hologram behind him changed to an image of a rocky barren planet.

"To start with, you can breathe the air on the planet, it is similar to galactic standard so you should not have any serious problems. Please note though that the oxygen level is a little lower than normal and you may get a bit short of breath if you're doing physical work.

OK, now to the mission. You are all here because you have all terrain vehicles. We have tried to map the planet from orbit but there are certain areas that have a new type of ore deposit that absorbs our scans. Therefore, we need you to go into these areas and map them for us. These areas may contain alien artifacts and remains. Please make sure you record every detail of anything you find."

He pressed the button again and a holographic map appeared behind him with large black flat sections.

"These black sections are some of the areas that are absorbing all of our scans. Our base of operations is here." He said pointing to an area near one of hills.

"It has a large landing area for your ships so pick an open area and set down. Please don't all crowd in near the camp's buildings as it will make getting your vehicles out an issue."

He pressed another button and a starship similar to the Carpaycus appeared behind him.

"There are no flight controllers on the surface. You will be guided down by the orbiting IPSF starships. On entering the system, you are to contact the Mellardrew. That is the ship which is responsible for our part of the expedition. It will guide you down to the camps location. On arrival, we will meet up for final instructions before we let you loose on the planet."

He pressed the button again and another view of the barren world appeared on the stage.

"Weapons. We are pretty sure that nothing is alive down there as the planet has been wandering through the depths of deep space for thousands of years but keep a weapon handy just in case. We may have missed something very alien on our scans."

He pressed the button again and A hologram of the IPSF logo appeared in the centre of the stage and started rotating. At the same time the other scientists walked up to the podium.

"These are my colleagues, Dr Thas, Dr Hissy, Dr Donet and Dr Jassen. They will be coming around to each of you in turn to go through the mission brief with you and give you your section of the map."

The scientists spread out across the room.

"Well, this looks like this will be fun. Everything we find will be new." Said Krissy.

"Yes, but it's not a city." Said Rosey who was slightly disappointed.

"It might be. They haven't been able to map the areas we're going into." Said Datch.

"Yes, we don't know what is there. It could have all sorts of ruins waiting to be discovered." Added Dapo.

"Strange how the ships were unable to scan the planet though." Said Datch.

"Yes, the ore must be really weird for the scanners not to be able to get an image." Added Carina.

"Well, we'll find out soon enough." Said Datch.

They started to go through the pack again and after a while Dr Donet came walking over.

"Good Afternoon, I'm Dr Donet. I believe you are The Datch Thome party?"

"Yes, Sir. I am Datch Thome and this is Carina, Krissy, Tish, Rosey, Dapo and Hagger."

They all said hello.

"Ok, your part of the mission is to explore the mountain plateau area two hundred and fifty kilometres to the northwest of base camp. The vehicle specs you gave us means you are more than capable of navigating the area whereas, some of the smaller vehicles may struggle with the terrain."

"If we are mapping the area won't our sensor have problems?" asked Datch.

"Yes. Active scans will be absorbed by the ore so you will need to set your terrain scanners to passive mode. Bio scanners seem to work ok though and vid systems as well. The black ore just seems to stop us scanning it."

"So, we just head to the plateau and look around?"

"Yes, we have a number of beacons that we need you to drop off at set points so we can start to get the terrain mapped correctly. Of course, if you see any structures please investigate them making sure to record every detail. We believe there may be some buildings to the east side of the plateau near some caves. One of the planetary probes picked up a visual of it on a flyby."

"That's cool. We'll look forward to examining them." Said Rosey smiling again.

"If you do find anything of interest, call it in. We will be giving you a comms unit to boost your normal signals as the ore also seems to reduce the range of the comms systems."

"Does that connect to the vehicle comms system?" asked Datch.

"It sits on your roof next to your comms transceiver and plugs into its auxiliary port boosting its output. We will have an engineer on the surface fit it for you."

"Cool, No probs."

"Ok, according to the probe's images the quickest way to get to the start of the mountains is this way."

He started to show them on the map where the best routes were and how they could get access to the plateau. Some of the route was ok, but going up the mountain was going to test the vehicle's abilities.

Datch had been doing some training using a simulator running on the solar ball console. He had got the hang of it easy enough and Dapo had been training along side him.

"Ok, folks just keep looking at the information pack while I go and see the next group. We will be uploading the details to your vehicle on the planet so don't worry too much about remembering all the details."

"Ok, Thank you sir."

With that he moved to the next group leaving the Pack to study the data.

Fifty minutes later Dr Geeson walked back up to the podium.

"Good afternoon again. You have all been briefed on you tasks planet side. When launching your ships tell the stations controller that you are heading to beacon 009. Also, switch your ships communications system to dual band, the primary will be for ship-to-ship communications and is band 7delta7. From there we will be heading the three-point-three light years to the planet at interspace fourteen. The trip should take about two hours and then after planet fall, we'll meet up in the camp operations centre for some last-minute updates. That will be followed by some food before we head to our beds ready for following days exploring. Right, that about wraps everything up. Please head back to your ships and get ready for departure. We leave in two hours!"

Everyone started to get up and head towards to door, the Pack got up and started to follow the rest.

"I'm getting very excited." Said Krissy.

"Me too." Said Rosey.

"Ok, just settle down. It's at least four hours before we get there." Said Datch trying to calm them down a bit but Krissy and Rosey were starting to look like they had eaten way to much sugar.

They made their way back to the Raven via another shop for more supplies. These consisted of cookies, Jeader slices, cake and then more cookies. Rosey said you can never have too many cookies.

Finally, they reached the Raven and went inside.

They spent fifteen minutes putting things in the newly named Blackbird. Krissy had insisted giving the vehicle a name and as the ship was the Raven the vehicle had to be a bird as well. They had managed to just about get everything in it that is apart from bedding, coats and cookies. They didn't what to crush them. There was no room for anyone to sit apart from Datch, but once it opened out into its operational configuration, they would have lots of room.

They headed to the rec room for a coffee before going to the cockpit. Datch and Dapo had to stay in the pilot's positions for this trip as there were going to be a lot of ships travelling in close proximity to each other and they needed to stay alert.

"How long?" asked Dapo getting comfortable.

"Err, about twenty minutes till we leave. As soon as we have done the pre-flight check I'm going to launch. It should give us about ten minutes to wait at the beacon."

"Ok, cool."

"Check the plasma confinement systems and the thruster controls. I'll do the interspace and flight controls."

They put on their headsets and set about pressing virtual buttons.

It took them about five minutes to finish the checks.

"OK, folks. Next stop Omega Theta." Said Datch.

There was a small cheer from the seat behind Datch. He opened the comms channel.

"Artemis station, this is the Raven, ready for launch. Requesting beacon 009 on departure from the station."

"Raven, that is the beacon for Omega Theta. Please confirm."

"Confirm control. We're heading there with research mission."

"Copy that, Raven. Launch will be in three minutes. Prepare for lift operation."

"Ready when you are control."

Then the Raven started to move as the lift systems engaged underneath it.

The beacons target appeared in their heads-up display.

The Raven started to rise up through the station to the launch bays. It emerged into a large long tube with an exit at the end. Around them were a large number of other ships waiting to launch. One by one the ships started to leave their pads.

"Raven, thirty seconds. Beacon will activate on exit from the station."

"Copy that control."

Datch put his hand over the power control for the engines.

"Raven, launch."

Datch increased power and the Raven started to move forwards and up at the same time. He fell in behind another ship heading for the exit. His heads-up display was showing twenty or thirty other ships with proximity alerts.

"Control, Raven is underway and heading for the exit."

"Copy that, Raven. Systems show exit in one minute."

The rectangular exit got bigger and bigger until they started to pass through it. From the launch pad, it had looked small, but now they were going through it. Its depth was about the size of a stadium, and every hundred meters there was a forcefield. Finally, they exited the station into space.

A red arrow appeared in Datch's display.

"Control, Raven has exited the station and has locked onto the beacon."

"Copy that, Raven. Safe travels and enjoy the new world."

"Thanks control, Raven out."

Datch, switched channels to band 7delta7.

"Omega Theta fleet. This is The Raven heading to Beacon."

"Good afternoon, Raven. This is the IPSF starship Tycon. We are your control point for the trip. Switch to beacon 009.37. That will guide you to your position. Be aware there are three hundred ships in the fleet. Stay on your position until told to move. You will drop in behind the transport ship Darkmoon."

"Copy that Tycon. Heading to 009.37."

Datch pressed some virtual buttons and the beacons number changed to 009.37.

He adjusted the Raven's course and headed out into space. In the distance pin points of light could be seen. Datch could also see at least twelve other ships heading to the fleet. Then the fleet started to appear in his heads-up display.

"Wow, look at all the ships." Said Dapo.

"Yeh, that's a lot." Said Datch.

"Where?" asked Krissy who along with Carina and Rosey were now craning over Datch's and Dapo's seats to get a better look.

"They will be visible shortly." Said Datch.

Behind the Raven another ten ships launched from the station. Heading towards the fleet.

In front of them the lights started to get brighter and then a large white starship appeared followed by lots of smaller ones.

Datch was watching the ships in front of him as well as heading for the beacon.

"Dapo, keep an eye on the ships behind. I'm focused on the ones in front."

"OK. will do."

"Why are they not automating it?" asked Tish.

"I think it's because we're in deep space. The automated beacons will be at the space station. All the ones out here will be virtual beacons." Said Carina.

"Wow, Look at that." Said Krissy.

Coming into view ahead of them was a fleet of ships surrounding a large white starship. There were all shapes and sizes. Freighters both large and small, star liners and a myriad of smaller ships.

Datch followed the beacon past a number of smaller ship and then down in between two freighters to where it was showing it was showing green. He brought the Raven to a stop and let out a sigh.

"Tycon control. Raven is at beacon 009.37."

"Thanks, Raven. Departure will be in twelve minutes. Ship to ship comms are on 7delta75. Please feel free to say hi to your neighbours."

Datch pressed some virtual buttons.

"Good afternoon all, This is the Raven." Datch said.

"Hello Raven. Welcome to the party and nice paint job." Came a voice from the cockpit's speakers.

In Datch's heads-up display Datch could see who was transmitting and the voice had come from the freighter next to them on the right called Grey Lady.

"Thank you, Grey Lady."

"Yes, it looks great." came another voice that was identified as The Singularity which was the freighter on the left.

"Where you from Raven?" asked Grey Lady.

"Bellatrix five." Replied Datch.

"Wow, you've come quite a way. How long has is taken you to get here?"

"About a week at interspace seventeen. And only stopping for fuel."

"That is a powerful little ship you have there. What is it?" asked The Singularity

"It's a Starbird."

"They cost a packet. I only ever seen them on the vids."

"We sort of got it as a present from a friend of mine."

"I need friends like that." Replied the Grey Lady.

"I was going to ask if you could keep up but by the sounds of it, you would leave us standing still." Said The Singularity

"The Raven looks after us well. She's a good ship."

At that point the mains comms channel burst into life.

"Tycon to the fleet. Prepare for interspace. All Ship lock on to sync signal on band 7delta71. It is counting down to the interspace jump and also contains the flight coordinates for Omega Theta. Set interspace drive to fourteen. 2 minutes to go."

"Raven, lock on to sync signal on channel 7delta71 and set course using coordinates in the sync data. Destination is Omega Theta. Set the interspace drive to factor fourteen and jump to interspace when sync reaches zero. Keep current distances from the other ships during interspace journey."

"Coordinates for Omega Theta have been laid into the navigational system and drive is set to interspace fourteen. Do you wish count down?"

"For the last ten seconds please."

"Count down will start in one minute."

"Looks like its show time." Came the voice of The Singularity

"Yes, time to rock and roll!" Said Grey Lady.

Datch decided he should stay something.

"It's Party time."

There was the sound of someone laughing from The Singularity.

"Ten, Nine, Eight," said the Raven

"Here we go folks." Said Datch

"Three, two, one."

Outside Ships started disappearing and then the stars winked out and started to flicker. This time all around them other ships were phasing in and out of normal space as their drive systems opened the interspace holes and went through them. The sight was almost hypnotic to watch. When The Pack had gone to Arcaneus all the ships had been inside the same field. Here, every ship was using its own drive systems that were not all in sync. Therefore, ships would disappear and then reappear like ghosts in the night.

"How you doing over there?" came a voice from The Singularity.

"We're good thanks. Just watching the interspace effects."

"They are kind of nice Raven. But just keep an eye on your interspace drive. Being this close to other ships can cause strange things to happen to the field strengths." Said the Grey Lady.

"I'll keep an eye on them." Said Datch.

Datch put up the interspace systems on the vid screen in front of him. Then Krissy leaned over and whispered in Datch's ear.

"Err, someone with me want to ask a question. Is that ok?" asked Datch.

"Sure, Put them on." Said The Singularity

Datch pressed a couple of buttons and nodded to Krissy.

"Hi, I'm Krissy and still a little new to travelling between worlds and I was just wondering where you were from?"

"Oh, a lady. You can stay on the channel for as long as you want. I'm from Jupa in the Antia star system. Where are you from?"

"Oh. I'm from Earth but live on Bellatrix with Datch."

"Earth, not sure I know that planet." Said the Gray

"It's the Sol star system. Sol Three." Said Krissy

There was a pause and then the Grey Lady spoke.

"That's not made contact yet."

"No. But I'm here. Sort of a long story."

"Well, we have an hour to kill and hearing a story from a lady will sure pass the time."

"Ok, it all began in the jungle on Earth aka Sol three."

Krissy started to tell the story and the next hour went by with the occasional bit of laughter. A number of other ships said hello during the story and were listening to it to pass the time.

It finally came to the end. The other ships all said they had enjoyed it and were looking forward to the vid of it if it was ever made.

Omega Theta

Then the control channel burst into life.

"This is the starship Tycon. Five minutes to Omega Theta. On exit from interspace please hold position until you are instructed to move. This may take a few minutes. Thank you for all following instructions and have a great adventure."

"Looks like we're almost here." Said The Singularity.

"Yes, I expect it will very busy there." Said Datch.

"The system is full of ships. This it my tenth trip hauling supplies for the IPSF base there." Said the Grey Lady.

"Wow. What's it like?" asked Krissy.

"I won't spoil it for you. Just wait a few minutes and you'll see for yourself. We drop out of interspace quite close to the planet." Said the Grey Lady.

"Awesome." Said Krissy.

"This is the starship Tycon. On exit from interspace, we command all ships to come to a stop. Interspace drives will disengage in thirty seconds."

Datch put his hands on the controls just in case they needed to move quickly for something.

"Ten, Nine, Eight.."

Krissy was leaning so far over the top of Datch's seat she was nearly in his lap.

"Three, Two, One."

Outside the stars stopped flickering and the stars light flooded in. Out of the window on Dapo's side was the bright shining crescent of the new world. The surface was shades of black and brown with a vast ocean in the centre. The waters were still thawing out with large sections still frozen ice. Strom systems could be seen in some areas of the planet with bolts of lightning flashing in the clouds. One of the launch sites for the exit of the planets race was also visible with a large black scorched area in the centre that was supposably where their exodus ships set off for their journey across the stars.

The IPSF were still trying to work out where the planets race had gone to as none of the current races in the galaxy had any records of a migration from a doomed world.

Above the world, a large moon orbited the planet causing strong weather systems. It had kept the core of the planet warm during the planet's long wanderings through space.

"All Ships. This is the Starship Tycon. Please change bands to 91Beta and contact the starship Mellardrew for further instruction. Thank you for a safe trip and enjoy your stay."

Datch pressed some virtual buttons and then opened a comms channel.

"Starship Mellardrew, this is the Raven requesting landing instructions."

There was a moments pause before the Mellardrew responded.

"Starship Raven, this is the Mellardrew. Please hold position. You are currently number one hundred and twenty fifth in the que."

"Copy that, Mellardrew. Holding position."

Datch relaxed a bit.

"Look at the planet." Said Krissy who was now along with Rosey peering out of the window over Dapo's head.

"It looks really cool. I can't believe we're going to be walking on ground no one has walked on for thousands of years." Said Rosey.

"Look at that storm."

"Wow. It looks very fierce."

"Yes, the weather systems are being driven by the thawing of the planet. The climate section says it should calm down in about a year or two." Said Carina who was the atmospheric and climate analyst for the adventure.

"Cool." Said Krissy.

The Comms burst into life.

"Raven, this is the Mellardrew. Prepare for planet fall. Set navigational vector for 124.34, 72.34 and descent vector 332.3. One minute to planet fall."

"Copy that Mellardrew."

Datch entered the data into the navigational array and then turned to Dapo.

"Dapo, you watch the other ships, ok?"

"No Probs."

"Folks, you had better sit down. This could get bumpy."

Rosey and Krissy sat back down in in their seats ready for planet fall.

"Raven, This is Mellardrew. You have a green light for planet fall."

"Commencing Planet fall now."

Datch piloted the Raven down towards the upper atmosphere following the navigational markers in his heads-up display. The Raven started to hit the atmosphere and the shields started to glow with plasma as the friction heated the atmosphere up to super high temperatures.

The ride became a bit bumpier as they reached the top of the storm front. The Raven jolted as the clouds reacted with the plasma. Then they were in the storm. Datch followed the navigation data sent from the starship above, as there was no visual outside. Just dark clouds. A lightning bolt struck the front shield, lighting up the cockpit. The Raven shook with the strike but continued to plough through the clouds. Another strike hit the Raven.

"Wow this is scary!" said Rosey.

"I've been in worse." Said Datch.

"Worse, when?" asked Dapo who was looking worried.

"Asmove, with my dad."

"And you flew though this?"

"Well. My dad did. Hold on."

The ship shuddered again as another bolt of lightning hit the shields.

"Oh!"

Then almost instantly they were out of the clouds and in clear sky. They were now only about six kilometres from the surface.

"Raven, landing site is in three hundred kilometres. Slow to five hundred KPH and landing is at your discretion on the two kilometre marker."

"Copy that Mellardrew. Slowing."

Datch slowed the Raven down.

In the distance in amongst the barren landscape were a number of large white buildings. They were nestled in a small valley towards one of the hillsides and consisted of six large buildings that looked like housing for the bases crew along with dorms for the volunteers. A large dome structure in the centre had a lot of people going in and out and then another large building that had a number of large transmission towers on it. In front of the buildings was a large flat area about two kilometres square.

"Mellardrew, this is the Raven. We're on final, three kilometres out and slowing to fifty KPH."

"Copy that, Raven. Please state when landed."

The Raven slowed right down. Below them was the landing field. It was a large open area that had a number of ships scattered about it. Datch spotted a clear area that was a good distance from any other ships and brought the Raven in for a soft landing. As it's thrusters fired black and brown dust was blown into the air. There was a small bump as the landing feet touched the ground.

"Mellardrew, the Raven has landed."

"Copy that, Raven. Enjoy your stay. Mellardrew out."

Datch shut down the engines and turned to the others.

"Well, we're here folks. Let's get the vehicle."

Krissy was giving him a hard look.

"Sorry, the Blackbird out and stow our gear in it."

They headed down to the cargo bay and Datch dropped the ramp and opened the main doors.

"Dapo, can you stand at the bottom of the ramp and make sure I come straight down."

"Sure."

Datch put a Comms earpiece in and climbed inside the Blackbird. Inside he went across the cabin and sat down in the main driving seat.

"Ok. let's see." He said under his breath.

He pressed a couple of buttons and the turbines started to whine. He pressed a few more buttons a number of indicators appeared on the vid screen.

"Right, should be good." he said to himself.

He took hold of the control column and slowly increased power by pressing a peddle under his foot. The Blackbird started to move slowly backwards. Datch edged it on to the ramp.

"Keep coming Datch. Your good so far." Came Dapo's voice in his earpiece.

"Ok."

Slowly he backed the Blackbird down the ramp and on to the planet's surface.

"Tell everyone stand back!" Datch said.

Outside the Pack who were all standing on the bottom of ramp stepped to the side a bit more.

"We're good, Datch." Said Dapo into the comms unit."

Datch pressed a number of buttons and then entered the security code which he had been sent with all to owners' information.

Outside, a warning siren sounded and then the Blackbird started to expand. The front wheels started to move forward and the rear wheels moved backwards while the centre set of wheels stayed still. As they moved the chassis expanded and the main support tubes became telescopic and started to expand tripling their length stretching the concertinaed hull of the vehicle into a flat skin. As it did four angled tubes extended from each section forming large steel triangles in the chassis super structure.

Inside Datch was glad he hadn't been drinking as the walls and cabin started expanding around him. He watched as the rear moved away from him and became a number a bunk beds with storage next to them and the bathroom popped into existence in the very rear.

The centre section became a large room and a number of chairs popped out of the floor. The small table in the centre became a large circular table with three vid screens in the centre. Then a small gally appeared in the corner and a number of storage units appeared in the walls. A ladder folded out of one of the walls leading up to a hatch that had magically popped into existence when a bank of vid screens had dropped down and locked into place.

The main cabin where he was sitting stretched outwards tripling in size. The various stations which had been all folded up and squashed next to each other now became spacious workstations. Even the space around his seat expanded and the chair itself grew arms with padding and he could swear the padding under him had got more comfortable.

Outside a large communications array popped out of the roof and a large clear observation dome appeared on the top of the centre section with a number of seats in it with a table in the centre.

Finally, there were a number of loud clanking noises as everything locked into place.

Datch sat looking around at the new interior. The amount of space was incredible considering how small it was before. There was a beep from the console in front of him and it said all systems ready.

He got up and headed for the door. The small ladder that had been outside was now a set of narrow stairs. He walked out the door and stood at the top of the steps looking towards the Raven.

"All done folks. Let's get our stuff!"

"Yeh, we're getting our coats too."

"It is a bit nippy isn't it." said Datch and headed back to the Raven in a hurry.

The next twenty minutes were spent ferrying stuff from the Raven to the Blackbird. Soon, everything was stowed away in various compartments and the bunks all had names placed on them.

Datch fetched the Pack's pistols and rifles from the storeroom and after putting the Raven into sleep mode, he headed over to the Blackbird. When he arrived there, he placed the weapons in a locker in the centre room. The others were just finishing sorting their stuff out.

"Ok folks. Get to your places. Let's do a couple of scans to try the systems out while we head to the bases centre."

The others went over to their places and sat down. This time they were able to power up the stations.

Krissy pressed the power button and the vid screen lit up in front of her. She had been learning all about the environmental station from her implant and had also done an online course to verify it for the IPSF. It had taken five weeks to complete it. The others had done the same.

They were not processing the results as the systems AI's did that as they went. All data was relayed back to the scientists at the base and they did the hard work in terms of detailed analyst of the AI's results.

She pressed a few buttons on the screen and it started showing her data.

"Environmental online and looking good." She said feeling pleased with herself.

"Topographic mapping online." Said Tish

"Power systems green across the board." Said Dapo.

"Organic detection systems are good." said Rosey.

"Mineral survey and language translation systems are online." Said Carina.

"Communications are good. The base has verified the data feed." said Hagger.

"Ok. let's move out."

Datch put on a headset and a view of the outside of the Blackbird appeared in front of him.

He slowly increased power to the drive systems and the Blackbird started to move. Its massive black wheels kicking up dirt as they went. The dusty makeshift roads that crisscrossed the landing field were quite narrow and the Blackbird was hanging over both sides of them kicking up dust as it went.

"How are we looking?" asked Datch.

"Very good." said Carina.

It didn't take long to get to the base HQ. Datch slowed down so he wouldn't run anyone over and then came to a stop at the back of the parking area.

"Base camp this is The Datch Thome Party are we good to park at the back?"

"Good evening. This omega seven, you are ok to park there. There will be a meeting in the main dome in about an hour. Do you have a name for your vehicle or do you wish to have us allot a call sign to you?"

"Could we be called Blackbird please?"

"Sure thing. Blackbird you are. Assigning that ID to your party. Do you need any supplies?"

"Negative, we brought everything with us."

"Copy that, Blackbird. We will be sending a crew out to attach your Comms booster and beacon deployment system shortly."

"Do we need to stay with the vehicle?"

"No Blackbird. The systems are external and should show up on your systems automatically. All you'll need to do is enable them on your systems when you get back."

"Ok, thanks Omega seven."

"No Problem. Omega seven out."

Datch took of his headset and shut down the engines.

"Let's head over to the dome and see what's going on." He said.

They left the Blackbird and stood at the bottom of the steps, looking across the sea of vehicles and equipment to the main dome.

"You know, next time, could we please park closer?" Rosey asked.

"It didn't look that far when we were inside," Datch said.

They turned and looked at the Blackbird. It was towering above them, and had expanded vertically as well as out. Now that they came to look at it, it was nearly two stories high. The wheels were as tall as they were, and you could walk underneath the main sections without having to duck down much at all. They had gotten two months of supplies on board, and there was still room for more.

"It is very big." Said Carina looking at it.

"Just a bit." said Krissy.

"Ok, next time I'll park closer and try not to squash anything in the process." Said Datch.

They looked at the wheels again and then at some of the vehicles in the parking area. Some were quite small by comparison.

"Yes, don't squash anything." Said Rosey looking concerned.

"Ok. Come on. It's going to take us ten minutes to cross the parking area." said Krissy.

They set out in the direction of the main dome. The ground was black and brown with a lot of dust. It had nothing growing in it that they could see, and it looked almost sterile.

The parking area was very busy with large numbers of vehicles sitting in staggered rows. There were small ones, large ones, some with large antennas, some with tracks, while others had wheels. There were even a couple of core drilling rigs to sample the rock structure below ground. To one side, there were a number of aircraft and transports ready to do reconnaissance or to transport people to remote dig sites.

As they approached the dome, the makeshift streets became very busy. The dome itself was at least three stories high and about two hundred meters wide. It had two large airlocks on the front of it, with rows of small windows going around the outside. The airlocks had been set up so that one was for going in and one was for coming out. They walked up to the one marked "in" and waited their turn to go through. The airlock held about thirty people at a time, and the air was filtered and pressurized to keep the dust out of the dome.

"How come they have airlocks?" Krissy asked.

"It's mostly for safety reasons," said one of the people standing next to her. "If there's a biological hazard detected, the dome is a safe haven. I think it also helps to keep the dust out a bit."

"Thank you," she said.

The airlock doors opened and they went in. It was a large glass tube with doors at either end. There was a large metal grid in the celling and the floor.

The airlock door shut, and warm air started to blow down from the grid in the ceiling. The air in the chamber was sucked out through the floor. The process made their ears pop with the pressure difference, and Rosey was not impressed as her hair was blown all over the place. Finally, the air flow stopped, and the inner doors opened.

The inside of the dome had a large central area that was a large circle with doors going off to various places, such as a restaurant, shops, and a bar. There were two sets of stairs leading up to a first-floor balcony that ran around the whole of the dome. It had a number of rooms and corridors running off of it, and another set of stairs ran up from the first-floor balcony to a second-floor balcony.

They stood looking around, and then Tish spotted a sign.

"Look, over there," she said.

They all followed where she was looking. There was a sign that said, "New arrivals – This way," with an arrow pointing up the stairs.

"Come on, let's go," said Datch.

They headed across to it and up the stairs. There was another sign pointing down a corridor. They followed it, and halfway down the corridor was a man standing at a counter with "New Arrivals" written on it.

"Good evening. Can I help you?" he said as they walked up.

"Hello sir, we are the Datch Thome party from Bellatrix." Said Datch.

"Welcome Omega seven."

The man looked down at his list.

"Ah yes. Seven of you. Is that correct?"

"Yes, sir."

"If you would like to head into that room over there and find yourself a seat. One of the officers will be with you shortly. There is a table with hot and cold drinks and also some snacks to eat. Feel free to help yourselves."

"Thank you, Sir."

They headed across the corridor and into the room. It was quite a small room with only about thirty chairs and a desk at the front. They got themselves a coffee and went and sat down. A few moments later, another group of eight people came in and sat down. Then, the door opened and an officer came in and walked to the desk at the front.

"Good evening, everyone. Welcome to Omega Theta. I'm Officer Jamster. I just need to go over a few things with you before we let you loose on the planet.

First, please only follow the instructions in the pack you were given on the space station. Everyone who comes to the planet is given set tasks. If you want to deviate from the instructions given to you, make sure you get clearance from the base first. I can't emphasize that enough. Is everyone clear on that?"

"Yes, sir." Said Datch and the rest all nodded.

"Good. The dome has some of the comforts of home, and also a few shops in case you forgot anything or you run out of things. Have a look around before you set out and familiarize yourselves with it.

There is a weather front coming across us in about an hour. The weather can be quite nasty, so if you need to get to your vehicles, do it as soon as we finish. Otherwise, you'll need to wait a couple of hours until it passes. Please watch out for the weather. Trust me, you don't want to get caught out in it.

Now, please do not leave rubbish about. It could contaminate the planet's surface. We're trying to detect the remnants of this planet's life, not what you had for breakfast. Keep all waste with you.

The air is breathable, but the atmosphere is still changing. So, watch your environmental sensors for any sign of bad air. The base will issue warnings on the alert frequency for any large anomalies. So, make sure your comm units are always active after you leave the base.

That's about it. Any questions?"

"Sir, do we need to carry oxygen with us all the time?" asked one of the members of the other group.

"It's a good idea, but as long as you can get to it quickly if you need it, you should be okay. As I said, the air is breathable, but it's slightly low on oxygen. It just means you might get tired quicker."

"You said there could be nasty weather?" asked Tish.

"Yes, storms can be fast and powerful. They can bring lightning, freezing torrential rain, and in higher areas, ice storms and blizzards. All of which have very strong winds. They come in fast and leave fast, most only last an hour or two. So, stay safe and protected."

"Any more questions?"

There was silence.

"Okay, go have fun exploring the planet and remember, if you have any issues, contact the base for instructions. Enjoy your evening, folks."

They all got up and headed back to the central area.

"Well, I don't want to drive in the dark until I get used to the Blackbird, and I've also been up since five this morning. So, let's have some food in the restaurant while the storm goes by, and then go and get some sleep," said Datch.

"Sounds good," said Carina.

The restaurant was more like a canteen, with plastic chairs and tables. There was an area where you collected a tray, and then you went along a counter in front of the serving area, collecting the food you wanted. It did have a small selection of wines and beers from a small bar at the end of the counter.

There was no need to pay, as this was an IPSF operation and they were supplying the food. The only reason the Pack had brought their own was that they wanted a bit of luxury while exploring.

Datch picked up a Hacks stew with rice and a small beer. They took the food across and found a couple of tables and sat down. They had gotten about halfway through their food when the lights started to flash amber.

"What's going on?" asked Rosey, looking a little worried.

One of the people sitting at the table next to her overheard her.

"It's the storm warning. It will be over us in about fifteen minutes. The lights will flash red when we're in it."

"Oh, we're okay in here though?" asked Tish.

"Yes, but they will close the airlocks except for emergencies while we're in the storm."

"Okay, thank you," said Rosey.

"Looks like we're here for a while," said Datch.

They were just finishing their food when the lights started flashing red. Moments later, they started to hear the howling of the wind outside, followed shortly after by the sound of rain hammering on the shield outside. They got up and headed towards the airlock to try and see the storm, but night had fallen outside and all they could see was the rain hammering down in the floodlights and flashes of lightning in the darkness.

"Wow, that's like the winter storms on Bellatrix," said Carina.

"Yeah, but it looks a lot colder," said Dapo.

"We don't want to get caught out in that," added Datch.

They watched it for a few minutes before heading to the bar. The bar also had plastic seats and tables, although there was music playing, which was drowning out the noise from the storm.

"What time are you thinking of moving out?" asked Dapo.

"I don't know, around 9ish?" said Datch.

"Sounds good. I'm ready for bed."

"Yeh, it's been a long day." Added Tish.

"Me and Datch were up earlier. We had to land the Raven," pointed out Dapo.

"Yes, but you woke me up at five in the morning and I couldn't get back to sleep," said Tish.

"Oh, sorry," said Dapo.

"It's okay. It was the door that woke me when you left our room."

"So, how long to get to the start of the survey area?" asked Carina.

"Hopefully about a day and a half, depending on the weather and the terrain," said Datch.

"Well, there are some makeshift roads for about two hundred kilometres, according to the maps," said Tish.

"Okay, if that's the case, we may get close tomorrow," said Datch.

"I can't wait to start exploring," said Krissy.

"Me neither," said Rosey.

They had another couple of drinks, and the lights stopped flashing red.

Outside, the storm disappeared into the darkness, leaving large puddles of water across the landing area. The dust had formed lakes of mud along the sides of the roads that crisscrossed the site.

The Pack got up and headed to the airlock. The doors were now operating again, and a trail of muddy footprints led across to one of the sets of stairs.

They went outside into the darkness and then quickly zipped up their coats. It was very cold, and they could see their breath as they breathed out.

"Wow, it's cold," said Carina.

"Just a bit," added Krissy.

"Come on, let's hurry back to the Blackbird," said Datch.

They hurried across the parking area to the Blackbird. When they reached it, Datch ran up the stairs and opened the door. Inside, it was nice and warm.

They took off their coats and sat down at the big table. Datch fetched some hot drinks from the galley area to warm everyone up. After the drinks, it was time for bed.

Each of the bunks had its own privacy screen so you could get undressed without being seen. However, The Pack were so used to getting changed with each other that the boys got ready in the main room and the girls all went in the bathroom.

Soon, everyone was in their bunks.

"So, who's going to put the light out?" asked Carina.

There was a long pause.

"Okay, I'll do it. Computer, lights off!" said Carina.

The sleeping cabin went dark apart from the light that was coming from the night lights in the main cabin.

Let's Roll!

The next morning, the Pack woke up all at the same time, thanks to a scream as Hagger fell out of his bunk.

After a bit of muttering, he picked himself up and then realized that everyone was staring at him.

"Err, sorry. I forgot I was in the top bunk."

They continued to stare at him with bleary eyes.

"Err, breakfast anyone?" he said, trying to appease the stares.

"You know, tonight I'm sleeping in your bunk and you can have mine," said Rosey, who had the bunk under his. "That way you have less distance to fall!"

They got up and Hagger made them all breakfast. It was eight in the morning when they finished breakfast, and they made Hagger wash up for waking them.

"Well, I think we might as well get moving. No point sitting here for an hour. Anyone need anything from the base before we leave?"

"I think we're good," said Rosey.

"OK, everyone, get to your stations."

They all got up and headed to their stations. Datch sat down and powered up all the systems. The turbines started to whine.

Datch put his headset on.

"Good morning, Omega Seven. This is the Blackbird. Ready to move out."

"Good morning, Blackbird. Data feeds are good, you're cleared to depart. Enjoy yourselves out there."

Datch increased power to the drive systems and the Blackbird started to move. He turned onto the main road heading to the mountains in the distance. There was a bit of traffic, but most of it was heading to some ruins a few kilometres up the road. Datch slowly picked up speed as he got the feel for the Blackbird.

After thirty minutes, they had cleared the traffic to the ruins and had a clear road.

"Okay, let's see what she can do," he said, and opened the power control.

The Blackbird accelerated down the road, kicking up gravel as it went. The turbines' pitch increased, and soon they were doing sixty kilometres per hour.

"Wow, this is so cool," said Datch.

"Yeah, this is fun," added Dapo.

"I was going to sell it to the IPSF base when we're ready to go home, but I think I'll take it home with us. It'll be so much fun in the desert."

"Hey, we could take it to Soto and chill next to the river."

"Yeah."

"You want to take a four hundred and fifty thousand credit vehicle dune racing?" asked Carina.

"Yes, why not?"

The girls just looked at each other and shrugged.

"Whatever," she said.

The Blackbird went speeding down the road, its large wheels tearing up the gravel as it went. Inside, Datch put some rock tunes on the music system.

Two hours later, the road started to get smaller. Datch slowed down to thirty kilometres per hour.

"Datch, we're going to run out of road in about ten kilometres," said Tish.

"Okay."

He watched the road intently. The surface was rougher here and looked unfinished. There were small holes in the road, but they were no problem as the wheels just rolled over them. But big ones would mean they needed the thrusters to keep the Blackbird level.

"One kilometre," said Tish.

"Okay."

Then, up ahead, there were some warning beacons. Datch slowed down and stopped next to them.

"Okay, no more road, folks. Let's have a break here before moving on," said Datch, getting up and stretching.

"Sounds good, I'll sort us out some Jeader rolls," said Carina.

Datch walked across the cabin to the door.

"I'm going to have a look outside. Are you coming?" he asked.

"Yes. A bit of fresh air would be good," said Krissy, getting up.

They all headed outside and down the steps.

There was nothing but rocks and dirt as far as the eye could see. The ground was mostly brown here, with the occasional boulder or two. Just across from the road was a small ravine with a stream flowing through it. The water was crystal clear and glistening in the midday sun. The sun was bright and warm on Datch's skin but it was not quite Bellatrixian temperatures though. According to Krissy, the temperature was twenty-six degrees Celsius and the oxygen level was good.

After a couple of minutes, Carina came walking down the steps carrying a tray of rolls.

"Here you are, folks," she said.

They stood looking across the landscape to where they were heading.

"How much further until we start sending data back?" asked Tish.

"We are doing now," said Hagger.

"Yes, I know, but I meant new data."

"Oh, about another fifty kilometres. But it's going to take a while." said Datch.

"Well, that terrain is going to give the systems a workout," said Dapo, looking at the rocks and gullies ahead of them.

"Hmm," said Datch, looking at the small gully the stream was following down.

"So, how long do you think?"

"Maybe five or six hours. We're going to have to go slow." said Datch, still looking at the non-existent road he was about to drive along.

They finished eating their rolls and then went back inside.

Datch sat down and got ready.

The turbines started to whine and the drive systems all showed green. He put his heads-up display on and the landscape in front of him showed a set of lines displaying the route the vehicle wanted to take. He set a waypoint marker for the start of the unknown area so the computer could plot a course. The lines could then be seen heading into the distance across the rocky terrain.

"Everyone ready?"

"Yep," came Krissy's voice from behind him.

Datch increased power to the drive systems and the wheels started to move. This time, however, the vehicle was rocking about a bit as it crawled its way across the uneven ground.

Datch could see rocks highlighted and was following the path the computer was selecting. The vehicle came to the stream. Datch followed the plot and the huge wheels rolled through the water, causing the stream to stop flowing for a moment as each blocked the path of the water. The truck carried on making its way across the landscape.

"This is hard work. Any chance of the coffee?" said Datch.

"Yes, I'll get one for you," said Rosey.

She got up and started to head across the room to the galley when the Blackbird lurched to the left.

She ended up sitting down on the table unexpectedly. "Ouch," she said.

"Sorry!" said Datch, who was trying to wrestle with the controls.

"I'll get you one with a straw," she said sarcastically.

She made her way to the galley and held on to a rail that someone in the development phase of the vehicle had kindly thought to put there.

The cupboard with the cups in had some with lids on. Another thoughtful touch by the designers.

"Anyone else want a drink while I'm here?"

There was a consensus that coffee would be good.

She stood there making the drinks and putting them in cups, then on the counter, which she had discovered was magnetic and stopped the cups from falling over.

Finally, she stuck a number of straws in the small holes at the top of the cups. She picked up a tray and started putting the drinks on it.

"Try and keep us level for a minute, can you?" she said just as the Blackbird lurched to the left and dipped down at the front.

It was then that Rosey found out that the cups were magnetic, not the counter.

"Sorry."

"It's okay. Am I safe to bring your coffee over?"

"One sec."

There was another bump as the Blackbird went over another large rock that had decided to sit in its path. The route looked fairly clear for a short distance.

"Okay, now would be good."

She made her way across the cabin, handing out drinks as she went. Datch took his drink and placed it in a thoughtfully positioned cup holder for easy access while driving.

They ploughed on through the terrain, hour after hour, bump after bump.

Then the comms burst into life.

"Blackbird, this is Omega Seven. Come in please?"

Datch pressed the comms button.

"Omega Seven, this is the Blackbird. We copy you loud and clear."

"Blackbird. Our systems are showing you nearing your exploration area. Please confirm?"

Datch looked at the waypoint. It was showing five kilometres.

"Copy that, Omega Seven. Looks like we're about five kilometres out."

"Thanks, Blackbird. Please be advised that comms will start to decay when entering the zone. Make sure your booster is active."

"Will do, Omega Seven. We'll notify you on zone entry."

"Copy that, Blackbird. Omega Seven out."

"Hagger, activate the comms booster please."

"Okay, Datch."

Hagger pressed some buttons and the booster appeared on his vid screen along with the beacon deployment system.

"Comms booster and beacon systems Active."

"Thanks."

They pressed on and came to a stop at the foot of a hill rising high above them to a ridge.

"Why have we stopped?" asked Krissy.

"Just checking the hill out. The sensors are having a little trouble with it," said Datch.

"My scanners are having issues with it too," said Tish.

"My systems are good," said Krissy.

"Mine too," said Carina.

"Okay, this must be the ore they were talking about. The ridge looks black at the top. The start of the mission is on the other side," said Datch.

"What are we going to do?" asked Rosey.

"What we're here for. Hold on!" said Datch.

He increased power to the drive systems and brought the thrusters online.

The Blackbird started to make its way up the hill to the ridge at the top. The thrusters were working hard and the turbines were screaming as they pumped hydraulic fluid to the drive motors. Bit by bit, it edged its way around rocks and boulders until it reached the top.

The top of the ridge was quite narrow, and Datch had to carefully balance the Blackbird as it came over the top. The thrusters were running, lifting the rear end up and the front started to drop down the other side. What greeted them was a vast flat valley stretching out for twenty to thirty kilometres to the foot of the mountain in the distance.

The Blackbird came to a stop on the other side of the ridge, facing down and across the valley.

"Wow! Look at that!" said Datch.

The sun was just starting to drop in the sky, and ribbons of gold, orange, and red stretched across from the mountains like fire in the sky.

"You can say that again. Can we get to the bottom before the sun sets?" asked Krissy.

"I'll try."

The turbines whined and the Blackbird shook as Datch tried to get them down. This side of the ridge was surprisingly smooth, with not many boulders or rocks, and the Blackbird was trying to accelerate down the steep slope. Datch was having to apply a lot of reverse power to stop it running out of control. The Blackbird shook as they descended the slope, and everyone was being shaken in their seats.

"It's a bit bumpy!" said Rosey.

"Yes, just a bit," added Carina.

"Almost there, folks," said Datch, fighting with the controls.

The descent was quite quick, and it wasn't long before the Blackbird reached the bottom. Datch waited until they were on the flat and then came to a stop.

"Phew!" he said, exhaling.

The valley ahead of them was mostly flat and covered with black sand. There were not many features, just mounds of black sand stretching in front of them.

"Hagger, launch one of the beacons, please."

"Okay, Datch."

Hagger pressed a few buttons, and there was a thud from above them as the beacon launched itself.

Outside, a small sphere hovered in the air for a moment before extending three small legs and landing about thirty metres to the right of the Blackbird. A small antenna deployed from the top, and a small light started to flash once every five seconds.

"Omega Seven, this is the Blackbird. We have entered the zone and have released the first beacon," said Datch into his headset.

"Copy that, Blackbird. We are receiving telemetry data."

"We are going to stop for the night now. We'll contact you in the morning."

"Okay, Blackbird. Have a good evening. Omega Seven out."

Datch shut down the drive systems.

"Dapo, are the power systems, okay?"

"Yes, green across the board."

"Well, let's stretch our legs." Datch said, getting up.

Krissy was out of her seat like a rocket and beat everyone to the door.

They headed down the steps just in time to see the sun dropping down behind the mountains, sending beams of red light across the valley. The sight was stunning, and they stood watching as the sun disappeared, plunging the valley into semi-darkness as the mountain became a silhouette against the darkening sky.

"Okay, let's get some food and review the data," said Datch.

"Can't we relax?" asked Hagger.

"Yes, after we review the data. It's part of our job."

"Okay."

They headed back inside the Blackbird and sat down around the table in the centre section of the unit. Dapo went and sorted out the food while the others looked at the data.

"So, what have we found out so far?" asked Datch.

They all looked at him blankly.

"Okay, Krissy. Any environmental data?"

Krissy pressed a few buttons on a keyboard that was part of the table, and the screens showed a number of fairly flat graphs.

"Not a lot," she said. "The environmental data has stayed pretty much the same since we left the base. The oxygen level has dropped a little as we have climbed up into the mountains, but other than that, everything is stable."

"Carina?"

"Everything was showing normal until we came to this side of the ridge. Now the systems sensors seem to be having a bit of trouble analysing anything beyond one metre down. I'll try and boost the sensors' resolution in the morning."

"Tish?"

She pressed a few buttons on her keyboard, and the mapping data appeared on the screen. The maps showed various points marking their path from the base.

"The mapping systems were okay until we got to the ridge. Now the sensors are having a few issues mapping the surface. Using a combination of the visual data from the vid cams and passive scanning data, I've been able to make a map of sorts. It only extends to the edge of the visual range, but we are making maps of the areas as we go."

"Cool. Rosey?"

"I haven't picked up any organic material so far, but the black ore is interfering with the sensors."

"Hagger?"

"Communications are good, but the signal strength has dropped quite a bit since we entered the valley."

"Okay, cool."

At that point, Dapo came walking across with some plates of food.

"Okay, folks. Feeding time."

"Dapo, all good with the power systems?"

"Yes, everything is working within normal parameters."

"Cool."

The food was a Jaxx stew with various vegetables, and Dapo had also gotten some bread to go with it. They all tucked into the food before cracking open a beer and watching a movie.

Outside, darkness descended on the valley. In the distant mountains, a light flashed for a moment before disappearing and a bright glair appeared as something shot out of the mountain, then it was gone.

The next morning, there was a queue for the bathroom. Rosey and Carina were in pink dressing gowns with furry slippers, Tish was in pyjamas with a big white squirrel on the back, and the boys were all in shorts and T-shirts. Everyone was carrying a toothbrush and a towel. Krissy was singing in the bathroom.

They all stood looking at the door.

"Err, I think I'll go and get some food started while we wait," said Datch.

"I'll have some pancakes please," said Carina.

"That sounds good," added Tish.

Datch headed off to the galley to make the food.

The singing stopped and Krissy came walking out and looked at the que.

"Oh, sorry. I didn't mean to be so long." Said Krissy.

"All's good." Said Carina wanting to get in the bathroom.

She ran inside quickly and shut the door.

A few moments later they could hear more singing and Dapo and Hagger let out a big sigh.

After breakfast, they got dressed and headed for their stations ready for their first full day at work.

Datch put on his headset and his heads-up display came online. He powered up the drive systems and got ready to move out.

"Omega seven. This is blackbird about to move out."

"Good morning, Blackbird. Data feeds are looking good. We picked up an anomaly last night forty kilometres north of your position and want you to take a look."

"An anomaly?"

"Yes, it was only for few moments and most likely was a static discharge. But keep your eyes out for anything unusual. We'll send you, its coordinates."

"Copy that Omega seven, we're heading that way."

"Ok Blackbird, Hope you have a good day's hunting. Omega seven out."

"Did you hear that, folks?"

"Yes, let's see if we can get near it today." Said Krissy.

"Hagger, you got the coordinates?"

"Yes, feeding them into the navigation system now."

A red cross appeared in Datch's heads-up display.

"Ok, here we go."

Datch increased power and the Blackbird started to move. The valley's floor was easy to drive on and Datch was able to get up to twenty-five kilometres an hour. The Blackbird thundered across the valley and black dust was thrown into the air making it look like they were trailing smoke behind them.

The ground here was very flat, in fact, too flat.

The console in front of Rosey started to beep.

"Datch, slow down," she said.

Datch dropped the speed down to ten kilometres per hour.

"What's up?"

"I'm getting some readings from just up ahead."

"Okay, tell me when we get close and I'll come to a stop."

They carried on moving forward.

"Okay, one hundred metres, ninety, eighty, seventy..."

Datch slowed the Blackbird to a crawl.

"Thirty, twenty."

Datch brought the Blackbird to a stop.

"Okay, it's about ten metres in front of us," said Rosey.

"I'll grab a hand scanner," said Krissy, jumping out of her seat.

They all got up and followed Krissy and Rosey outside to see what it was.

Krissy walked slowly forward, holding the scanner in front of them.

"It's just here," she said, kneeling down.

In the dirt was a tiny little patch of what looked like moss.

"Is it alive?" asked Carina.

Krissy handed the scanner to Rosey so she could look.

"I'm not sure yet," Rosey said.

After a few moments of pressing buttons on the scanner, she came to a conclusion.

"Yes, I think it's growing."

"Is it alien?"

"Hmm. The scanner can't identify it, so yes, but I need to enter these scans into the Blackbird's systems to be sure, and I think we need to contact the base."

"Okay, everyone back inside. We don't want to disturb it."

They went back inside, and Rosey fed the data from the scanner into the Organic Detection System.

Datch put his headset on.

"Omega Seven, this is the Blackbird. Come in, please?"

There was a short pause, and then the comms burst into life.

"Blackbird, this is Omega Seven."

"Omega Seven, we have found a life form growing on the surface. It appears to be some sort of moss."

"That's great news, Blackbird. Can you send us the data and place a beacon next to it so we can send out a drone to do a detailed analysis of it?"

"Sure thing. Hagger, Rosey. Can you do the honours, please?" said Datch.

"Sending data now," said Rosey.

There was a thud from above their heads as the beacon deployed. This time, however, the beacon was guided down by Hagger so that it landed next to the moss, but far enough away from it so that it wouldn't disturb it.

"This data is taking a while to send." Said Rosey.

"Yes, the comms signal strength is down to 38%," said Hagger.

When the data had been sent, Rosey nodded at Datch.

"Omega Seven, data has been sent. Please be advised that our signal strength is down to 38%."

"Copy that, Blackbird. If you lose signal, make sure you store all data."

"No problem. We have plenty of onboard storage. We'll try to connect again this evening unless we find anything else."

"Okay, Blackbird. Well done. Omega Seven out."

"Okay, folks. Let's move on. I want to try to get near the coordinates of that energy spike as soon as we can."

Everyone nodded and turned to their stations. Datch backed the Blackbird up a bit and then went around the opposite side of the beacon to the moss, making sure that he didn't disturb it in any way.

As soon as he had cleared it, he increased speed again, and it wasn't long before they were racing across the valley again at the ultra-fast speed of thirty kilometres per hour.

Ten minutes later, Rosey shouted again. Datch slowed down again and came to a stop. They all got out and walked to the front of the Blackbird. This time, there was more than one little tiny patch of moss. It was a large area about six metres across.

Datch looked further ahead.

"Err, folks?"

They followed his gaze.

Further on, there were a lot of areas with moss. In fact, pretty much the area from where they were standing to the mountains had moss growing.

"How come they didn't see that?" asked Dapo.

"It's the black ore. The orbital scans couldn't detect it, and it may only have been tiny bits when the probes flew over, so they didn't see it," said Rosey.

"Well, there's a lot of it now. We'd better report it."

They went inside and opened the comms.

"Omega Seven, this is Blackbird."

"Blackbird, this is Omega Seven."

"Further to our last report, we have discovered a lot more of the moss. It looks like it stretches from our current position towards the mountains."

"Say again, Blackbird?"

Datch repeated the message.

"Okay, Blackbird. We will be dispatching a biological team as soon as one is available."

"How do you want us to proceed?"

"Please hold while I ask."

"Okay, standing by."

Datch launched a small drone to fly in front of them, scouting the valley ahead of them.

The ground ahead of them was covered with the moss, almost to the point that it looked like a carpet.

"Omega Seven, I am relaying the vid stream from a drone I've launched."

"Receiving the stream now, Blackbird."

There was silence for a few minutes while the drone flew across the valley and then returned to the Blackbird. It landed on the top, in front of the dome, where another mini-dome closed over it.

"Blackbird, this is Omega Seven. You are cleared to proceed to the mountains, but try to keep a straight line and see if you can disturb as little as possible. We are dispatching a biological survey team to your current position now. Fantastic work, folks."

"Thanks, Omega Seven. We're moving on. Blackbird out."

Datch increased power to the drives, and they headed towards the mountains. He took his time, trying to run over as little as possible, although, looking at the amount of moss around them, a few tyre tracks were not going to make much difference.

"Folks, I'm picking up an increase in temperature outside," said Krissy.

"How much?"

"Nearly eight degrees Celsius."

"How much?" said Datch again.

"Make that nine. Also, the atmosphere is changing."

Datch brought the Blackbird to a stop.

"Should we go outside?" said Carina.

"No! Rosey, anything on the organic scanners?" asked Datch.

"Just moss, I think."

"Is the air okay to breathe still?"

"I'm not sure. The oxygen content is actually better, but there is another substance in it that I can't identify."

"Hmm..." said Datch as he peered out of the front windows.

"I'm going to carry on," he said after a moment's thought.

They carried on across the valley. Outside, the moss was everywhere. The Blackbird was fully self-contained, so they would be safe even if the moss was toxic. They could even park underwater if they wanted to and it wouldn't make any difference to it.

"Datch, the temperature is at 30 degrees and rising. I'm also getting a large temperature spike up ahead," said Krissy.

"Okay."

Datch brought the Blackbird to a stop. They were only about a kilometre from the foot of a large vertical cliff stretching up the side of the nearest mountain.

"I'll send the drone up."

They watched as the drone flew over a very large black area ahead of them. There appeared to be smoke or steam coming off of it.

"What is that?" asked Hagger.

"I'm not sure, but whatever it is, it's hot," said Krissy.

"Yes, but if these readings are right, most of the heat isn't going up. It's just spreading out across the valley."

"What?"

"The drone is over it and it's reading 5 degrees."

"Err, isn't that impossible?"

"It's very weird, I'll say that." said Rosey.

Datch pressed the comm channel.

"Omega Seven, this is Blackbird. We have found an anomaly."

The comms were so crackly that they could just make out a broken voice.

"Black erd, say a n. we'r hav n trouble he in yo."

"Hagger, can you boost the signal?"

"I'm trying. One second."

Hagger pressed some buttons and the console beeped.

"Ok, try that."

Datch tried the comms again.

"Blackbird, we hear you now. But your signal strength is quite low."

"We have come across a large black area that seems to be very hot. Also, the external temperature is up to thirty degrees. But the heat is not going up."

"Say again, it sounded like you said the heat isn't rising?"

"Omega Seven, I say again, the heat seems to be spreading out across the valley floor and not going into the atmosphere."

The drone flew back to the Blackbird, and as it dropped down towards the Blackbird, its temperature sensors detected an increase in temperature. Datch pressed a few buttons, and the drone's data was transmitted to Omega Seven.

"Omega Seven, we are sending you the footage from our drone."

"Datch, the temperature of the rocks ahead of us are nearly three hundred degrees," said Carina.

"Thanks, Carina."

He pressed a few more buttons.

"Omega Seven, please review the data currently being sent."

"Copy that, Blackbird. Please stand by."

Datch muted the comms channel.

"Well, folks, we wanted to find something, and I think we just did."

"Well, it sort of looks volcanic in nature," said Carina.

"What? You mean like from a volcano?" asked Krissy.

"Yes, but if there had been an eruption, we would have felt it."

"Hmm... maybe it happened before we got here?" said Rosey.

"Yeah. Then the moss would have had a chance to grow because of the heat."

"Hmm... maybe?"

"Err... one question. Where is the volcano?" asked Tish.

They all peered out the front windows.

"Err... I don't see it."

"Let's go up the stairs to the dome."

They all headed up the stairs to the large dome on the top of the Blackbird and stood looking out.

"I still can't see it," said Krissy.

Then it dawned on Tish where it was.

"Err, guys, we're in it. It's the valley!"

"Ahh. In which case, I think we'd better move, and quickly."

They all headed back down the steps and to their seats in a hurry.

"I think we need to go up!"

"Why?"

"It's a long way back, and if it decides to go bang, the higher the better. Dapo, you do the rear thrusters, and I'll do the front."

"OK, but where are we going too? The thrusters are only good for a few hundred feet."

"We'll go to the top of that cliff to start with. Then we'll work out how to get higher. If we can get further into the mountains, they should protect us a bit."

Datch started to increase the main thrusters. The Blackbird started to shake and shudder as it slowly lifted off the ground. It was slow going, and the vehicle was shaking all the way.

"See if you can give me more power," said Datch.

"Trying!"

The Blackbird lurched to the right and then to the left.

"Can we not do that please? I think I'm going to throw up," said Hagger, who had gone green.

Finally, Datch landed the Blackbird on the top of the cliff, and the shaking stopped.

"Wow, that was a bumpy ride!" said Rosey.

Hagger ran for the bathroom.

"This isn't meant to fly!" said Dapo.

Just then, the comms burst into life.

"Blackbird, this is Omega Seven. We are advising you to move away from the hot spot. We believe it may be volcanic."

"No shit!" said Rosey.

"Blackbird, please repeat?" said Omega Seven.

"Copy that. We have already done so, Omega Seven."

"We have dispatched a drone to your approximate position to monitor the situation. It should be with you shortly. Please advise us of its location when it arrives, as the local interference is making our sensors pretty much non-operational."

"OK, we're safe at the moment, and as long as the thing doesn't erupt under us, our shields will cope with it."

"Copy that, Blackbird. Stay safe. Omega Seven out."

Datch turned to face the others.

"Krissy, what's the air like outside?"

She looked at her screen.

"It looks fine. It's the same as it was a kilometre or so back."

"So, no heat is rising?"

"No. It's about ten degrees outside."

"Hmm. Carina?"

"My sensors are pretty much nonfunctional, though what information I'm getting looks okay."

"Tish?"

"Same here."

"Rosey?"

"Same."

"Okay, and the air is good?"

"Yes," said Krissy.

"Okay, let's go and have a look outside."

Datch got up and headed over to the door.

"You coming?" he asked.

The others got up and followed him out the door and down the steps.

They were sitting on top of a very large and very flat cliff. It was about the size of a football field and had a surprising geometrical shape about it. The edges dropped vertically down towards the pool of what they were now calling lava.

"Okay? Is the top of this cliff weird or what?" asked Tish.

They walked around to the other side of the Blackbird, which was facing the mountain. The rock face stretched up about the same distance as it was down to the lava. They stood looking at it for a moment.

"Err, what's that?" said Carina, pointing.

In the cliff face, there was a round hole.

"Maybe a cave? Let's have a look."

"I'll grab some flashlights," said Dapo.

He headed inside the Blackbird and came out a few moments later carrying the lights. They were passed around.

"Okay, let's go have a look," said Datch.

They started to walk towards the cave.

"Is it just me or is that cave round?" asked Krissy.

"Err, it looks round," said Rosey.

"Yes, very round," added Tish.

Datch and Dapo were at the front and stopped.

The cave was about four metres wide and was a perfect circle. It didn't look like a cave now they had gotten close to it. It was more like the end of a pipe.

"Err, you wait here," said Datch.

"Wait..." said Dapo.

Datch took no notice and walked up to the cave's entrance. He looked inside. It was jet black and stretched deep into the mountain. The surface of the tube was also so smooth it was almost like polished glass. Datch looked at it and then touched it. It was very cold, almost icy to the touch.

"It's okay. Come and see this!" he said.

They all came over and looked into the hole.

"That's not a natural cave," said Carina.

"No, it looks like it was made. Did the lava come out of it?" asked Rosey.

"No, it's cold, feel it," said Datch.

They all started to feel the tube.

"Let's check it out," said Datch.

"Are you sure?"

"Yes."

"What about the drone?"

"Okay. Let's wait for the drone and check out the area as best we can with the sensors while we wait."

They went back inside and sat down around the large table. Each of them started to pull up information from the sensors, checking the data as it appeared.

"Datch, err... I can't see the cave," said Tish.

"What? It's there," said Datch, looking out the window.

"Yes, I can see that, but according to my sensors, that is a solid cliff face."

She pressed a few buttons, and the image from the sensors appeared on the large screens in the centre of the table.

They looked at it and then back outside. The image on the screen showed a solid rock wall with one or two small, jagged rocks sticking out, but no hole.

"That's really odd," said Carina.

"You're telling me," said Rosey.

"Okay, let me try something," said Dapo.

He got up and went outside. Then he walked over to the hole. The image on the screen showed him standing next to a rock wall. He then put his hand out into the hole and waved it about. The image looked like he had his arm chopped off. Then he carefully stepped just inside the cave and this time waved his hands outside it. This had the effect of just being able to see his hands on the image sticking out of a rock face and waving. He stopped and walked back to the Blackbird.

"That is pretty amazing. The sensors can't see inside the cave," said Tish.

"Mine said his biosignature almost totally disappeared," said Rosey.

"It's as if the detection systems are being blocked by something."

"The black ore?"

"No, that absorbs the signals. In this case, they are being reflected back by something we can't see."

At that point, Dapo came walking back into the room.

"So, what happened?" he asked.

"You disappeared from the sensors, but we could see you out the window. Did you feel anything?"

"Not really, the cave is a little warmer on the inside, but not by much. Other than that, nothing!"

"What, nothing?" asked Tish.

"Not even a tingling?" asked Rosey.

"No, not a thing."

"Okay, so something is stopping our sensors from seeing the hole. That is so weird," said Krissy.

Outside, they heard the sound of thrusters. Datch got up and walked to the window. About 300 meters from the cliff, a drone was hovering in mid-air. Datch picked up his headset.

"Omega Seven, this is Blackbird. We see your drone about 300 meters out. It is about 100 meters away from the pool of black ore that we suspect to be volcanic."

"Okay, Blackbird. We're having comms issues with it. Can you deploy another beacon so we can use it as a relay for the drone?"

"Sure thing."

He nodded at Hagger, who pressed a few buttons and there was a thud from the top of the vehicle. The beacon landed on the edge of the cliff and deployed its antenna.

"Beacon deployed, Omega Seven."

"Thanks, Blackbird. We're getting data now."

"Err, Omega Seven. Can the drone see us on the cliff?"

"One second, Blackbird."

They watched as the drone turned in the sky.

"Yes, we see you, Blackbird."

"Do you see any caves behind us?"

"No, just a solid rock wall. Why?"

"We can see a cave, but our sensors can't."

"That's strange. Can you see if you can get readings inside the cave with hand scanners for us?"

"Sure, will do. We're going to take a look now."

"Okay, Blackbird, but be careful and take oxygen suits with you in case the air is bad."

"Copy that, Omega Seven. We'll call you back shortly."

"Okay, Blackbird. Omega Seven out."

"Looks like we have a mission directive," said Datch, grinning.

"Yes. Let's get the oxygen gear."

Hagger got up and went to one of the cupboards. Inside were a number of masks with a small life support system attached to each of them. He handed them out, along with flashlights and handheld scanners. Datch fetched a floating light out of one of the cupboards and placed it in a backpack along with a pack of location markers for pinpointing valuable finds.

"Okay, let's go and take a look inside," said Datch.

"Do you think someone should stay here?" asked Carina.

Datch looked around at the others. Everyone was looking excited about going in the cave. He didn't want to say no to anyone.

"No, we'll just go in a little way to start with to make sure it's safe. Krissy, Carina, and Rosey, you come with me, and Dapo, Tish, and Hagger come in a couple of minutes later. That way, if anything happens, you can raise the alarm."

"Okay. Are you sure you want to do this?" said Rosey.

"We've been given orders," said Datch.

"Okay."

They followed him outside towards the cave. They all put on their oxygen masks and formed up into the two groups at the cave entrance.

"Dapo, I'm going to try the comms when I'm inside. See if you can hear me."

"Okay."

Datch stepped through the invisible wall. He then pressed his comms badge.

"Dapo, can you hear me?"

There was no response. Datch tried again with the same result. He walked back out.

"Hmm, the comms doesn't seem to work."

"What about inside?"

Both Dapo and Datch stepped inside the cave, and Datch tried again. The comms seemed to work inside. They came back outside.

"Hmm, the comms work inside and they work outside, just not from inside to outside."

"That's just plain weird," said Rosey.

"You can say that again."

Hagger looked thoughtful for a moment.

"If I get the emergency antenna from the Blackbird and put it inside the optical link, it should allow us to communicate through whatever it is."

"Okay, Hagger. Go and get it."

Hagger went back inside and a few moments later came back out with a box and a long optical cable. He plugged one end of the cable into a connector on the underside of the Blackbird before walking over to the cave mouth carrying the box.

"Okay, I'll put this just inside the cave, and we'll see what happens."

Datch went back inside the cave.

After Hagger had placed the box inside the forcefield and stepped back outside.

"Can you hear me now?" Datch said into his comms unit.

"Yes, loud and clear," said Dapo.

"Awesome. Okay. Blackbird, connect me to the comms system please."

"Connected," came a voice in his earpiece.

"Omega Seven, comms check please?"

"Blackbird, comms at forty-three percent."

"Thanks, Omega Seven. Blackbird out."

Datch walked back out to the others.

"The comms are working inside now. Let's go see what we can find."

"Are you sure it's okay?" asked Krissy.

"Yes. Right, you folks follow us in a couple of minutes."

"Okay, Datch."

Datch walked into the cave, followed shortly afterwards by Carina, Krissy, and Rosey, albeit a little apprehensively. The cave was very smooth and was almost perfectly round; the only imperfections were small channels running along the bottom and top of the tunnel.

They stopped ten metres in.

"Can you still hear us?" said Datch.

"Yes, loud and clear."

They started to move further into the tunnel. The walls were jet-black and glistened in the light from their torches as if they were made of glass. As they reached about two hundred metres in, they came across a number of sections cut into the walls, forming large rectangular alcoves. They were about two metres wide and three metres high, and went back into the rock about two metres. They stopped and climbed inside one. The wall at the back had some strange markings on it in bright colours, and Rosey took a close look at them. They were some sort of writing and symbols, judging by the shapes of them. She took some images with her scanner in the hopes that the computers on the Blackbird could decode them.

"What do you think?" asked Datch, looking at Rosey.

"Hmm... I'm not sure what they mean, but my scanner is working properly when I point it at them."

Datch tried his scanner and found that the area around the markings could be scanned and was showing a hollow space in the wall behind them.

"I'm detecting a space behind them, but if I try to scan the tunnel, it absorbs the scans."

"This tunnel is not natural, that's for sure."

"The people who lived here must have made it for some reason."

"Hmm... Let's carry on and see what else we can find."

Datch hit his comms badge.

"Guys, this tunnel has been made by aliens, and we have found some sort of panel with markings."

"Wow, we're on our way," said Tish.

"OK, we're going to move further inside. I'll leave a marker for you."

"OK. Thanks."

Datch fetched one of the markers from his backpack and placed it on the floor in front of the panel. The marker was a tiny little flashing light that could be attached to things or, in this case, placed on the floor. They climbed back into the main tunnel and looked up towards the entrance. They could make out the silhouettes of Tish, Dapo, and Hagger as they started to head into the tunnel.

It was almost pitch black now, and they were moving deep into the mountain. The alcoves were about every hundred metres, and they appeared to have the same markings in them. After about five hundred metres, they reached a junction in the tunnel where it split into two. The tunnel went to the left and to the right, and then after five metres, it curved downwards into a vertical shaft.

Datch fetched out a small marker and dropped it down one of the shafts. It fell for a very long time before disappearing from view.

"Wow, that's a long way down," Datch said, pulling out a floating light from his bag.

He turned the light on, and it illuminated the area around them. The end of the tunnel was basically a V shape, with the centre of the V having an alcove in it. The markings were different here, and there appeared to be some sort of control panel on the side of the alcove.

Datch placed his hand on it, and after a moment, the panel started to glow.

"Wow. It's lit up and seems to be working," he said, pulling his hand away.

There was a small display with symbols on it, and some of them were changing at regular intervals.

"Yes, that bit seems to be updating every second or so," he said.

Datch turned to look up the tunnel and pressed his comms badge.

"Guys, we've found the end of the tunnel, and there's a control panel of some type that seems to be working."

"Working, did you say?" came Dapo's voice.

"Yes, working. I touched it with my hand, and it lit up."

"Oh, wow. The scientists are going to go nuts when we tell them."

"I'll contact them. Blackbird, please connect me to the communication system."

Rosey started recording what the panel was doing. Krissy and Carina were studying the back of the alcove for clues. Then, the ridge running along the centre of the tunnel lit up brightly.

"Omega Seven, this is Blackbird. We think we may have found your power anomaly."

"Blackbird, say again."

"We have found that the cave is a tunnel, and at the far end there is a panel which seems to have power to it. I touched it with my hand and it lit up."

"Blackbird, please get some images of it."

"We are recording it now and will upload all data to you on return to the vehicle. We ran an optical repeater into the mouth of the tunnel, and the comms now work inside, although the data rate is quite slow."

"You're in the tunnel now, Blackbird?"

"Yes, Omega Seven. We are recording everything we find as we go. However, we have reached a dead end now that has two vertical shafts that drop a long way down, so we're going to head back out shortly."

"Copy that, Blackbird. Well done again, and we look forward to the data."

"Ok, Blackbird out."

They carried on recording the panel for a few minutes and scanning the tunnel.

"Guys, let's head back to the Blackbird folks and start to process the data," said Datch.

They headed back towards the daylight. It was starting to lose some of its brightness now, and the darkness was on its way. They reached Hagger, Tish, and Dapo.

"Guys, you ready?"

"I just want to carry on for a few minutes. There seems to be a small gap in the corner of this wall," said Tish, pointing to a section at the back of the alcove.

"I'll stay with her," said Dapo.

"Okay. Don't be too long though. It looks like it's starting to get dark."

"No probs. We should only be another couple of minutes."

Hagger followed the rest of them back to the entrance of the tunnel.

The Loss

Outside the cliff was in semi-darkness as the shadows of the mountains stretched out across the valley below. The sight was breathtaking, with the dark silhouettes of the mountains surrounded by an orange light from the setting sun. The blackness of the ore and the light from the sun caused a stark contrast between darkness and light. Another three hours and it would be dark.

They stood looking at the view in awe of its beauty.

"Come on, the scientists will be wanting their data," said Carina.

They headed inside and sat down at their stations to start processing the data. Datch went and fetched everyone a beer before sitting down at the console in the centre of the room. There wasn't much for him to do as he was the pilot, and his job was driving. He fiddled with his drink a bit before getting up and going to bug Carina.

He was just about to lean over her shoulder when an alarm started to beep on Krissy's console.

"What's up?" he asked.

"I'm picking up a large energy distortion outside," she said.

Datch hit the comms.

"Tish, Dapo, get your asses back here now!"

"OK, we're just..." said Dapo, and the comms cut off.

In the tunnel, Dapo looked down the tunnel. There was now a red light running along the top and bottom channels, and where the V was, a bright glow started to appear in the shafts coming up from the depths of the planet. The glow got brighter and brighter, and then lava came rushing up through the tubes and hurtling down the tunnel. Dapo jumped on top of Tish to protect her from the lava as it reached them. The wall behind her moved.

The lava came rushing past the alcove, incinerating everything in sight. At the end of the tunnel, it carried on in an invisible tunnel, forming a perfect cylinder of molten rock a metre in the air that shot off the end of the cliff. The stream of molten rock then poured down into the pool at the bottom of the cliff.

"Dapo! Tish!" Datch screamed into the comms unit.

There was just a hiss from the unit. He tried again and again.

"Datch, it's no good," shouted Hagger. "The relay's been destroyed. If they're okay, they can't hear you."

Outside the tunnel, the flow of lava emptied and the flow vanished over the cliff. The area outside returned to a state of tranquillity, apart from a flashing light above the tunnel exit. After a few moments, it stopped.

"I need to go look," said Datch.

"Don't be stupid. That tunnel's got to be at over a thousand degrees."

"I need to find them."

The others looked at each other. They all had the same thought in their minds, and that was Tish and Dapo were gone.

Datch got up and ran out the door and down the steps.

"Datch, wait!"

"I'll go after him," said Carina, getting up.

"Okay, I'll call it in," said Hagger with a very sad look on his face.

Carina ran down the steps and across the cliff top. She finally caught up with Datch at the tunnel entrance. He was staring into the tunnel.

"Datch? Wait."

He stepped inside the tunnel. The tunnel was cold like before the lava came out. He carefully touched the inside of the tunnel and to his surprise it was almost icy cold.

"The tunnel's cold." he said quietly.

"What?" Asked Carina.

"The tunnel. It's cold!"

"Cold?" Asked Carina.

"Tish! Dapo!" he shouted.

"I'm going to see if I can find them. You stay there."

"Datch, No!"

"Look, I have to know!"

He stated to walk into the tunnel. Then his walk then turned into a trot and then a run. The tunnel still had the light running along the bottom of it but now it was green not red.

Datch approached the alcove where he thought they were. There was no sign of them, not even charred remains. Maybe this wasn't the one. He ran to the next one and then to the next. Final he reached the end of the tunnel. He looked back towards the entrance and started to walk back.

They were gone, incinerated by the lava. He screamed "No!!!!"

He walked back tears running down his face. His thoughts were ones of sadness and loss. His heart felt like someone had pieced a dagger through it. It took fifteen long and painful minutes to get back to the tunnel mouth where Carina was standing waiting for him.

She looked at Datch as he emerged for the tunnel. His cheeks were stained with tears and the look on his face said it all.

"Did you find them?" she asked already knowing the answer.

"No." Datch said shakily.

She put her arm around him and helped him back to the Blackbird. The others looked at Carina as she came in the cabin. She just shook her head.

Rosey grabbed the bottle of Old Man's Boots and handed everyone a glass of it.

"I think we need these." She said in a quiet voice.

They all took a drink and sat there, looking into their glasses. It was a while before anyone spoke.

"Datch, did you find anything at all?" asked Hagger.

"No, nothing. The tunnel was empty."

"Datch, what do we do?" asked Krissy.

Datch looked up at them. They were all looking at him. He tried to get the thoughts out of his head. These were his team and his friends and they needed him now more than ever. They were all very upset and were looking to him to guide them. He was struggling with his emotions, but they were on an alien world, a long way from help.

He shook his head and took another gulp of Old Man's Boots. How did Rosey and Hagger drink this stuff? He shook his head again and tried to think.

"Okay, Hagger, did you tell the base what's happened?" he asked in a shaky voice.

"I tried to call it in, but I can't get through to the base. The energy field seems to have stopped the comms from working."

"What about the emergency unit?"

"It was in the tunnel, remember."

"Oh, yes. Well, we need help. We need to get the comms working."

"Okay, Datch. I'll try."

Hagger got up and went to his console and started pressing buttons.

"I need some fresh air to clear my head. Let me know when the comms are back up and running."

He filled his glass with Old Man's Boots and headed back outside.

"I'll go make sure he's okay," said Krissy, sensing that Carina was very upset herself.

"Okay, Carina, can you check the relay systems in the back? Panels C3 to C21. I'll help Hagger," said Rosey, pulling herself together.

Krissy got up and headed outside to Datch. He was sitting on a rock, looking into his drink. She went over and sat next to him.

In a dark tunnel in the mountain, something moved, and then something moaned.

"That hurt!" came a voice in the darkness.

"Sorry," came another voice.

"Can you get off me?"

Dapo climbed off of Tish.

"Well, at least we know what the writing says," he said, standing up.

"What?"

"Emergency exit."

Tish stood up and dusted herself off. There were tiny little lights and things glowing dimly in the darkness.

"Are you okay?"

"Yes, I think so. Where are we?"

"We seem to have fallen into a side tunnel. I've got a light in my pocket. One sec."

He fished out the light and turned it on.

They were near the end of a long tunnel heading into the mountain. There were what looked like huge power cables running along the walls, and here and there were small panels displaying information in some alien language. The small lights appeared to be power indicators of some kind.

Dapo walked over to one and touched it. The panel lit up brightly, and then lights started to come on along the tunnel.

"What did you do?" asked Tish.

"Err, I found the light switch, I think."

"Wow, this place is huge. We'd better call the others."

"Yeah, they'll be worried."

Dapo pressed his comms badge.

"Datch, you there?"

He waited, but there was no response.

"Datch, can you hear me?"

Nothing.

"The lava must have taken out the comms repeater. They won't be able to hear us."

He tried the door they had fallen through. It was locked, and there was no handle that he could see. He tried pressing a few things, but couldn't find a way to open it.

"Hmm, we're not getting out that way."

They looked in the direction of the Blackbird and found it was a dead end.

"Let's see if there's another way out, then."

They set off down the tunnel.

Outside, Datch was staring into space.

"I can't believe they're gone," he said.

"No, me neither. I've only known them for a couple of years, but it's horrible. You'd have thought we could find something," said Krissy.

"Yes, there should have been something."

He said, and started staring into the distance. After a couple of minutes, he turned to her.

"You know, there should have been something."

He got up and walked back over to the Blackbird.

Krissy got up and followed him. He ran up the stairs and came back out a moment later with a hand scanner.

"Datch! What are you doing?"

"I need to check," he yelled as he sprinted over to the tunnel.

When he reached the tunnel entrance, he stopped and stared into it.

Krissy caught up with him and followed his stare.

"Err, how did you turn the lights on?" asked Krissy.

"I didn't. I didn't even know it had lights," said Datch.

The tunnel was now brightly lit, with sections of the wall glowing like floodlights.

They stood there, looking into the tunnel.

"Do you think we should go in?" asked Krissy.

"Err, yes. The lights were off when it happened. So, if the lights go out, we run for the entrance. Okay?"

"Yes."

They started to walk inside, and had gotten about halfway towards where Tish and Dapo had been working when Datch's comms badge came on.

"Datch!"

Both he and Krissy almost jumped out of their skins.

"Hagger?"

"Yes, where are you?"

"Err, halfway down the tunnel."

"That's impossible. The comms relay was destroyed."

"Well, we are, and the lights are on."

"What lights?"

"Err, the tunnel, it has lights."

"Oh, well, we have local comms back, but there is still too much interference to talk to the base."

"Okay, me and Krissy are just going to scan the area where Tish and Dapo were."

"Why?"

"I don't know, but I need to be sure."

"Well, if the lights go out, don't hang around."

"We won't."

They carried on down the tunnel to the spot where Tish and Dapo had been.

Datch looked closely at the alcove. It was lit up brightly now, and you could see footprints in the bottom of it. He pressed a few buttons on the scanner and pointed it at the wall. The scanner beeped. He looked at it and pressed some more buttons. It beeped again.

"What is it?" asked Krissy.

"Err, I don't know, their DNA is all over this wall and the alcove."

"Shouldn't that have burned along with them?"

"Yes, this area should be sterile. But it's not."

"What's that mean?"

Datch looked deep in thought.

Inside the mountain, Tish and Dapo reached the end of the tunnel, where there was an open area with a flight of stairs leading down into the darkness.

Dapo walked over to the top of the stairs. There was another panel next to them. He pressed it.

The lights behind them turned off, and the stairwell lit up. They looked down the stairwell.

"How many flights do you think?" he asked.

"Twenty or thirty, maybe?"

"Hmm."

He pressed it again, and the tunnel lit back up.

"Well, it looks like the lights switch from one set to another."

He pressed it one more time, and the stairwell lit up again.

"Looks like we go down." said Dapo.

Datch looked up as the light went out.

"Let's get out of here." he said.

Both him and Krissy started to run up the tunnel. They got about twenty metres before the lights came back on.

They slowed down.

"Err, that's weird." said Krissy.

They had just come to a stop when the lights went off again.

"Screw this, let's get out of here." said Datch.

They pounded their way to the exit and outside, stopping just to the side of the tunnel to get their breath back.

"Err, that was weird." said Krissy.

"Yes." said Datch.

Just then, Carina, Rosey, and Hagger came running down the steps from the Blackbird.

"Are you guys okay?" shouted Carina as she ran across to them.

"Yes, just out of breath." said Datch.

"What do you think you were doing?" asked Rosey.

"I needed to know."

"Know what? They died."

"I had to do a scan!"

"We can't afford to lose you too. You're the only one who can get us out of here." said Rosey in a tone that shook everyone.

"Come on, let's go back inside the Blackbird." said Hagger.

They headed back inside and sat down around the big table.

"So, what did you find?" said Rosey, who was still mad at Datch.

"Err, Tish and Dapo's DNA was all over the back of the alcove but it wasn't damaged. The heat hadn't affected it."

"That's crazy. The scanner must be wrong. The temperature of that lava was over a thousand degrees. It would have melted it."

"Well, it didn't. Also, there were traces of fibre from their clothes on the wall at the back."

"So, the heat didn't get in the alcove?" asked Carina.

"I don't think so."

"So, where are they?" asked Rosey.

"I don't know, but I don't think they were incinerated.

Inside the mountain, Tish and Dapo started to head down the stairs.

The steps were about the same size as the stairs they had at home. Another set of lights came on down below them.

"Err, did you just touch something?" asked Tish.

"No, did you?"

Dapo and Tish both looked over the edge of the stair well and looked down.

Far below them, a set of lights were illuminating four floors of stairs.

"That's a long way down." said Tish.

"Good, because if they're coming for us it's going to take them a long time to get here if they don't have a lift."

The lights went off again.

"Okay, let's check if there's a lift!"

"Err, why?"

"One, if they're coming up, I want to go to another floor, and two, I'm fed up with walking down these stairs."

"Okay, good point."

They started to look around and after another flight of stairs, they found a door leading to another room with what looked like lifts.

Dapo walked up to one and put his hand over the panel next to it. The doors opened and they went in. A panel next to the doors lit up with an arrow pointing up.

"Well, that seems to be working."

"Yes, but how do we tell where the lift goes to?"

"Hmm. I didn't think of that."

Dapo had just assumed that they could just tell it a floor but in this case, they would have to work out a manual way.

He touched the panel on the right, and it lit up with symbols. It had four columns of blue circles with alien writing after each. Each column had about forty rows of buttons. Halfway down the first column was one surrounded by a red box.

"Okay, I think we're here," he said, pointing to the one with the red box.

"Err, there are more floors above us than flights of stairs we've come down. We only came down seven floors."

"Hmm. Let's try going to the top one then. Maybe it will be the way out."

"Yes, and it's the opposite direction to where the lights were."

Dapo pressed the top blue icon.

The doors closed, and a speaker said something in a strange language.

"Do you think that was 'mind the doors'?" Tish asked.

"I hope so."

The lift started to move upwards.

In the Blackbird, the rest of them were all sitting around the table with a drink. It had been an hour since Tish and Dapo had vanished. Hagger was still trying to contact the base, but the electromagnetic interference was still blocking the transmissions.

Datch was looking at the data from the scanner he had used in the tunnel.

"I still can't understand this. The data shows no damage to any of the DNA or fabric samples in the alcove," Datch said.

"Yes, we know. You've said that, but if that's true, where are they?" Carina said.

They were all clinging to the hope that somehow they had survived, but at the same time, part of them was saying that they were dead.

"I don't know," Datch said reluctantly.

"Maybe the IPSF will be able to find them," Rosey said.

"Yes, they have better scanners than us," Hagger said.

The lift came to a stop, and there was a ping before the doors opened.

"Well, looks like we're here," Dapo said.

He stuck his head out of the lift. The lift opened into a corridor. There were a number of rooms leading off of it here and there, but more to the point, Dapo could see light coming in from outside.

"Look, daylight," he said.

"Cool, let's go," Tish said.

They left the lift and started to head along the corridor. Pieces of lighting and ceiling tiles littered the floor. Thousands of years of disuse had caused the internal structure to degrade.

"This is odd, the rooms in the lower levels were spotless, but this floor is a mess," Tish said.

"Maybe whoever they are, they're staying deep down in the planet. It's been travelling through the emptiness of space for thousands of years."

"That's true," Dapo said, stepping over a pile of rubble.

They finally reached the end of the corridor and went through what was left of the door into another room.

Inside was a large viewing gallery, well, what was left of it. It looked across the valley through windows that stretched from the floor up to where the ceiling would have been. The roof was almost totally missing, and if the windows had glass in them, it had long since been lost to space. In the corners of the room, large blocks of ice were slowly melting, forming a small trails of water running across the floor and out of the windows.

They moved closer to the windows and peered out. The mountain dropped down sharply away, and way down below them, they could just make out the back of the Blackbird sitting on the cliff.

"Wow, that's a long way down," Tish said.

"Yeah, just a bit. Well, we're not going to climb down there, that's for sure."

"Does the coms work? We're outside."

"Hmm, don't know."

Dapo pressed his communicator.

"Datch, can you hear us?" he said.

There was no response.

"Try again."

"Datch! Can you hear us?"

In the Blackbird, Hagger screamed.

"Dapo! Is that you?"

The others all jumped off of their chairs.

"Err, yes. I think it's me. Why?"

"Put him on speakers," Datch said.

Hagger pressed a couple of buttons and nodded at Datch.

"Dapo. Are you and Tish okay?" Datch asked.

"Yes, we're both fine. We found out what the symbols on the wall meant," Dapo's voice came over the comms, a bit hissy.

"What?"

"Emergency exit. It opened when the lava came rushing up the tunnel and we fell through."

"You did? Where are you?"

"We're about twenty stories higher up the mountain looking down on you. We can just see the back of the Blackbird."

"Can you get down to us?"

"Err, not a chance unless you have a shuttle inbound."

"One second, I'll come outside and see if I can see you."

They all went running outside and looked up. Dapo peered over the edge again and waved. High above the Blackbird, Datch could just make out an arm waving.

"How the Jaxx did you get up there?" Carina asked.

"Err, we used the lift!"

"The lift?" Datch asked.

"Yes, the lift. It sure beats using the stairs." Tish's voice came over the comms.

"What stairs?"

"The ones inside the complex."

"What complex?"

"Okay. We fell into a service tunnel, I think, that then led to a very large flight of stairs. Then a light came on way below us. We then found a lift, and as the light was below us, we headed up to the top floor and here we are."

"You mean there are aliens inside the planet?" Rosey asked.

"Maybe, we didn't want to wait and find out."

"Okay. I'm not sure we can get to you. I would need you to help pilot the Blackbird up there. Can you take the lift back down and come out of the emergency exit?"

"No. It only seems to open from the outside."

"Oh. We're trying to get through to the base camp, but the interference is stopping the signal."

"Will you be okay up there until we can make contact and get a shuttle here to get you down?"

"Err. We can go back inside out of the cold and the weather, but we might bump into something or someone."

"Okay, do you still have your pistols?"

"Yes, we both have them."

"Cool. We'll go back inside and try to make contact with the base. I'll let you know as soon as we find out anything."

"Okay, we'll have a look in the other rooms up here and see if we can find a spot for the night. Dapo out."

They all headed inside the Blackbird, now very relieved that their friends were alive.

"So, how can we get them down just in case we can't get through to base?" Datch asked when everyone had sat back down.

There were a lot of puzzled looks.

"Can I suggest that we have something to eat now before we have any more issues? I'm quite hungry," Rosey said.

"Okay. We'll have some food and then try to raise the base again. It will be getting dark soon, and with the weird interference, I doubt they will send a shuttle until dawn."

Rosey got up and went to make some food while the rest of them sat thinking about Tish and Dapo.

"How are we going to get Tish and Dapo their food?" Krissy asked.

"Hmm... Hagger, how difficult would it be to send a beacon up there?" Datch asked.

Hagger pulled up some information on the screen and activated the targeting system. He fiddled with the controls a bit and then looked up.

"I can get one up there. It's quite close to the height limit, but it would make it."

"If we could just find something long enough to attach to it, we could send stuff up to them."

They all sat pondering it while Rosey finished making the food.

They had the food and then tried contacting the base again. There was still too much interference to get through, but the static was starting to clear a bit.

"What about the emergency fibre-optic cable? The drum contains a thousand metres of fibre," Hagger suggested.

"Is it strong enough?" Carina asked.

"Yes, I think so. It's designed to be launched up into the air with the emergency relay beacon. We might be able to attach it to one of the beacons."

"Cool, we have a plan. Hagger, come with me, and we'll attach the fibre to the beacon. Carina, see if you can get through to Dapo or Tish, and Rosey, you run outside and throw the broken end of the fibre up to us."

"Err, what can I do?" Krissy asked.

"Err..." Datch thought for a moment. "The washing up. It's your turn."

"Oh."

She started collecting the dishes up.

Hagger and Datch disappeared up the steps leading to the dome on the top. It had a hatch that led outside to the beacon launch system. Rosey ran outside and found the end of the fibre.

They set about making their creation.

Further up the mountain, Tish and Dapo were working their way through the rooms. Some of the lights still worked, and as it was now almost dark, they were glad to have them.

Most of the rooms were empty apart from a desk or two. They had found one near the gallery room that was still intact. It also had some seats to sit on.

Nothing had come out of the lift and it had been over an hour now since they had seen the light below them. Dapo put a seat with a load of plastic on it leaning against the lift door so if it opened there would be a loud noise as everything fell into the floor.

"Tish, are you there?" came Carina's voice through the comms unit.

"Yes, Carina. What's up?"

"We still haven't got through to the base, so we're sending a beacon up to you and a cable attached to it. We can then send things up to you like dinner."

"Dinner would be good. How long?"

"Datch, Hagger, and Rosey are working on it now, so hopefully not long."

"Okay, give us a shout before you launch it."

"Will do. Have you seen any signs of life?"

"No, nothing since the light came on below us. It may have been an automated system of some kind."

"Let's hope so. Did you do any scans inside the mountain?"

"Yes, if everything works and you can get stuff up to us, you can send another scanner up. I'll send this one down."

"Okay, no probs. I'll go and see how they are getting on."

Carina got up and went off to find Datch.

He was on the roof with Hagger. Rosey had passed the fibre up to them, and they were busy attaching it to the beacon.

"How's it going?" Carina asked, walking out of the dome.

"Okay, I think," said Datch.

"Yeah, we just have to hope the fibre doesn't break when we launch the beacon," added Hagger.

"Will it?" asked Carina.

"Well, it is designed to be launched with the emergency beacon, so it should work, but this beacon launches at a higher speed."

Hagger clipped the beacon back into the launcher with the fibre trailing out of the top launch tube.

"I think we're good," said Hagger.

"Okay, let's give it a go," said Datch.

They headed back inside the dome.

Krissy was sitting at the big table waiting when they climbed down the ladder.

"Can I do anything to help?"

"Not at the moment. I think we're good to give it a try," said Datch who followed Hagger over to his seat.

Datch pressed his comms badge.

"Dapo, you there?"

There was a short pause.

"Yes, Datch. What's up?" came Dapo's voice.

"We're ready to try the beacon."

"Oh, cool. We've cleared an area in front of what's left of the windows. I'm hoping the beacon will see it as a good place to land."

"Sounds like a plan."

"OK, we're ready when you are."

"Hagger."

Hagger pressed a few buttons and took aim using a small joystick. It was a bit tricky to target the spot twenty stories up and on top of what was effectively a cliff top. He finally found a spot he was happy with and pressed the launch button.

There was a thud from the top of the Blackbird as the beacon left on its journey up the cliff face. They could hear the cable drum whirring around above their heads as the fibre was pulled out. Hagger gently guided the beacon as it went.

Dapo and Tish watched it from the door, ready to run into another room if things went wrong.

Outside, the beacon got higher and higher, dragging the cable behind it into what was now darkness. Soon, it reached the ledge with the broken gallery on the top. Hagger made a few more adjustments and managed to get the beacon to deploy in what was left of the gallery.

It touched down and anchored itself firing steel bolts into the floor.

"Dapo, is the beacon secure?" asked Datch.

Tish and Dapo went over to it and looked at it. The beacon was flashing a small red light on the top of it. It sat on four metal legs that it had embedded in the floor. Dapo tried to move one of them and found it was solid.

"Yes, looks good," he said. "Can we have dinner now?"

Datch laughed.

"Yes, you can have dinner now. We'll send it right up."

"I'll get it," said Krissy, eager to help.

She sorted out some food and drinks and placed them in a bag. They went back up to the roof and tied it to the fibre as it came out of the cable drum.

"Okay, Dapo. Ready when you are."

Up on the platform, Dapo attached a rock to the end of the cable after passing it around the back of the beacon's legs. He then slowly let the rock go and the cable started to move. He had wrapped his coat sleeve around the cable so he could control the descent.

"We're dropping this end down with a rock on it, so look out for it," said Tish.

"Okay."

Datch went back into the Blackbird and turned the external lights on. Outside, bright lights lit up the cliff face and the area around them like daylight. Above them, Dapo and Tish had to look away for a moment while their eyes got used to the glare. They carried on feeding the cable down and the food slowly headed upwards.

Deep inside the planet, a light started flashing and a panel made a beeping noise. Something moved in the semi-darkness and silenced the alarm. A screen lit up, showing a view down a tunnel. At the far end, light was flooding in from the entrance. This was the second strange thing to happen on this cycle. The first was when one of the exit doors had momentarily opened when the magma had been vented. The being looked at the display thoughtfully and decided to investigate.

Camp Out

It took about ten minutes to move the food to the top, but Datch had found out there was enough fibre on the drum to go up and down. After Dapo and Tish had eaten, Datch and Hagger started to send camping gear up a bit at a time. It was slow work as they didn't want to overload the cable. They also sent all the climbing rope they had up in the hope that it would reach the ground when tied together.

Inside the mountain, three beings came out of the lift at the top of the stairs where Dapo and Tish had been earlier. They made their way across the landing to a panel on the opposite side of the stairwell and the leader put his hand on the panel. A hatch opened and the three of them stepped inside.

The inside of the room was full of equipment with various lights flashing on it. They moved across to the other side of the room and the leader touched some more buttons on another panel. He looked at it and said something in an alien tongue before he pressed another panel next to him. A hatch opened looking down the vent tunnel towards the bright light flooding in. They stood looking for a while before one of them started to move up the tunnel towards the exit. The other two stood watching him go. It was a slow and deliberate pace so he was ready to run back if the aliens started to come inside the vent.

Outside, Datch and Krissy were placing camping supplies on the fibre ready to go up to Dapo and Tish. They had already delivered food and a new scanner to them along with some inflatable bedding. It was now the turn of the sleeping bags.

The creature in the tunnel got close to the end of the vent and looked back down towards the other two. One of them put his arm up. The creature cautiously moved to the mouth of the vent. Outside, he could see two of the alien creatures placing things on the end of a cable of some sort. There was also a vehicle of some sort parked on the cliff top with very bright lights on it. He stood watching them for a few moments.

Krissy had just attached the last sleeping bag when a shiver ran down her spine. It felt like something was watching her. She looked around but couldn't see anything.

The creature spotted her looking and headed back in the tunnel.

The sudden movement caught Krissy's eye. It was only a shadow but it moved.

"Datch!" she shouted.

"What's up?" he said, noticing the look on her face.

"I think there is something in the tunnel."

Datch looked across at the tunnel. He couldn't see anything.

"Let me get my pistol and I'll have a look."

He hit his comms badge.

"Carina. Grab your pistol and mine and bring them outside please."

The creature was careful, peering around the edge of the vent tube and decided to make a hasty retreat as both of the creatures were looking at the vent's exit. 'Had they noticed him?' he wasn't sure but wasn't going to wait to find out. He hurried down the vent tube to the first emergency exit point while waving at the others to go back through the hatch. He reached the emergency exit point and hit the release system.

Carina came running down the ladder with the pistols.

"Datch, what's up?" she said, reaching them.

"Krissy thinks she's seen something at the tunnel mouth."

"Yes, it was like a shadow or something."

"Could you make out what it was?" asked Carina.

"No, it was only there for a brief moment. I only turned to look as I felt something was watching me. Then I spotted something move backwards into the tunnel."

Datch took his pistol from Carina.

"Come on, let's have a look."

"Are you sure?"

"Well, I can't get us out of here until we figure out how to get Dapo and Tish down and I don't fancy sleeping here not knowing."

"Hmm. I see your point. How do you want to do it?"

"If you keep a little bit back from me. That way if something goes to grab me, you can shoot it."

"Oh thanks." Said Carina sarcastically.

Datch lifted his pistol and started to make his way slowly towards the tunnel mouth. Carina stayed about a metre behind him, holding her pistol in front of her.

Datch looked over his shoulder to see where Carina was, and then crept up closer to the entrance. He cautiously looked into the opening. The tunnel looked empty.

"Krissy, pass me the flashlight please," Datch asked.

She brought the flashlight nervously over to Datch and Carina.

Datch took it and shone it down the tunnel. It was empty. The light in the channel was now a green strip light that ran all the way to the junction at the far end. There was no sign of anything between the entrance and the junction. Datch shone the light's beam up and down.

"Well, if there was something there, it's gone now," he said.

"I'm sure there was something there," said Krissy.

"Okay, let's go back inside and check the sensors and see if they picked up anything."

Datch gave the tunnel one last look before heading back towards the Blackbird.

He hit his comms.

"Dapo, you two okay?"

"Yes, we're just pulling up the sleeping bags. Why?"

"Krissy thinks she spotted something in the tunnel. There's nothing there now, but keep your pistols handy."

"I will. We'll hear them if they come out of the lift. We piled a load of stuff in front of it just in case."

"Sounds good. I'll talk to you soon. We're just going to review the data from the sensors in case they have detected anything."

"Okay, Datch."

The comms closed.

Datch followed Krissy and Carina inside the Blackbird. Haggar and Rosey were sitting around the big table when they came in, looking at sensor data.

"Did the sensors pick anything up?" asked Datch, walking through the door.

"Err, the entrance to the tunnel has disappeared again. It vanished about twenty minutes ago, according to the data."

"What, before Krissy spotted the shadow?"

"As far as I can tell. It was about ten to fifteen minutes before it."

"Oh. Why didn't we notice?"

"Err, we were watching you and Krissy put things on the cable."

"Oh."

"On the bright side, I can see both Tish and Dapo on the sensors now. Also, I've started getting signals from the base again. They're quite weak, but we may be able to talk to them."

"Okay. Let's give it a try. Patch me into the comms system."

Hagger pressed a couple of buttons.

"Okay, you're in."

"Omega Seven, this is Blackbird. Come in please."

There was static with a very quiet voice embedded in it.

"I'll see if I can filter the signal a bit more."

Hagger pressed some more buttons and then nodded at Datch.

"Omega Seven, this is Blackbird. Come in please."

The static cleared a bit.

"Blackbird, this is Omega Seven. We can hear you, but your signal is very low."

Datch breathed a sigh of relief.

"Omega Seven, this is Blackbird. We have found a complex of some kind inside the mountain that still seems to be operational. However, two of our people are now stuck about twenty stories above us and we need a shuttle to get them down."

"Blackbird, did you say a complex in the mountain?"

"Yes, and it's operational. We also need a shuttle."

"Copy that, however it's going to be about twenty-four hours before we can get to you as we're under a storm front that has grounded everything unless it's a life or death situation. Is that the case?"

"No, they're okay and are inside part of the alien complex at the top of a cliff. They just can't get back down to us."

"Blackbird, please be aware that the storm front is also heading your way. We suggest you stay inside as it's a very nasty one. The comms are also going to be heavily affected, so you may not be able to contact us. If you do have an emergency, then contact the Mellardrew on channel zero for emergency evac."

"Copy that, Omega Seven. We should be alright."

"Do not send us data at the moment as the comms feed is not stable and we may get data loss. Stay safe."

"Copy that, Omega Seven. Blackbird out."

He turned to the others.

"Well, looks like we're on our own for a bit."

"I hope so," said Krissy. "Why didn't you mention the shadow and the lights?"

"The shadow was just that, and the lights may have been automatic. At this point, all we know is that the complex is active and venting lava every now and again."

"But I did see something."

"I'm not saying you didn't, it's just I think we need to be sure before we bring half the IPSF fleet down here to say hi to them."

Krissy thought about this.

"Well, I hope they don't eat us." She added.

"Eat us?" said Carina, slightly worried.

"Yes, haven't you seen the movies?"

"Err, not those ones." Said Datch.

She looked at them for a moment. They were all staring blankly at her.

"Never mind, it's an Earth thing." she said.

Datch pressed his comms badge.

"Dapo, you there?"

"Yes, Datch. What's up?"

"You need to make sure you're under cover. There's a storm coming in."

"Okay, I hope the roof doesn't leak."

"Is it likely to?"

"Judging by this place, it might."

"Oh, we've been in touch with base and they can't send a shuttle until after the storm has gone by. We can call for emergency evac from the Mellardrew if we need it."

"Ok, we'll try not to need it."

"I think we need to keep watch tonight. Just in case."

"OK, I'll get Tish to go sleep now."

"I'll leave the comms open so you can hear us and we can hear you."

"OK."

Datch turned to the others.

"OK, I'll stay up and keep watch first, Haggar if you go and get your head down and take the second."

"No probs, what time do you want me to take over?"

"Say, four-ish. That should give you about six hours."

"Sounds good. See you at four."

He got up and headed for his bunk with Rosey in tow.

"Ok folks, let's see what's on the scanner." Said Datch.

Carina connected it to the Blackbird's computer and downloaded the data. It took a few moments for the data to download and by the time it had finished Rosey was back.

They replayed the images from inside the mountain. They showed large power cables carrying huge amounts of power to and from the bowels of the planet. The alien signs, the lights coming on and off. The place looked very alive.

"Wow. This place looks almost lived in." Said Rosey.

"Yes, very." Added Carina.

Datch sat back in his chair with a ponderous look on his face.

"Hmm." he said after they had watched the whole thing twice.

"Hmm what?" Asked Carina.

"Hmm, I don't think this is a dead world."

"What? It has been flying through deep space for years, frozen solid." Said Rosey.

"Yes, along with its moon. The moon is the key. It stayed with the planet and kept the planet's core hot all this time."

"Yes, but the planet's inhabitants left." Added Carina.

"Did they?"

"What do you mean?" asked Rosey.

"We have seen the launch pads for the fleet of ships that left the planet. They were meant to allow the population to leave the planet."

"And?"

"What if they weren't launch pads but thrusters to launch the planet and its moon into space?"

"Why would they even do that?" said Carina.

"Ok. What if the star was dying and they did not have interspace drive systems. There was no way they could escape their star. So, I think they moved the planet."

"That's nuts." Said Rosey.

"Ok, the planet has been travelling for thousands of years and just happens to enter the correct orbit of this star to make the planet's climate perfect for life."

"So, you are saying the planet was piloted here?"

"Yes, and I think the planet's population is still here."

"Ok. if that's true, why haven't they contacted us yet?"

"I don't know. But I'm starting to think they are here watching us."

"So, they moved the planet?"

"Yes, why not?"

They all sat looking at the data on the screens. The complex inside the mountain was not dead that was for sure and the shadow, the lights bellow Tish and Dapo, it all added up.

"Ok, so what if they are inside. What do we do?"

"You have all read the first contact information. That's what we do."

"OK."

They all nodded.

Aliens

Deep in the planet, the three creatures left one of the lifts and headed into a large room with a number of other aliens. One of them walked over to them.

He looked at them and then spoke.

"So, I understand there are aliens on the surface?" he asked.

"Yes, sir, there appears to be a number of aliens on the surface in some sort of vehicle."

"How many are they?"

"The number is unknown as all of the surface sensors have been destroyed during the journey."

"Are they hostile?"

"Not that we can tell at this point. Although, we have not had any direct contact with them."

"Have any of them entered the lower levels yet?"

"No, sir. We detected an entry in the exhaust vent and started tracking the aliens, but they headed up to the old observation gallery. None of the sensors are working up there either, but power is being drawn by the lighting system in parts of it. We therefore think they are still there."

"So, aliens have access to the top of the mountain. What about the ones at the end of the exhaust vent?"

"They seemed to be trying to help the ones at the top of the mountain in the observation gallery. The vehicle they had seemed to be land-based, so we are thinking they have a spacecraft of some sort somewhere else on the planet."

"What level of technology do you think they have?"

"It's hard to say for sure, sir. But from the sensor readings we took using the vent's exit, it appears to be at our level of tech or higher."

"You think they are part of an advanced race?"

"I believe so, sir."

"Okay, I'll go and consult the council about this issue. Go to the level below the gallery and see if you can get some sensor readings and report back. Do not make contact with them unless you don't have any choice. We are still reviving the population and a lot of our people are still waiting for bodies. We cannot afford a confrontation at this point."

"Understood, sir."

"Okay, carry on."

"Yes, sir."

The three aliens turned and left the room, heading for the lifts.

The alien who had spoken to them turned to the others in the room.

"Everyone, focus on getting the defensive systems operational. We may need them."

The aliens started to hurry about, trying to repair systems that had been built thousands of years ago and maintained by an army of robots throughout the journey. The robot's numbers had dropped over time as the resources were used up. When the planet finally arrived at its destination and the population started to be awakened, there were only a few hundred still operational.

On the mountain top, Dapo and Tish had settled down for the night. Tish had already fallen asleep, and Dapo was sitting in a chair playing on his vid com that Datch had sent up with the bedding. He had positioned himself so he could see the corridor through a clear panel in the door. Outside, the wind was getting up, and he could hear the thunder getting closer.

There was a loud thunderclap outside, and then it started to rain. Within minutes, it was hammering down. Dapo got up and went to the door. Along the corridor, he could see the rain cascading down the beacon and flowing across the floor, and then flowing through the remains of the gallery and down the mountain side.

"You ok, Dapo?" came Datch's voice on the coms.

"Yes. The water's pouring out of the gallery, and so far, the roof seems to be holding up."

"Good. It's really coming down out there."

"What you doing?"

"Oh, just looking through the data from your scanner. It's quite something you have found."

"We found? We just found the inside the mountain bit."

"Ok, we found it. Talking of which, any sign of life?"

"Only Tish snoring in her sleeping bag." He joked.

Datch laughed.

"Good, let's hope it stays that way."

They carried on chatting.

Down below Dapo and Tish, a lift was ascending through the lift shaft. Its occupants carried pistols and a box of scanning equipment. The lift started to slow and then came to a stop. Dapo looked down the corridor towards the lift.

The lift doors opened, and the aliens stepped out into a dark corridor. The leader touched one of the panels next to the lift and the lights tried to come on. There was a small bang from up the corridor, and two lighting panels fell out of the ceiling, followed by a lot of water.

"Well, at least we know where the water was coming from in the bottom of the lift shaft." Said one of them.

"Yes." Said another.

They made their way up along the corridor and stopped at about halfway from the lift.

"This looks like a good spot, let's set up the equipment here."

Up above, Dapo had heard what sounded like a bang. It was hard to tell because of the storm outside.

"Datch, you there?"

"Yes, Dapo. What's up?"

"Did you just hear a bang?"

"I can hear lots of bangs from the storm."

"No, not that sort of bang."

Datch looked down towards the back of the Blackbird.

"Well, everyone is still in bed."

"That's not helping."

"Sorry. But you're twenty stories higher than us. How is the lift looking?"

Dapo gave the corridor another glance.

"It looks okay."

"It may just have been the storm. It's pretty rough out there. If you're bothered, just do a quick scan."

"Hmm, maybe I will."

He got up and went over to a bag with the hand scanner in it and fetched it out. Datch decided to run a scan just in case.

He went back over to the door and turned it on. The little screen lit up and it went through its startup routines before showing ready. He pointed it down the corridor and pressed the trigger button. The scanner started showing the power cables and the lift shaft, but there was nothing unusual. He turned and pointed it to the gallery. Still nothing.

He sighed and sat back down.

"The scanner didn't find anything."

"It must have been in the storm. Just relax."

"Yeh, I think the storm is making me jumpy."

He was bored and decided to scan Tish for a joke.

The scanner beeped and he looked at it expecting to see Tish. The display did show Tish, but it was also reading something else. He looked at it again. It was showing something down. He pointed the scanner down towards the floor and pressed the trigger again. The scanner beeped again. Dapo looked at it. It was showing three lifeforms eight meters below them.

"Datch! We're not alone!"

"What?"

"I have three lifeforms on the floor below!"

"Are you sure?"

"Yes, they are about in the centre of the corridor and one floor down."

He walked over to Tish and shook her, putting his finger to his lips.

She looked at him and blinked. He pointed to the scanner's screen.

"Oh crap," she said quietly.

"I can't see them on the scanners down here. The rock must be shielding them. What are they doing?"

"It looks like they're standing still in the corridor."

"See if you can get some detailed scans and I'll try to contact the Mellardrew."

Datch shouted down the Blackbird.

There was a loud bang and a moan as Rosey fell out of her bunk.

"What's uuppp," she said, getting up.

"Wake the others. There are aliens one floor below Dapo and Tish."

"Oh crap," said Rosey, and set about upsetting everyone else.

The aliens stood looking at the piece of equipment. There was power to it, and it had been working before they got in the lift. However, now it was refusing to work.

"I think we should give it a kick," said one of them.

"The state this is in, if we kicked it, there would just be a pile of parts on the floor."

"Let me have a look."

One of them bent down to the equipment and pressed a button on the side. Nothing happened. He poked it. Still nothing, so he did what any intelligent being would do and smacked it on the side with his hand.

There was a strange gurgling noise from the device followed by a strangled beep. The screen then lit up.

"See, it just needed a gentle prod," he said triumphantly.

The other two just looked at him.

"Well, it worked!"

"Okay, let's see what we have upstairs."

The scanner beeped and started showing two lifeforms above them.

"Well, they are humanoid and quite similar to us, if this thing is working right."

"Do they have any weapons?"

"They have something that looks like it may be weapons of some sort. But it's something I've never seen before. Also, there is a large probe of some sort in the gallery."

"What are they doing?"

"Well, it looks like they are standing together looking at something."

In the Blackbird, Carina, Krissy, Rosey, and Hagger were trying to wake up after about two hours of sleep. It was not a pretty sight.

"Mellardrew, this is the Blackbird. Do you copy?"

"This is the Blackbird, please come in!"

"This is the Mellardrew. Please state the nature of your emergency?"

"Err, we have found aliens."

"Say again Blackbird."

"We have just found aliens. They are in the complex we found earlier and informed Omega Seven," said Datch very fast.

"Blackbird. CALM DOWN!"

Datch stopped. People didn't normally shout at him unless they were asking him if he wanted a beer at a noisy party.

"Sorry, Mellardrew."

"Okay, now say again and give us as much information as possible."

Datch started to recite the story. It took him a couple of minutes to give the short, short version.

"Okay, Blackbird. Don't panic. What are they doing now?"

"One second, tying you into the local coms." He pressed a couple of buttons.

"Dapo, you are being relayed to the Mellardrew."

"Dapo, this is the Mellardrew. What are the aliens doing now?"

"Err, they seem to be looking at something."

"Are they doing anything hostile?"

"Well, no. Not that I can tell."

"Okay, try to stay calm. They are most likely just as curious about you as we are about them. They are probably using some sort of scanner to find out more about you. Just sit tight and we'll decide what to do."

"Okay."

"Datch, please switch channel to 772 delta 2 and wait while I inform the operations commander. If the aliens make contact, please follow first contact protocols as laid out in document FCP132."

"Okay, switching channels." Said Datch.

He pressed a couple of buttons on the screen.

"Mellardrew, do you copy?"

"Yes Blackbird, we copy. Please stand by."

"Dapo? You two, okay?"

"Yes, we're good I think."

Datch was feeling strange. Normally he was the one in control, but this time he wasn't. His friends were trapped at the top of the mountain and were being watched by the aliens, and there was no way to get to them.

The three aliens were staring at the scanner.

"What do you think?" said one of them.

"Looking at all the data I think they are camping out."

"What? No, I meant, do you think they are hostile?"

"Well, they both have some form of side arm, but I would say it was for their personal protection. Also, one of them has a cuddly toy."

"Cuddly toy?"

"Yes, a furry one. So, they can't be dangerous."

"How does having a cuddly toy mean they're not dangerous?"

"Well, if I was going to invade a planet, I wouldn't take a cuddly toy with me. It might get hurt."

"You know when you were reintegrated into your new body, did they miss anything by any chance?"

"No, I'm a hundred percent me. Why?"

"I just wondered." And gave him a hard stare.

"So, what are they doing now?"

"They appear to be looking into a device that's pointed at us."

"So, they are looking at us and we're looking at them."

The alien holding the scanner looked at the ceiling and waved.

"Err, why did you do that?"

"I thought it would be a friendly thing to do."

"The commander said no contact."

"Yes, but it was only a wave."

He let out a sigh.

Up above them, Tish and Dapo were staring at the scanner.

"Did that alien just wave at us?" said Tish.

"Err, I'm not sure, it looked like it," said Dapo.

Tish waved at the floor.

"What are you doing?"

"Waving back."

"Ohh, ok."

Dapo now waved at the floor.

At that point, Datch picked up that something was going on.

"Guys, what are you doing?"

"The aliens waved at us so we're waving back."

"Okay. I'll relay that to Mellardrew when they come back to us."

The alien in charge looked in disbelief at the scanner.

"I think we need to call this in. They know we're here now."

He walked down the corridor to the comms panel.

"Command, please patch me through to the commander."

"He is currently with the council."

"Yes, I understand, but I really need to talk to him now."

"Okay. Please wait."

There was a short pause, and then the commander's voice came through the comms.

"Yes, what is it?"

"Err, we have sort of made contact, sir."

"Sort of? You have or you haven't."

"Well, they are waving at us and we've waved at them."

"I thought you were on the floor below them?"

"We are, sir. They can see us through a scanner of some kind, and we can see them, sir."

"And you're waving at them?"

"Yes, sir."

"I would say that is contact. What else do you have to report?"

"We think they are just exploring and found the complex by accident. They appear to be having a camp out in the gallery, sir. Also, they only have small sidearms, possibly for their own protection."

"Okay, please stand by."

The commander turned to the council members.

"I take it you all heard that. How do you wish to proceed?"

"Commander, do you think they are a threat?"

"I'm not sure. The aliens don't seem to have any backup, or they would have been rescued by now. So, we are likely to be dealing with six or seven aliens in total. However, I cannot be certain of that without planetary sensors."

"Hmm, I think we should bring them inside. We need to know what we're dealing with. This star system was deserted when we started our journey, but by now, we may have entered an inhabited system."

"Understood, sir."

He turned and left the room.

Up on the surface, Datch was looking worried. Outside, the storm was still hammering down, and even if the Mellardrew sent a rescue shuttle down, it would have one hell of a time getting Dapo and Tish off the top of the mountain. The others were looking at him, waiting for him to decide what

to do. He was out of ideas, and the storm was set to keep
going for at least a day.

"Blackbird, this is the Mellardrew. I have the Operations
Commander for you."

"Blackbird, I am Commander Santiny. I have been briefed
that you have made alien contact."

"Yes, sir," said Datch. "We have two members of our party
stuck on top of the mountain in an alien complex, and there
are three aliens on the floor below."

"How have you made contact?"

"They are waving at each other via scanning equipment."

"Okay. Have you read the first contact protocol
document?"

"Yes, sir. We have all downloaded it into our implants
before we left home."

"Good to see you came prepared. We will be sending a
shuttle down to you shortly, but the weather on the planet is
making flying difficult in your area at the moment, so it could
be a while. I've checked our records and you have a track
record when it comes to alien cultures, so I'm okay with you
making contact if needed."

"Thank you, sir. We will try our best."

"Just try not to get shot, won't you."

"We don't plan to, sir."

"I've instructed communications to keep this channel open
and to record any activity."

"I understand, sir. We will relay all that we can."

"Okay. Mellardrew standing by."

"Dapo, did you hear all that?"

"Yes, we heard."

"What are the aliens doing now?"

"One is at the end of the corridor near the lift, but the other two are still watching the scanner."

"Okay."

The comms panel next to the alien burst into life.

"Zark, this is command. The council has decided we need to talk with the aliens. We want you to bring them to the lower levels to meet with us. Do not be hostile towards them. They are as yet unknown in numbers and we may even have invaded their solar system. So, try to explain that we are friendly."

"Understood, sir."

"We suggest you use the scanner to try and work out some of their language."

"Okay, sir. We will try our best."

He turned to the others.

"Guys, we've been told to go and meet with the aliens and then ask them to come with us to meet the council."

"Oh crap," said one of them.

"I think this is cool," said the other.

"You would, Plark," said Zark.

"How are we going to talk to them?" asked the other.

"I'm not sure, Quark. I think Plark should do it, as he started it."

"Thanks, I would love to," said Plark, who now had a very big grin on his face.

"Try not to look too happy about it, please!"

"Yes, sir," said Plark, still grinning.

"Come on then, let's go see them."

They picked up the scanning equipment and headed for the lift.

Upstairs, Dapo looked at the scanner.

"Datch, they're moving towards the lift."

"Okay. If they come up, keep the comms channel open so we can hear everything."

Dapo pressed another button on the side of his comms badge and it beeped.

"Okay, comms channel is open."

"Are you getting this, Mellardrew?"

"Yes, Blackbird. Loud and clear."

Dapo's scanner showed them entering the lift and it coming up to their floor.

"They're coming up! Datch!"

"Yes, Dapo. Calm down and go into the corridor and stand near the door. I'm going to try boosting the signal from your hand scanner so we can see what's going on."

"Okay."

"Tish, you follow him and tell the scanner to link to the Blackbird. We should be able to get a data feed because of the beacon."

Datch looked at Hagger, who was busy pressing buttons. He nodded and an image of the room with Dapo and Tish in it appeared on the main screen in the centre of the large table.

"Okay, we can see you. Go and say hi."

"Remember, first contact protocols," added Carina.

"Okay," said Dapo and sighed.

He walked out the door, followed by Tish.

The lift doors opened and a number of bits of metal crashed to the floor.

"What was that?" asked the Mellardrew.

"Err, my door alarm," said Dapo.

"I'll patch the feed to the comms, Mellardrew. You should get visual as well as audio." Said Hagger.

Hagger pressed a couple of buttons.

The last of the door alarms rolled away from the lift doors and the three occupants stepped out.

They were humanoid in shape and had pale skin. They were all dressed in light blue uniforms and each had a sidearm. Their faces were quite thin with pronounced cheekbones. Their mouths looked quite slim with red lips and they had quite small ears.

The one in the middle took a step forward and waved.

Dapo looked him up and down and then waved back.

"Hello," said Dapo.

The aliens looked at the scanner.

"Do you think that was hello?" said Quark.

"Might be."

"Hello," said Plark.

The alien made a noise that sounded like "tarar." Dapo glanced at Tish, who was looking at the scanner. The aliens were looking at him.

He tried to make the same sound.

"Tararr. I am Dapo," said Dapo, pointing at himself.

"Tish, you do the same," he whispered.

She stepped out from behind him and said,

"Tararr. I am Tish."

The aliens looked at her and then back at Dapo.

"Okay, do you think he is Dapo and his mate is Tish?" whispered Quark.

"Hmm, might be, and they seem to have said hello. Plark, introduce us."

The alien at the front pointed to himself and said "Plark," and then pointed to the alien on the left and said "Quark," and finally to the alien on the right and said "Zark."

Dapo very slowly removed his sidearm and put it on the floor. The aliens watched him very carefully.

"What is he doing? Surrendering?"

"No, I think he's trying to show us he's peaceful."

"Should we do the same?"

"Let me," said Plark.

Plark removed his sidearm and placed it on the floor.

"Tish, you stay there. I'm going to take a few steps forward."

"Be careful."

Dapo took a couple of steps forward and waited. Plark watched him.

"I'm going to do the same," said Plark.

Plark moved a few steps closer to Dapo. Dapo did the same. They moved closer and closer until they were a metre apart. Dapo held out his hand.

The Plark looked at it and then at his hand. This must be some form of greeting, he thought. He put his hand out and Dapo put his hand in it and shook it up and down slowly, smiling at him. Plark smiled back.

Everyone now relaxed a bit.

Dapo led Plark to Tish, who smiled and held out her hand.

"Tararr," she said.

"Tarar," said Plark.

Plark shook her hand and smiled.

"Tararr. Hello," she said.

He looked at her.

"Hell lo," he said.

"What are they doing?" asked Zark.

"Saying 'hello,' I think," said Plark.

Plark then gestured to Dapo and Tish to move to the others.

"Hold out your hands like they did and say 'Hell lo,' like I did."

Dapo and Tish followed Plark to the other aliens. They held out their hands.

Dapo went to each of them and said "Hello," and Tish did the same.

Plark pointed at himself and said "Plark," then at Quark and said "Quark," and finally at Zark and said "Zark."

Dapo pointed to himself and said "Dapo," and then at Tish and said "Tish."

"Now what?" asked Tish quietly.

"We show them things. Hopefully the translator can find a common link."

Plark looked at them, wondering what they were saying. Dapo looked at him and beckoned him to follow. He picked up his gun and made sure Dapo could see him holster it, and then followed him. Dapo stopped at his pistol and did the same. They moved into the room with their camping stuff.

Dapo stopped and pointed at a table.

"Table," he said.

Plark looked at him.

He pointed again and said "Table."

"Polus," said Plark.

"What is he doing?" asked Zark.

"I think they are trying to get a common frame of reference, sir," said Plark, and pointed at a chair.

"Tave," he said.

"Chair," said Dapo.

They then proceeded around the room, pointing at things and saying what they were called. Everything from sleeping bags to the dust on the floor.

Datch and the rest of the pack looked on as the Blackbird's computers worked overtime trying to find a common structure in the language.

Then Dapo turned back to the table.

"This is a table," he said. He pointed at the chair. "This is a chair." And then he put the two together. "This is a table and a chair."

Plark realized what he was doing and did the same. Slowly, they worked up to complex sentences, and then the computer on the Blackbird bleeped It had got a translation.

"Dapo, we have a basic translation matrix. Sending it to the scanner." Said Datch.

"Okay."

The aliens all looked at him when they heard Datch's voice.

Dapo pointed at the scanner. The scanner showed a bar going across the screen and then it beeped.

"Tish, press the translate button."

She did, and the screen showed "ready."

"Hello, my name is Dapo," he said.

The scanner then converted it to the alien language.

The three aliens looked at it and Plark said something.

"I am Plark, and this is Zark and Quark."

Dapo smiled.

"Can you take us to our friends?" asked Dapo.

Plark looked at him puzzled. The unit had said "can you take us to" and then stopped.

Dapo noticed.

"Follow me," he said.

The scanner translated.

They followed Dapo to the gallery and Dapo pointed down. It was raining hard, and they ran out and then back under cover, but it was enough.

"Friends," said Dapo.

Plark said "friends" to the unit.

It beeped.

"Can you take us to our friends?" asked Dapo.

This time the scanner got it.

"Yes, but they want to meet up down unknown," said the scanner.

Plark looked at Zark and Quark.

"Command said they wanted to meet them, so I think we should take them all?"

The scanner tried to translate, but only got half of it.

"Okay, that would make sense," said Zark.

Plark turned to Dapo.

"Yes, we can, but we want them to come to." He said.

"Come where?" asked Dapo.

"To meet."

Dapo looked at Plark. Plark smiled.

"Datch, they will bring us to you, but they want us all to follow them back inside to meet. I'm assuming they want us to meet their leaders."

"Okay, but bring them to us first. We will see if they can add to the translation algorithm."

"Okay."

Dapo turned to Plark.

"Yes, let's go to our friends," he said and gestured to the door.

"Yes," said Plark.

Dapo and Tish picked up their belongings and headed to the lift with the aliens.

"Mellardrew, looks like we are having visitors."

"Yes, we were following the comms. The command staff are all listening. Can you put your internal vids on the comms so we can see them?"

"Okay, adding the vid feeds."

"Err, Blackbird. It may be an idea to get dressed."

Datch turned around and realized that the others had just come straight from their bunks.

"Ah. Guys, get dressed in a hurry."

There was a sudden flurry of activity as everyone rushed off to get dressed.

The lift came to a stop and Zark led the way across the landing to the small hatch of the opposite side and pressed the panel next to it. The hatch slid open and Dapo and Tish followed Zark inside and across the little room to the other hatch.

When Plark and Quark had entered the hatch, the hatch closed and the one on the other side opened. Through the second hatch was the exhaust vent. Zark stepped through it and waited for Dapo and Tish.

"Please lead the way," Zark said.

"Please lead," said the scanner.

The party followed Dapo and Tish up the exhaust vent.

Datch sat inside waiting. Outside, the rain suddenly stopped. He looked up and realised it hadn't stopped, but it was now being diverted by some sort of forcefield.

"Can you still hear us, Mellardrew?"

"Yes, but your signal strength is very low. We're going to use the beacon as a relay."

Datch looked at Hagger, who was fully dressed and back at his station, although he did have his T-shirt on backwards. Hagger pressed a few buttons and nodded at Datch.

"Mellardrew, how's that?"

"Much better, Blackbird."

"Hagger, T-shirt."

"What?" He looked down. "Oh, I see."

He stood up and turned it around just as the girls arrived back at their stations.

Then, in the tunnel mouth, Dapo and Tish appeared followed by three aliens.

"Guys, the aliens are coming. Hagger, put your pistol close at hand just in case." Said Datch.

"Okay, Datch."

Dapo and Tish led Zark, Plark, and Quark across the cliff top to the Blackbird. Zark looked up at the vehicle and paused for a moment. This craft was very high-tech, and it also looked very new.

"Come on," said Dapo and smiled.

Dapo went up the steps and entered through the door. Datch and the rest of them turned to look at the door.

"Hi guys," said Dapo stepping through the door.

"Hi Dapo, are you okay?"

"Yes, we're good. Let me introduce our new friends."

Zark, Plark, and Quark stepped through the door into the bright interior of the Blackbird.

"This is Zark, Plark, and Quark."

Datch stood up and walked over to them and held out his hand.

"Hello. I am Datch," he said.

Zark put his hand in Datch's and shook it.

"Tarar. Pan wsa Zark," he said.

The scanner said, "Hello. I am Zark."

"Dapo, feed the scanner data into the main system please."

"Okay, Datch."

Zark looked around. The alien's vehicle was very advanced. He could see the scanned images on the displays in the centre of a large table that appeared to be streaming all of the data.

Dapo put the scanner in a holder, and then after a few seconds, it beeped.

Datch pointed to each of the Pack in turn.

"This is Carina, Rosey, Krissy, and Hagger."

Zark nodded to each of them.

"Please come and sit," said Datch heading over to the large table.

Zark followed him and sat next to him.

"Computer, please run the translation program to set up a basic translator for our guests."

The screen showed a picture of a chair.

"Chair," Datch said and pointed at it.

Zark looked at it for a moment and then said, "Tave."

The image changed to a table.

Zark realized what they were trying to do. He said his name for a table.

"Table," he said.

The screen changed again and again, displaying image after image. Plark and Quark were shown to seats and the same happened with them. After about five minutes, the screens flashed up "Processing - please wait."

Zark looked at Datch. Datch smiled.

"Processing complete - basic matrix ready."

"Please transfer to three earpieces for the aliens and upload to our implants."

Three earpieces that had been charging started flashing green. Datch fetched them and handed one to Zark.

He looked at it and then back at Datch. Datch picked up another one and placed it in his ear, and gestured to Zark to do the same. Zark looked at it again and put it in his ear.

"Can you understand me now?" said Datch.

At the same time, the earpiece relayed it in Zark's language.

"Yes," he said.

Datch handed them to Plark and Quark.

"Put them on," said Zark.

The aliens were very advanced. These little units were already translating for them, he thought.

"Okay, these earpieces may miss out the odd word, but they will try to translate for you," said Datch.

"These are very good," said Zark, not wanting to say how advanced they were.

"Why are you here?" asked Quark.

"We are part of a planetary expedition to study your world. We thought it was dead and wanted to know more about who lived here," said Datch.

"There are more of you?" asked Zark.

"Yes, lots more, and a number of starships in orbit," said Carina.

Zark looked worried.

"Do not worry. We are not invading you. We thought it was a dead world and wanted to explore it," said Krissy.

"Yes, we are here peacefully."

"Our council wishes to meet with you and ask you a few questions."

At this point, the comms system spoke.

"Blackbird, this is Mellardrew. Please may we speak with your guests?"

"Zark, these are the leaders of the expedition, and they wish to talk to you."

"Mellardrew, we are putting you on the main screen."

Datch pressed a couple of buttons, and an image of a man wearing an IPSF uniform appeared on the screen.

Zark looked at him.

"Hello Zark. I am Commander Santiny. I would first like to say sorry for not meeting you in person, but due to the current weather on your planet, it is not safe to bring a shuttle down from orbit. I would like to reassure you that we mean no harm to your world and only wish to learn about yourselves and your culture. Please can you convey that to your leaders and inform them that if you need any help, we will be more than happy to discuss it. The crew of the Blackbird has agreed to act as ambassadors until we can come to meet you in person. Datch, please can you take a copy of this to show their council."

"Yes, sir," said Datch.

"Now I will leave you in their capable hands."

Zark looked at the image and waited for the full translation. "Thank you, commander." He said after a few moments.

"Datch, may I speak with you privately for a moment? I just need to brief you on a few things."

"Excuse me for a moment, Zark."

Datch went over to his seat and sat down. He pressed a couple of buttons and put on his headset.

"Yes, Commander, we're now on private comms."

"Datch, I know you like helping people and saving just about anyone, but do not agree to anything without talking to us first. These are an unknown race. They are going to want to know everything they can about us. The last thing they need to know is that there is a fleet of ships sitting above their planet. Be careful what you say."

"Yes, sir, understood."

"Okay, be careful. We expect to lose comms when you enter the complex, so do not be alarmed. We will come looking for you if you have not contacted us by the time the storm clears. Okay?"

"Yes, sir."

"Oh, and don't sing to them, please."

"Okay, sir."

"Right, go be nice."

"Yes, sir."

Datch took off his headset and got up.

Dapo was showing the aliens around the Blackbird and explaining things. The computer was also updating the translation matrix as they went.

"Krissy, go get a bag and put some food in it, please. Carina and Rosey, grab a couple of scanners and a couple of extra memory crystals. Tish, do you want to freshen up?"

"Yes, please."

Zark and Plark watched as Tish disappeared into the back and closed the door.

"It's the bathroom," said Dapo, noticing them looking.

"Bathroom?"

"Computer, display pictures of bathrooms and restrooms on the monitor." said Dapo.

They looked at the images and said something in their own language. The computer updated the matrix.

"Wow, good job we caught that one," said Krissy.

"Computer, add toilet to the restroom update," said Datch.

"Okay, folks, we'd better move out or I'm going to be asleep," said Datch.

"Do you want something to keep you awake?" asked Carina.

"I'm okay at the moment, but I may need something later."

"I'll grab some caffeine tablets in case we need them."

"Caffeine?" asked Quark.

"Yes, it helps keep us awake."

He looked puzzled.

"Computer, show sleep and awake. Then add caffeine tablet and show awake."

Quark watched the screen and smiled.

"What? No, how long awake?" he asked.

"One daylight cycle and half a night one," said Datch.

He looked puzzled again and Datch got the computer to show more images.

"So, you up late?" asked Plark.

"Yes, very. So, it would be nice to hurry up a bit."

"Okay."

Tish came out of the bathroom.

"Are we all ready?" asked Datch.

They all nodded.

"Commander, we are heading inside the mountain now so comms will be unlikely to work."

"Okay, Datch, good luck."

"Thanks, commander."

Datch turned to Zark.

"Okay, Zark. Take us to your leaders."

Zark looked at him. Datch smiled and point to the door.

They followed Zark outside and over to the vent. The vent was brightly lit, and the lights in the channel were showing green.

The party headed inside the mountain to the far end of the vent. Zark pressed a couple of buttons on the panel, and the hatch opened. Moments later, they came walking out onto the landing with the lifts. Datch looked at the stairs which disappeared down into the darkness.

"How far down?" asked Datch.

Zark looked at him for a moment and realized what he was asking.

"Err, I think it is 235. Err."

"Floors?" said Datch.

Zark looked at him.

Datch pointed to the floor.

"Floor." He said.

"Yes, cerave is floor. 235 floor."

The translator beeped.

"That is a lot of floors."

He led the way across the landing and into a smaller room with lifts.

"Now we go down."

"How many floors?"

"Floor 40." He said.

The lift arrived, and they went in.

When they were all in, Zark moved to the left side of the lift and pressed the panel. It lit up, and he selected a button right a third of the way down the last column. The lift doors shut, and the lift started to drop down the shaft.

"Well, they don't have AG in the lifts." Said Hagger and burped.

"A G?" asked Quark.

"Artificial Gravity." Said Rosey.

Quark and Plark looked puzzled.

"Hmm. Lift is made. Tree is not. Artificial is made and Gravity is," she stopped and thought for a moment and then dropped her scanner from one hand into the other. "This," she pointed to the path the scanner had taken.

"The thing that makes things fall?" Plark asked.

"Yes, gravity is the thing that makes things fall."

The lift was falling at quite a speed, and the lights on the panel were going down quickly. Then, a few moments later, it started to slow down. The lift came to a stop, and the doors opened. Dapo got out a scanner and pointed it out the lift.

Zark looked at him nervously.

"Just checking the air is okay for us." Said Tish.

"Ok. Follow me please." He said.

Outside of the lift, there was a large open area with a number of exits and various pieces of equipment on the walls and some very strange looking machinery. The far wall had a number of clear panels in, and behind them was the glow of molten rock. There were a number of aliens manning the systems. They stopped and looked at the Pack as they came out of the lift.

"Is that molten rock behind there?" asked Hagger.

"Yes, the planet's core powers all our systems. The vent we came in through is a pressure release system to stop excess heat in the core." said Zark.

"Why were parts of the top of the mountain still frozen then?" asked Tish.

"The vent has only been active since we came into orbit around this star when the planet had started to defrost. Until then, all the excess temperature was used to heat the upper levels." Said Plark.

"Wow." Said Hagger.

They followed Zark across to another set of doors and entered a long corridor. The air was warm and pleasant with bright lighting in the ceiling.

"I just want to warn you. We will be arriving at centre command shortly, and they are... hmmm. A little nervous. So please do not be offended." Said Zark.

"Okay. We can understand that." said Carina.

"Err, can you please explain to them that we mean no harm." Said Datch.

"I will try."

"Thanks."

They came to another set of doors.

These led out into a large open area. There were a number of armed troops standing in two lines, one on either side of the door, forming a wide corridor. At the far end were three aliens, two were dressed in robes and the third was in a similar uniform but with a little more frilliness. The Pack stopped and looked at them.

"It's good," said Zark, noticing their apprehension.

"If you say so," said Hagger.

They followed Zark, Plark, and Quark past all the troopers to the three people at the far end.

Zark stopped and the other two stepped to the side.

"These are the aliens, sir. Their commander has told us that they are ambassadors for their race and they are to help 'beep' 'bleep' in opening a dialogue between our two races."

The commander looked at the small scanner that beeped.

"What is that?"

"It translates our language to theirs and back again."

"Why did it beep?"

"It does that when it can't translate words."

"Oh."

The commander looked at the other two aliens and they nodded. He stepped forward.

"Greetings to you from our world of Marduk. I am Commander Natuk. I am pleased to introduce two of our council members, Othred and Kratos."

The two other aliens now stepped forward. Datch smiled at them and stepped forward himself.

"I am Datch and these are my fellow travellers, Carina, Krissy, Tish, Rosey, Hagger, and Dapo. We bring greetings to you from distant worlds."

"Welcome. I know this is straight to the point, but why have you come to our world?"

"Our ships noticed your world coming into orbit a year ago, and the IPSF scientists came to see what we thought was a long-dead world. We wished only to explore your world and find out about the people who lived here if any, nothing more. We didn't realize you were still here as our orbital scans couldn't see through the black ore."

The council member looked thoughtful for a while.

"May I ask what planet you are from?"

"Yes, I am from Bellatrix, as are my companions apart from Krissy, who is from Earth."

"Bellatrix, hmm."

"Yes, Bellatrix. It's about two thousand light years away."

"Two thousand. How long did it take to get here?"

"Hmm, about eight days."

"Eight days to cover two thousand light years, that's incredible."

"Actually, that's slow for the intergalactic starships. They can travel that distance in less than a second." Added Hagger.

"How many vessels do you have?"

"There are two large science vessels in orbit and a stream of freighters and transports coming and going between your planet and the space station two and a half light years away."

The two council members looked at each other, and Datch noticed their alarmed expressions.

"Please don't be alarmed, though. Now that we know you're here, we'll cease operations. Also, if you need any assistance, I'm sure we'll give you anything you require."

"A fleet like that, and you could easily take our planet."

"We are not like that. We represent thousands of worlds who all live together peacefully. We grow and prosper together, and have developed a system of government that looks after all of our worlds."

"Doesn't your planet have its own government?"

"Yes, it does, and it has a seat in the senate on Olympus Prime. As do all the worlds that are part of the federation. I'm sure if you wish to join us, you will be made to feel welcome."

"Hmm. And if we said 'go away,' you would?"

"Yes, sir. We would leave your star system."

"Hmm. Would you mind excusing us for a short while? We need to have a talk. Commander, if you would please look after our guests. Zark, Plark, and Quark, if you could follow us, please."

"Yes, sir." said Natuk.

The council members led Zark, Plark, and Quark off to another room.

"If you would follow me, please. We have some drinks for you." said Natuk.

"Thank you," said Datch.

"Please don't be concerned when we scan them. We just need to make sure they are not toxic to us."

"I understand. We would want to do the same."

They followed Natuk across to a table with what looked like coffee machines on it.

"This is called Poely. It has a mild stimulating effect on our bodies. If you wish, we also have water and fruit juices."

Krissy pointed her scanner at the table. It beeped a number of times. She looked at its little screen.

"It all looks okay, folks. The Poely has a similar makeup to coffee and will have the same effect. The fruit juices are also okay to drink."

"Cool, I need a coffee. Err, Poely," said Dapo.

"Me too," added Datch.

They all went to get a large cup of Poely.

Next door, the two council members were with Zark, Plark, and Quark.

"Zark, please can you give us an assessment of the aliens and their technology?" asked Kratos.

"Well, sir, from what I've seen, they are very advanced by our standards. Their vehicle had some very advanced systems with a lot of information being displayed on the screens."

"Did they try to hide anything from you?"

"No, sir. They seemed to be very open with us."

"Did you see anything that concerns you?"

He paused for a moment before answering, his mind going through everything that had happened to them on the surface. Was there anything he had noticed? No.

"No, sir. I believe they mean what they say. And sir, if they wanted to, they could overwhelm us easily."

"Yes, I understand that. What about you two? Do you agree with what Zark says?"

"Yes, sir," said Plark.

"Yes, sir. They have done nothing to make me suspect they are anything more than what they say they are."

"Hmm. Can I ask you another question? Do you trust them enough to go with them to their starship?"

There was a pause, and then Plark spoke.

"Yes, sir, I would be willing to go with them."

"I would too, sir," said Zark.

"What about you, Quark?" asked Othred.

"I would go, but I don't like flying," Quark said.

"Really?"

"Yes, sir, I never have."

Othred looked at the other council member, who nodded.

"Hmm... I will need to talk to the council, but if they allow it, then expect a road trip, gentlemen."

"Please go back to the aliens and show them around a bit. Let me know if anything changes."

"Yes, sir."

The council members left the room and headed for the council chambers.

The three officers looked at each other.

"Which bit of 'I don't like flying' did he miss?" Quark asked.

"All of it, I think," said Zark.

"It will be fun," said Plark.

"You would say that. Come on, let's go."

They headed out the door and back to the Pack.

Othred and Kratos entered the council chambers. It was a large room with seating set out in a semicircle and had four tiers of seats. In the centre was a raised area with a podium on it. The chamber was half full and waiting for them.

Kratos walked up to the podium.

"Good evening, gentlemen. Myself and Othred have met the aliens. They are very similar to us in looks and appear to be quite friendly. They have offered a hand of friendship to us. From what I have been told, their technology is a lot more advanced than ours, and they seem to be able to travel the vast distances between the stars in a matter of hours.

They told us that they came to this world thinking it was dead, and apparently their sensors could not pass through the Crilium ore. They have a number of starships in orbit and a base of operations on the surface.

I believe that if they wanted to, they could easily take this world from us. They have told me, however, that if we ask them to, they will leave and not bother us again.

However, given our current issues with the power systems and the state of the planet, I would like to explore the possibility of a form of aid from them.

I am proposing that myself, Othred, and the three troopers who made first contact journey to their starship in orbit to explore the possibility of help. If we can get the other power systems running, it would help in reviving our race."

"Do you think they will help?" asked one of the council members.

"I hope so. If another one of our power systems fails, we could lose half of our people."

"I am a bit uneasy about putting our people in the hands of an alien race that we have just met and know nothing about. Are you sure they are not hostile?" asked another.

"I don't believe they are. Either way, they know we are here now. If we do nothing and they are hostile, we won't stand a chance. I believe meeting with them is the best policy."

"Does anyone else wish to ask a question?" said Othred.

There were a few murmurs, but nothing more.

"Okay, gentlemen, let's put it to a vote," said Othred.

A screen lit up behind the podium with the words "Agree", "Disagree", and "Abstain" on it. At the same time, a small post lit up next to each of the council members, with three small buttons on it: red, blue, and green.

"Please vote now," said Othred.

The screen showed the number of votes going up, and a timer counting down to zero.

When it reached zero, the results appeared. The motion passed by 57 votes to 25, with 8 abstentions.

"Thank you, gentlemen. We will ask the aliens to arrange to escort us to their ships tomorrow afternoon. The storm should have died down by then."

With that, Kratos and Othred headed back to the Pack.

Datch was leaning against a pillar, sipping his Poely, which by this point in the night didn't taste half bad. Natuk had been asking a few more questions about them and was chatting with Krissy and Carina. Zark was talking to Dapo, while Plark and Quark were chatting with Rosey and Hagger.

Every now and then, the scanner would beep and someone would correct it.

The doors opened and Kratos and Othred came walking through.

"Good evening again. We have been to talk to the council, and if you are happy to do it, we would like you to escort myself, Othred, Zark, Plark, and Quark to your ship in orbit tomorrow afternoon."

"We would be honored to. However, our ship is about a day's drive from here, near your ruined town to the south." said Datch.

"Hmm, near the launch thruster?" asked Natuk.

"Thruster?"

"Yes, it's about four kilometres wide."

"That was a thruster?"

"Yes, it is one of the planetary thrusters that launched our planet into the stars."

"Oh. Well, yes, our ship is at the base of operations about ten kilometres to the south of there, in a valley."

"Zark, would their vehicle fit in the maintenance tunnel?"

"Yes, sir."

"Okay, go with them and take them to the thruster. The tunnel exit there should still be operational. That should only take about two hours, maybe three. Then get back here and get some sleep."

"Yes, sir."

He turned to Datch.

"If you can get your vehicle down to the crater floor, Zark will show you the way into the tunnel network."

"Thank you. I might get some sleep after all," said Datch, smiling.

"Datch and all of you, it's been an honour to meet you, and I look forward to seeing you tomorrow. We will come to the tunnel exit at the thruster."

"We'll be waiting for you, sir, and it's been an honour to meet you as well," said Datch.

"Plark, take a shuttle car to the crater maintenance exit and then lead them to the thruster. You can bring Zark back then as well."

"Yes, sir."

"Shall we go?" said Zark.

"Yes, lead the way."

Zark led them back to the lifts and up to the exhaust vent. They all headed out and into the Blackbird. It was still raining quite hard, but at least it wasn't ice rain.

Datch sat down in his seat and started to power up the systems.

"Mellardrew, this is Blackbird. Come in please."

"Blackbird, this is Mellardrew. Glad to hear your voice. Is everything okay down there?"

"Yes, the meeting with the Marduk council went well. Tell Commander Santiny he will be having guests tomorrow. The council has asked if we can escort them to meet with you. We are now enroute to our ship to 'A' get some sleep and 'B' get some food."

"Blackbird, we were going to send a shuttle for you."

"No need. If you check your records, the Raven is no stranger to the IPSF ships. We have spent a lot of time on the Carpaycus for one thing or another. We will be going signal dark shortly as we're taking a shortcut to Omega Seven base camp, and it's doubtful if we'll have signal during the trip."

"Okay, Blackbird. I'll inform the commander. I will also inform the base that you're on your way."

"Thanks, Mellardrew. Blackbird out."

Datch turned to Zark.

"Zark, if you could sit down here next to me, please. Then you can guide us. Dapo, get ready on the rear thruster controls."

"Already on them."

Zark sat down next to Datch. Everyone else had sat down in their seats and were putting their harnesses on. Once everyone had gotten settled, Datch turned around.

"Everyone good?"

They all nodded.

"Okay, here we go."

Datch increased power to the turbines, and the Blackbird started to move towards the edge of the cliff. The external lights were brightly illuminating the area in front of them.

"Okay, Dapo, let's get airborne."

The thrusters outside started to roar, and then the Blackbird flew over the edge of the cliff. The vehicle was shaking under the stress, and then they started to descend towards the crater floor. Datch was watching his instruments and guiding the Blackbird to the left away from the magma pool.

Zark looked nervous.

"It's okay, Zark, this is normal," said Krissy.

"It is?"

"Yes. It's a land vehicle and shouldn't normally fly."

"Oh."

There was a bump as the Blackbird touched down on the crater floor. The floodlight outside lit up the area.

"Okay, we're down. Where to?"

Zark looked out the window and waited. Then, after a moment, a light flashed briefly on the cliff face.

"There, see the light? That's the entrance."

"Okay, I see it."

The Blackbird started to move towards the position of the light. It flashed again. The crater floor was smooth here, almost like driving on a road. In front of them, the cliff face reached up into the darkness. It looked like solid rock.

As the Blackbird approached the cliff, two enormous doors opened in the rock face. They seemed to be part of the rock itself and hadn't been there moments before. The entrance was huge. Inside, they could see a small vehicle sitting in the tunnel.

"That's the shuttle car with Plark in it. Just pull up behind it."

"Okay."

Datch took the Blackbird inside and stopped behind the small vehicle. Behind them, the doors closed with a thud.

"Coms are down," said Hagger.

"Thanks, Hagger," said Datch.

The little vehicle started to move off.

"Just follow him," said Zark.

"Okay," said Datch.

He started to follow the little vehicle down the tunnel. It was brightly lit with the walls themselves glowing. They were a metallic grey colour but seemed to be glowing white from within.

Then, up ahead, the tunnel intersected with another one that was even bigger. Datch followed the shuttle car as it accelerated down the bigger tunnel. The tunnel ahead of them disappeared into the distance.

"Zark, are we following this tunnel to the thruster?"

"Yes, pretty much all the way. At this speed, it will take about two hours, maybe a little more."

"Folks, if you want to get some rest, go for it."

"I'll stay with you, Datch," said Dapo.

"Me too," said Krissy.

The rest of them got up and headed to their bunks.

"What does 'get your heads down' mean?" asked Zark.

"It means 'go and get some sleep. When we leave the thruster, it will be about an hour's travel before we get to the ship in the storm."

"Oh, I see."

"Zark, tell me about what happened to make you launch your planet into space?"

"Hmm. It was a long time ago when our scientists found that our star was going to go... err, 'bang'?"

"That would be 'supernova' or explode," said Dapo.

"Yes, supernova. We had never really bothered much about space. There were far more important things to do, like feed the poor or make the world greener. We created a perfect world. Then they realized that the rockets we had could not reach the stars quickly enough and that life on our beautiful planet was going to come to an end."

"So, what happened?"

"We moved the planet. Our minds and memories were converted into data and stored for the journey while an automated system kept the planet going as we travelled to this star system. Then, when we arrived in orbit, the systems started to create new bodies for us and we have been slowly reviving our race since."

"Wow. That's impressive." Said Krissy.

"Now we need to make our world great again."

"How did you keep the planet on course for all that time?"

"We used the moon. It has acted as a stabilizer during the flight and was linked to the planet by an energy beam."

"Oh wow, our scientists were trying to work out how the moon had stayed with the planet."

"Well, now you know. Can I ask you something?"

"Sure."

"What is your world like?"

"Bellatrix Five. It's a bit bigger than yours and has slightly more gravity. It has a light green sky and is warm due to the weather being controlled."

"No, I meant what's it like?"

"Oh, I see. Hmm. Myself, Carina, and Krissy live on a ranch near a great desert to the north of Yuland City. We tend to spend a lot of time in a bar in the city called the Barbers Inn. We watch the sport on the vid and chill out with our friends a lot."

"Do you not work?"

"Oh, yes. We are all part of a rock band and are also part-time ambassadors to Welly Four."

"I thought you were scientists."

"No. We volunteered to come and explore this world as a sort of holiday. We got all the information we needed from our implants."

Zark looked at them hard for a moment.

"You won't see them. They are normally transported into our brains when we are little. They allow us to access the galactic database."

"I got mine a couple of years ago as I came from a world without them." Added Krissy.

"Do they control you?"

"No. They just allow us to access information so we don't need to learn everything. For instance, all the data for your world was uploaded so if we needed to reference it, we could." Said Datch.

"What about your world?" Asked Krissy.

"It was a wonderful place with lush forests and shining cities. There was a beautiful blue sky and a warm sun. That was until shortly before we left. The planet was starting to warm up. Plants and trees were dying and everyone retreated inside the planet to be converted to data."

"Converted, did it hurt?"

"No. All I remember is closing my eyes and falling asleep. The next thing I remember was waking up two hundred days ago in a revival pod."

"Wow. Imagine being asleep for that long." Said Krissy.

"Well, technically I was in storage, not asleep. Anyway, tell me more about your worlds."

"Hmm, I can do better than that." Said Krissy and went over to the big table.

She placed her vid-com on the table next to the large screen and pressed a few buttons.

The screen started showing pictures of Bellatrix.

Zark looked at the Images of the distant world that he was being told about.

"Wow, it looks very beautiful," he said.

Krissy carried on showing him her photo album. There were scenic views of various vistas of distant worlds and lots of alien cities. Also, quite a lot of swimming pools and beaches as well as a few blurry shots of the insides of bars. Then came the spaceships and orbital space stations.

The next two hours went by chatting about each other's worlds.

Up ahead, the tunnel had red flashing lights.

"Zark?" said Datch, looking out the window.

Zark looked up.

"We're approaching the thruster. We're nearly there," he said.

The little shuttle car started to slow down. Up ahead were two enormous doors with red flashing lights on. They came to a stop in front of them.

Plark got out and walked over to a panel in a small alcove in the wall. He pressed something and orange lights started to flash. He walked back to the shuttle car and got in.

"The doors will open in a second, allowing us to enter the thruster. We can follow the maintenance road up to the surface doors." Said Zark.

Then the two doors started to move apart, revealing an engine core that was still pulsating.

"It's still active?" asked Datch.

"Yes, we used them to slow our entry to the star system and make sure we entered the correct orbit."

"Is it safe?"

"Yes, the fusion core is still cooling down, so all the systems stay active until it goes cold. Just follow Plark."

The shuttle car went through the doors and started to head up the ramp at the side of the engine. It was huge, with glowing pipework and bright lights illuminating glittering metal. The centre core was pulsating slowly as they followed the little vehicle up and up the ramp that circled the engine core. Higher and higher they went.

"Wow, how high is this?" asked Dapo, who was watching the sensors.

"It's about four hundred floors. But we came in about halfway up."

"That is one hell of an engine."

"There were sixty of them around the planet that all fired in sequence, pushing our world out of orbit and into interstellar space. There are only eight still working. The safety margin was six. We needed them to keep working so we didn't overshoot the star system."

The little car came to a stop at the top of the ramp. Plark got out and went to another panel mounted on a post. He pressed a few buttons and the roof started to slide apart. Bits of rock and debris fell in through the opening, and then the rain and water came running in, cascading off the side of the platform and disappearing into the depths below.

"Coms are back, Datch," said Dapo.

"Thanks, Dapo."

Plark waved Datch to come past him. The Blackbird pulled forward towards the opening before coming to a stop in front of the little car.

"Well, folks, it looks like my stop. I'll be seeing you in about twelve hours. Land next to the exit doors, We'll wait until we see you before we come out." said Zark.

Datch reached across and picked up a comms badge.

"Take this," he said. "If you bring this with you and open the door a bit, we'll be able to talk to you when we're on our way."

Zark looked at the little badge.

"Just stick it in your pocket," said Datch.

"Okay. Thank you."

He got up.

"See you this afternoon," said Krissy smiling.

"Yes. I look forward to it."

He left the Blackbird and headed over to Plark.

Datch started to move forward up the ramp and out into the storm above. They came out onto a flat area to the side of the circular thruster cover. Behind them, the doors slid shut.

"Mellardrew, this is Blackbird. We are now at the thruster site, about an hour's drive from Omega Seven Base."

"Good to hear from you again, Blackbird. The base is expecting you and will require a report."

"It might have to wait until lunch time, Mellardrew. I need sleep before flying their delegation up to you tomorrow."

"We understand, Blackbird. Any information will be useful. Did you say thruster site?"

"Yes, the large black circular areas have planetary thrusters under them. That's how the planet got here. If anyone is trying to explore them, tell them to stop. There is a huge fusion drive underneath them, and they are still cooling down."

"Thanks for the information, Blackbird. We have already ordered all planetary operations to stand down."

"Copy that, Mellardrew. We are relaying all the information we have now."

"Data is being received. Have a safe journey back to base. Mellardrew out."

Dapo and Krissy were busy sending the data to Mellardrew while Datch found the road. The night vision systems made it look like daytime outside, and he brought the systems up to full power.

The Blackbird thundered down the road, spray shooting into the air from its wheels as it went. The vehicle's stabilizers were working overtime to keep the Blackbird stable as kilometre after kilometre went by. Water and ice covered some sections of the road, but the Blackbird powered across them as if it were dry land. Puddles on the road became jets of spray in the darkness as the wheels hit them. Datch was actually really enjoying himself, even though it was about three in the morning.

Then, up ahead in the darkness, lights appeared. He started to slow down.

"We're nearly at the base, folks," he said.

There was no answer. He glanced behind him. Both Krissy and Dapo had fallen asleep in their chairs. He smiled to himself.

The Blackbird came down the hill leading to the base, slowing as it came. The base was quiet now, as most people had gone to bed. A security guard waved at him to go to the base HQ. Datch sighed.

He brought the Blackbird to a stop right outside the main doors, blocking up half the road. He figured that they wouldn't want the Blackbird to be there for too long, and therefore he could go to bed. He put the systems in park and got up. Krissy and Dapo were both still asleep, and as there was no movement from the others, he figured they were out for the count as well.

"Computer, if the others wake up, tell them that I've just nipped into the base and to go back to sleep."

"Message set."

"Thanks, computer."

He headed outside and down the steps. It was still raining, but it was more of a light rain now. He hurried around the front of the Blackbird and into the base. The airlock hissed as he went in.

He could see inside the base, and there was a large group of people eagerly waiting for him. He sighed again and walked through the doors.

"Welcome back, Blackbird! Is it true there are aliens here?" said a scientist rushing over to greet him.

"Thank you. And yes, there are aliens here."

There then followed a barrage of questions all at the same time. Datch cleared his throat and was shocked to find it didn't work. Instead, they carried on. He waved his hands and yelled, "Stop!"

They finally stopped. He looked at the crowd. These folks had either had far too much coffee or way too much sugar. Then he corrected himself. Way too much coffee with loads of sugar.

"Thank you," he said. "Now, I am very tired and my team are all asleep, which is where I plan to be very shortly. I know you are all excited about this and want to know more, but it's going up for four in the morning. So, I'll just say this. They seem to be very friendly, and we have met with some of their council members. They are humanoid and similar to us, apart from having a very light-coloured skin. We are taking a small group of them to the Mellardrew tomorrow, err today to meet the operations commander. I'll be giving you a report around lunchtime before we go to meet them."

"Can you tell us anything else?"

"Not at this time of night. Sorry, but I really need some sleep."

He turned and walked away, leaving the crowd of scientists buzzing with excitement.

There was a lot of murmuring.

"Look, if you want to see them, go to bed and you might get a look at them tomorrow," Datch said.

There was a general consensus that sleep might be a good idea.

"Okay, folks. See you at lunchtime."

Datch turned and went back into the airlock. The crowd looked a little disappointed, but it was almost 4 am. The other side of the airlock opened, and he headed out and back into the Blackbird. Krissy and Dapo were still sleeping in their chairs when he came through the door. He went over and sat down in his chair. He took the Blackbird out of park and headed across the landing area to the Raven. It was good to see her sitting there waiting for them. Datch brought the Blackbird to a stop just to the side of her.

He debated waking the others, but decided that sleeping in the Blackbird was a better option at this point. Datch got up and walked over to Krissy and gently tapped her shoulder. It took a couple of moments for her to open her eyes.

"We're back at base. Go get some sleep in your bunk."

"Okay..." she said, getting up. She gave him a hug before heading to her bunk in the rear.

Datch did the same with Dapo, and they all headed to bed.

Ambassador Time

The next day, Datch was woken up by Carina offering him a cup of coffee. He looked at her for a moment, blinking in the light.

"What time is it?" he said, yawning.

"It's just after midday. Here, drink this."

He took the coffee from her and had a sip.

"Is everyone up?"

"Yes. Half of them are in the Raven, having a decent shower, and the rest are in the rec room."

"Oh, sounds like a plan."

"You could have woken us up when we arrived back at the base."

"I couldn't see the point of disturbing the rest of you. When we got back, I went into the HQ and told them I was going to sleep. Then I came out and parked next to the Raven and went to bed."

"So, do we all have to go over?"

"Yes, they'll want to know everything." He sighed. "Still, breakfast first."

"It's lunch time."

"Okay, lunch first."

Datch climbed out of his bunk and headed over to the large table and sat down with Carina. He was still wearing clothes from the day before.

"I think I'd better get a shower too, and at this moment the Raven's shower sounds very nice."

"You do need one." She said sniffing him.

Datch sniffed his armpit and wrinkled his nose.

"Yes, I do a bit. Would you get me some Jeader rolls while I get one?"

"Sure. What did you make of the Marduks?"

"I think they're a good race. I do think they're less advanced than we are. Zark seemed to be quite amazed by some of our technology." Datch took another large gulp of coffee.

"Yes, I agree, but they did pilot their planet through space."

"True." He took another gulp.

"Do you think they're advanced enough to join the IPSF?"

"Hmm, I'm not sure. Still, that's not for us to decide."

"Hmm..."

"Come on, I need a shower." Said Datch, drinking his last bit of coffee.

They got up and headed over to the Raven.

Three quarters of an hour later, Datch wandered into the rec room on the Raven. The rest of the Pack were there, sitting and watching a movie.

"Morning all."

"Afternoon," said Rosey.

"Ah yes, afternoon. We'd better make a move to the base HQ. They're going to need to know everything we did."

"That's going to take a while," said Dapo.

"Yes, and we only have about two and a half hours until we're meeting the council members at the thruster," added Krissy.

"Hmm. Let's go. We'll get the base to feed us while we tell them about the Marduks. Afterwards, we'd better put our ambassadorial hats on." Said Datch.

"Oh, and I've just done my hair," said Tish.

Everyone laughed.

"Come on, folks," said Datch, heading for the door.

The rest of them followed him out to the Blackbird.

Outside, the rain had stopped and the sky was starting to clear. Rays of light bathed the landing area with patches of sunlight. The air was damp and humid, with a fine mist rising from the wet ground. The air smelled fresh, and the sun was warm on the skin.

The Pack headed inside the Blackbird, and Datch powered up the systems.

Five minutes later, the Pack walked into the base HQ. It was very busy, as the dig sites had all stopped and everyone was waiting to find out what was going to happen next.

Several people came walking over to them.

"Hey, have you guys heard the news?" one said.

"Yes, we are the news," said Datch.

"What, is it true?" asked another.

"If you mean is the planet habitable? Yes, it is, and we have met them."

"You are the Blackbird crew?" asked another.

"Yes, we are. Now we need to talk to the scientists." said Carina.

The group of people started to get larger as the news spread through the building.

The Pack made their way to the bottom of the stairs, where four security officers were standing.

"Hi, we're here to talk to the scientists," said Datch.

They were taken up the stairs and into one of the rooms on the top floor. After they had been shown in and sat down, another group of scientists came in, followed by a couple of IPSF officers who stood by the door.

"Good afternoon, everyone. I am Dr. Draycot. The IPSF have joined us for this meeting, and the Mellardrew are listening in. We have been reviewing the data you sent to the Mellardrew and want to ask you what you made of the, err, Marduks?"

"Yes, this planet is Marduk, and so we are calling them Marduks. Err, before we start though, can someone go and get us some lunch as we are not going to get a chance afterwards?"

Dr. Draycot looked at them for a moment and sighed.

"Okay, what do you want?" he said, and nodded to one of the officers next to the door.

The Pack reeled off a list of various items, and the officer noted them all down. Then, when they had finished, the officer disappeared through the door.

"Okay," said Datch, "let's try and tell you everything we felt and what we thought."

The meeting took about 50 minutes, during which several trays of food were consumed and several large cups of coffee were downed. As the meeting was drawing to a close, Dr. Draycot summed things up.

"Well, from what we can tell, they are technology level 200 or thereabouts. This would mean that they could join the IPSF, but they would need to advance in interspace systems. Their technology level in planetary control systems, however, seems to be very advanced, as your scanners have detected. They are using the planet's core as a very efficient power source. You have told us that they are pleasant enough and seem to be understanding about us being here. Would you agree, Commander?"

"Yes, Doctor. I am looking forward to meeting them. Datch, please use the channel you were using last night for comms."

"Yes, sir."

"Okay, gentlemen. I think we're done for now."

"Err, I just wanted to ask, is it okay if a number of us could go with Team Datch? After all, we are in charge of the planet."

"Sorry, Doctor. The Blackbird's crew are listed as IPSF ambassadors and you are not. They call the shots."

"Oh." said the doctor, looking a little surprised.

Datch started to grin.

"Commander, we'll be seeing you in about an hour, sir. Err, you don't happen to have any ice cream up there, do you?"

There was a pause.

"Datch, I'm not sure. Why?"

"Everyone likes ice cream."

"Do you want some at the meeting?"

"It would be nice." added Krissy.

"I shall look into it."

"Thank you, sir." said Datch.

Datch started to get up.

"Err... where are you going?" asked the doctor.

"To the bar." he replied.

The rest of the Pack got up and headed to the door.

The doctor looked at the security guard next to the door who just smiled and opened it for them.

The Pack walked down the stairs and were greeted with a security detachment of twenty troopers.

The front officer stepped forward.

"Sir, we are here as your security detail."

"Thank you, I have a feeling we may need you. We're going to the bar." said Datch.

The officer looked at the bar and then back at Datch.

"Yes, sir!"

The bar was full of people, but that was only until the security detail walked in. Everyone then decided to stand to the side a bit as they looked like they meant business.

Datch walked up to the bar and ordered a round of drinks. There was no queue, at least in the part of the bar where the troopers were.

The Pack went over and found that a number of chairs had also suddenly become vacant. They sat down.

"How long have we got?" asked Dapo.

Datch looked at his vid com.

"About three quarters of an hour. So just long enough to have a drink to steady our nerves."

He turned to the lead trooper who was standing next to him.

"Lieutenant, it might be an idea to let your troopers sit down. The rest of the bar looks worried."

The Lieutenant looked around and then said something into his headset. The rest of the troopers started to sit down and the bar breathed a sigh of relief.

"Lieutenant, are you coming with us all the way to the Mellardrew?" asked Carina.

"Yes, ma'am. Myself and four of the troopers are the Marduk's honour guard. The rest will stay on the planet until a shuttle comes down to collect them after we leave."

"Oh, cool."

"Err, your men will need to sit in the rec room during the flight to the Mellardrew. That is unless they want to stand in the cargo bay." said Datch.

"I'm sure your rec room will be fine, sir."

"That's sorted then. Err, can you try and make the Marduks feel at ease if possible. We don't want to frighten them."

"We have all been briefed on the situation and have been told to follow your lead, sir."

"Cool."

"Do you think we should put our posh clothes on?" asked Tish.

Datch looked at them. They were all wearing jeans and sweatshirts.

"Hmm, maybe we should. Trousers and shirts would look better. Come on, let's drink up and get changed."

They finished their drinks and stood up. The troopers all stood up again and then followed the Pack outside to the Blackbird.

Datch looked at the Blackbird and then at the troopers.

"Lieutenant, this might be a bit of a squeeze."

"We're used to being in tight spots, sir."

"Okay, if you say so."

The Pack headed into the Blackbird, with the troopers following behind. Then a queue formed on the steps leading up to the door.

Inside, the Pack sat down in their seats and then watched as the troopers came in, slowly filling up from the back of the Blackbird. There was even one standing in the bathroom. The Blackbird got fuller and fuller, with the troopers shuffling about until they were all in. The lieutenant ended up squeezing in behind Datch's chair.

"Everyone in?" asked Datch.

"Yes, sir," said the lieutenant.

Datch powered up the drive systems.

"Okay, hold on, folks," he said and increased power to the turbines.

The Blackbird headed out across the landing area and over to the Raven. The whole trip took five minutes, and as everyone was jammed in like sardines, no one fell over.

Datch pulled up alongside the Raven and shut the Blackbird down.

"If you guys want to get out first, please," said Datch.

"Yes, sir," said the lieutenant.

There was a lot of shuffling about, and then one by one, the troopers exited through the door.

The Pack then headed outside, and Datch led the troopers into the Raven's cargo bay.

"If you will excuse us a few moments, Lieutenant, we'll go and get changed," he said.

"Yes, sir."

The Pack headed off to their rooms to put their posh clothes on. Ten minutes later, Datch stuck his head around the cargo bay door.

"Lieutenant, if you would like to follow me to the cockpit and tell your troopers to get ready for liftoff."

The lieutenant followed Datch up to the cockpit and Datch asked him to sit in a chair at the back. The rest of the Pack were sitting in their seats and were now looking much more official in their posh clothes. Rosey was still trying to sort her blouse out, and Tish was doing something with Krissy's hair.

"Everyone ready?" asked Datch.

There was a lot of nodding.

Datch put his headset on.

"Raven, please switch the coms channel to 772 delta 2."

Datch pressed a few virtual buttons and there was a beep.

"Mellardrew, this is the Raven, ready for departure to the Thruster site."

"Good afternoon, Raven. We copy you. Flight paths in your area have been cleared. You are cleared to launch."

Datch increased power to the engines, and the Raven lifted off.

"How are we looking for time?" he asked.

"We have about ten minutes," said Dapo, who was sitting in the co-pilot's seat.

Datch hit the ship's comms.

"Zark, can you hear me?" Datch asked.

There was a short pause, and then a voice came over the cockpit speakers.

"Err, is it on? I think so. Do I press something? I don't think so. Just try talking. Oh, okay. Datch, I hear you." said Zark.

"We're on approach to the thruster site now. Should be there in three minutes."

"Okay, Datch, we're ready. The council members are inside waiting for my go-ahead."

"Okay, please be aware, we have a squad of troopers with us as an honour guard, so please don't be alarmed. It's sort of a protocol thing."

"I understand. We would do the same."

"Okay, you should see us in a moment."

Zark looked into the sky. A dark spot could be seen in the distance. Then it started to slowly get larger, and as it did, the noise of the thrusters could be heard. Zark watched as the black dot turned into a large black craft shaped like a giant bird.

"Wow, that's a nice paint job," said Plark.

"Yes, it's quite a ship, isn't it?" said Zark.

Quark was very quiet.

"Quark, are you okay?"

"Yes, I just don't like flying," he said nervously while clutching a small bag.

The Raven slowed down and came to a stop a little way from them. It then turned in the air, pointing its rear towards Zark, Plark, and Quark. On its underside, three panels slid open and landing feet dropped down. Then, slowly, the craft dropped down to the ground. The engines shut down, and a ramp dropped down at the back.

"Okay, Zark, we'll be out in a few moments."

"Okay, Datch. I'll tell the council members."

He turned to Quark.

"Can you go and fetch them, please?"

"Okay."

Quark went over to a small hatch in the ground and climbed down inside.

The Raven's cargo bay doors opened, and a number of troopers came running down and formed two lines on either side of the ramp facing inwards. Datch and the Pack came walking down and stopped at the bottom.

Behind Zark, the ground opened up, revealing a ramp leading down into the thruster. Three shuttle cars came up the ramp and stopped next to Zark and Plark. Quark got out, followed by Othred and Kratos. The doors of the other cars opened, and a number of other people got out, including Commander Natuk.

Quark, Othred, and Kratos walked over to Zark and Plark.

"Hmm, interesting paint job," said Othred.

"Yes, very green," added Kratos.

"Shall we go, gentlemen?" asked Othred.

They started to walk over to the Raven. Datch stepped forward and met them.

"Good to see you again, Councillor Othred," said Datch and held out his hand.

Othred shook his hand.

"Thank you, Datch."

"Good to see you again, Councillor Kratos."

They shook hands.

"Thank you."

"Please, follow me," said Datch, and then led the Marduk delegation inside.

The five troopers followed them inside, and the rest formed up into a line and headed to the left of the thruster to wait for a shuttle.

Inside the Raven, Datch led the delegation through the Raven and up to the cockpit.

"If you would like to sit here, please," said Datch, guiding the council members to the seats behind Dapo.

"And if you three can sit here," he said, pointing to the seats behind him. "You should all get a good view out of the front of the cockpit on the way up."

Zark and Plark sat down, and Quark sat in the seat behind them.

"Err, don't we need restraints of some kind?" Quark asked.

"No, the Raven has a dampening field and stabilizers. You won't feel a thing."

Quark didn't look impressed.

"If it will make you feel better, there is a lap belt you can put on under your seat."

Quark fished it out and put it on.

When everyone was seated, Datch went and sat in the pilot's seat.

"Okay, gentlemen, time to go."

Datch put on his headset and brought the engines online.

"Mellardrew, this is Raven. The delegation is onboard and we are ready for launch."

"Raven, this is Mellardrew. You are cleared for launch, on reaching orbit, lock on to beacon MEL232 for automated approach."

"Copy that, Mellardrew. Beacon MEL232."

Datch turned to the others.

"Here we go, folks."

He turned back to the front and increased power to the thrusters. The Raven slowly lifted into the air and then pointed its nose upwards. Datch pulled back on the main engines power control and the Raven shot into the sky.

Inside, Quark was waiting for the Raven to move and gripping his seat. After a few moments, he opened his eyes. Everyone was looking out of the front windows. Clouds were moving past outside.

"Err... are we moving?"

"Yes, we are accelerating and currently at twelve thousand kilometres per hour," said Dapo.

Outside, the sky started to get darker and darker. Then the stars came out and the planet's crescent could be seen below them.

"Wow," said Plark.

"You can say that again," added Zark.

The Raven flew higher and higher.

"That's quite a view, Ambassador," said Othred.

It took a moment for Datch to realize that Othred was talking to him.

"Sorry, sir, I was concentrating. Yes, it only gets better."

Datch started to lower power to the drive systems.

"Mellardrew, this is Raven. We have reached orbit and are locking on to beacon MEL232."

"What, we are in orbit already?" asked Othred.

"Yes, we are currently at an altitude of five hundred kilometres and travelling at a speed of thirty thousand kilometres per hour," said Dapo.

"Mellardrew, locked on to beacon. Raven is yours."

"Copy that, Raven. ETA nine minutes."

Datch relaxed and took his hands off the controls.

"Err, who is flying us?" asked Kratos.

"The Mellardrew has control and will guide us in on autopilot," said Datch, turning around.

Outside, the planet dropped below them and then they could only see stars.

"Do all your ships fly on autopilot?" asked Othred.

"They do most of the time. With IPSF ships, it is mandatory when approaching them."

"Hmm, very interesting."

Ahead of them, a star started to get a lot brighter.

"What's that?" asked Zark.

"That is the Mellardrew," said Datch, looking at the navigation display.

The star got bigger and bigger before turning into a huge starship. It was about twice the size of the Carpaycus and had two rows of smaller ships to its left. The Raven banked to the left and lined up to fly through the centre of the ships.

"That ship is huge," said Othred.

"I have to agree. I have never seen anything this big. Datch, you said these were science vessels?" asked Kratos.

"Yes, quite small ones by fleet standards. I've seen the big ones and they make this one look like the size of a shuttle."

"Yes, and the intergalactic ships are almost the size of small planets," added Dapo.

"That is impressive," said Kratos, looking at Othred.

"Raven, this is Mellardrew, you're on final. A welcome party will be waiting for you when you land."

"Copy that, Mellardrew."

The Raven flew between the shuttles that were all facing inwards. A large landing bay lay ahead of them with amber lights strobing inside to the landing pads. The Raven slowed to almost a stop as it entered the bay. A flash of sparkles passed over the Raven.

"What was that?" asked Quark, a little alarmed.

"It's just the forcefield keeping the landing bays pressurized. We don't dock, we land," said Dapo.

In front of them was a huge collection of ships laid out across the bay. The Raven flew deep inside the Mellardrew and then up ahead of them was a party of troopers and officers all in dress suits. The Raven slowed to a stop in front of them and turned facing away from them before landing gently on the pad. There was a loud clunk as the landing pad gripped the landing feet.

"Raven, you are clear to shut down your systems. The captain and commander are waiting for you on the pad."

"Thank you, Mellardrew. Shutting down. Raven out."

Datch shut the systems down and got up.

"Kratos, Othred, and honoured guests. Please follow me."

The Marduk delegation got up and followed Datch to the cargo bay, with the rest of the Pack who were now in ambassador mode following behind.

The troopers had headed to the cargo bay and were standing in a line next to the door.

Datch turned to Kratos.

"Kratos, how would you like me to introduce you all?"

"I am the leader of the Marduk Council, and this is my leader of planetary affairs. This is our security detail. Is that okay?"

"Yes, thank you."

Datch walked over and pressed the door release. The ramp dropped down and the door slid open, revealing the party below. The troopers all stood to attention as they walked past.

Datch walked down the ramp, followed by the Marduk delegation. He reached the party below and they all saluted. Datch saluted back.

One of the officers stepped forward.

"Hello, Ambassador Thome. I am Captain Taper of the Mellardrew, and this is my operations commander, Commander Santiny, who I believe you have spoken to?"

"Yes, Captain, he has been a great help. Commander." Datch said, looking at the commander and saluting.

"Captain, may I introduce the leader of the Marduk Council, Kratos."

"Pleased to meet you, sir." The captain said, and they all shook hands.

"And his leader of planetary affairs, Othred." Datch continued.

"Pleased to meet you, sir." The captain said again, and shook his hands.

"These are their security detail: Zark, Plark, and Quark."

They saluted.

"And of course, you will know my fellow ambassadors, Carina, Rosey, Tish, Krissy, Dapo, and Hagger."

"Welcome, ladies and gentlemen." The captain said.

They all nodded.

Krissy turned to Carina and whispered in her ear.

"When did I become an ambassador?"

"Just now, I think."

"But I don't know what to do?"

"Just don't get drunk and fall under the table like you did last month at the Barbers." Carina said, smiling at the commander.

"Oh, I had forgotten about that. I'll try not to." Krissy whispered.

"Ladies and gentlemen, if you would like to follow me to the reception suite, we have laid out a buffet for you where we can get to know each other." The captain said.

They followed the captain and commander down the corridor to one of the pods. It was lined with the ship's crew, who all saluted as they went past.

They reached the pod and went in.

"Forward observation suite," said the commander.

The pod doors shut and it started to move.

"Captain, this lift feels very different from ours," said Othred.

"It is not a lift as such. It travels horizontally as well as vertically. The pod can take you to almost anywhere on the ship."

"Very impressive, Commander. How far are we going?"

"We will be going up forty-one decks and it is approximately two kilometres to the front of the ship. We will be arriving at our destination in fifty seconds."

"It doesn't seem like we are moving."

"All the pods have dampening systems in, so you do not notice the pod's movements."

"That's very fascinating, Commander."

"The dampening systems are similar to the ones on the Raven," said Datch.

"Yes, Ambassador. That was a very smooth flight. I have been into space a few times, albeit several thousand years ago. However, I do remember a lot more shaking involved."

The pod's doors opened.

"Ladies and gentlemen, if you would like to follow me," said the captain.

The captain stepped out of the pod into the corridor. It was lined with crew members all in dress uniforms. The Pack followed Kratos and Othred up the corridor, and the commander followed behind.

The commander tapped Datch on the shoulder. Datch slowed and fell into step next to him.

"Yes, Commander?" he said quietly.

"I just wanted to let you know that operations on the planet have been stood down, and if the Marduks wish us to leave, we will. It will take a couple of weeks, though, to get everyone off the planet. I also wanted to let you know that we are picking up some unstable readings in the planet's core. Please take this and have a look at it before we make any rushed decisions."

He handed Datch a small tablet.

"Thank you, Commander. Are you not going to be leading the talks?"

"No, Ambassador. The leader of Welly Four has said we should let you do it, as you are very skilled in these matters."

"He did? Hmm... Commander, please remind me to send Widfab a message after we're done."

"Yes, Ambassador."

Datch looked down at the tablet and started reading the information.

They reached a set of doors with two very smartly dressed officers standing next to them. The captain walked in, followed by the rest of the party.

The room was very large and had a window running the full width of the room. Outside of the window, the planet was shining brightly in the light from its new star. Along one wall was a long table with food on it and on the back wall, was a bar with two officers waiting to serve them. In the centre was a large table with the exact number of chairs for them.

"Before we sit down, if you would like a drink, just ask and the staff will get it for you. Then we can get the formalities out of the way." The captain said, looking at Datch.

"Thank you, Captain. Kratos, Othred, if you would like to follow me, I'll explain what we have available. Then, you can scan it to check that it is not harmful to your race. We have passed the scans we took on the surface to the ship's biologists, and you are very similar to us biologically speaking. However, I suggest you scan the food and drinks just to be sure."

They followed Datch across to the bar.

"Datch, what are you having?" asked Kratos.

For a moment Datch thought a shot of old man's boots would be good at this point but then figured the delegation would try it and then he would have to explain to rest of the planet why their diplomatic team all came back drunk.

"I'll have a coffee, milk and sugar please."

"Any particular coffee sir?" asked the officer.

"Just a medium roast please."

"Coming right up sir."

There was a humming from a machine behind the bar.

"Coffee is similar to Poely and has the same type of effects on you as it does on us. I like a medium roast myself, but there is mild and rich roast as well."

The officer placed a cup of coffee on the counter.

"Please scan it." said Datch.

"Thank you."

Kratos looked at Plark, who had been given the job of scanning things. He walked up to the bar and pointed the scanner at the coffee. After a few seconds, it beeped. He looked at the screen for a moment.

"It is very close to Poely. We can drink it," he said.

"Datch, you say this is a medium roast and the rich is a stronger one?"

"Yes, sir."

"I think I'll try the same as you then, but rich please."

The officer nodded and the machine hummed again. After it had finished, the officer placed the drink on the counter.

Kratos picked it up and sniffed it before taking a sip. He savoured the taste for a while and then smiled.

"This is very nice," he said.

"Othred, what would you like?"

"I will have the same please."

There followed a queue at the bar, and the coffee machine worked overtime. Datch led Kratos and Othred over to the table and guided them to their seats. He found his seat and sat down. When everyone had sorted themselves out, the captain cleared his throat.

"Okay, ladies and gentlemen. Shall we get started?"

Everyone nodded.

"I would like to start by apologizing once again for invading your world. We have ceased all activity on the surface and have recalled all of our science teams back to their bases. However, it will take a couple of weeks to remove them from the surface and move them back to the space station. We have about twenty thousand people on the surface currently, and they are spread out across thirty bases. So, I'm sure you can understand the logistics involved in removing them."

"Yes, Captain. Thank you," said Kratos.

"We have a relay device for you if you wish it. It will allow direct communication with us, and we can keep you updated as to how we are doing. It is ready to go and can be placed wherever you wish it. Please understand, however, that it cannot transmit through the black ore that covers sections of your planet."

"Thank you, Captain. Ambassador, you were able to communicate through it, weren't you?"

"Yes, Kratos, we used an optical fibre running inside the mountain past the ore and into a relay. May I suggest that the site on the top of the mountain where we first made contact would be ideal if you wish it? It would allow easy access to your control centre below, where we could set up some sort of interface for you."

"Hmm... What do you think, Othred?"

"I feel that no matter what the outcome of this meeting, we should have a direct line of communication. It would help in future discussions and increase a better understanding between our races."

"Yes, I agree. Ambassador, could we implement that?"

"Yes. I will start the process after the meeting," said Datch, who looked at the Captain. The Captain nodded.

"Now, we are curious to know more about this IPSF?"

"Hmm. Where do I start? Over fifty thousand years ago, there were a group of twelve star systems who were fed up with all the wars that broke out around them. They decided to group together and form an alliance. But to stop any issue between them, they formed a battle fleet to police all the star systems. It was independent of any one world and was charged with keeping the peace. Over the next thousand years, more and more worlds joined this alliance, and it was decided that none of the worlds should be the centre of power.

They decided to create a new world for the purpose of holding the seat of power. Olympus Prime was born. It is where all the worlds meet and create the laws that govern us.

The IPSF fleet grew with every star system that joined, and now it spans six galaxies. We all live in peace and prosperity, secure in the knowledge that the IPSF will keep us safe."

"You said that you still have a government on your planet?" asked Kratos.

"Yes, we do. All the worlds have their own governments and oversee their own worlds. The IPSF just makes sure everyone behaves, I suppose."

"How do you even manage to talk across that kind of distance?" asked Othred.

"Interspace nodes. Remember how I said we travel between the stars? The same technology is used to open tiny tunnels through the fabric of space. This allows for fast communication across the huge distances. For instance, my parents live on Bellatrix Five, and if I sent them a message, it would take about a week to get there. That's two thousand light years away. But if I sent a message to the space station two and a half light years away, the transit time would be about five minutes."

"Hmm… And you would share this technology with us?"

Datch looked thoughtful for a moment. "We would, depending on a number of things."

"Things?"

"Yes. We would need to know that you are not a warlike race and that you are not likely to become one. Also, the technology exchange would be in line with your technology level. What I mean by that is that we would help you develop new technology, but we won't just give it to you. If you can understand that?"

Kratos sat back for a moment and looked thoughtful.

"Hmm..." he said after a moment. "Yes, I can sort of understand that. We wouldn't want to give a less developed race our technologies."

Datch sat back in his chair and looked at Carina.

'Your turn,' came his voice in her head.

'Thanks.'

"Kratos, maybe you can give us a rundown of your recent history, as that may help us understand you as a people?" she asked.

"Yes. You have been very open with us. Why not? We have been asleep quite a while, but before then we were a peaceful race. Most of our efforts were on making our world a paradise. We did have some colonies on other planets in our system, but they will have been destroyed when the star went nova. We did launch two colony ships to nearby stars, but we could not send everyone on them. It was then we decided to move the planet. It was a final attempt to save everyone."

Kratos paused for a second and looked down. Datch was watching him.

"Kratos, you are not telling us everything, are you?"

Kratos looked at Datch, trying to work out what he knew.

"What do you mean?" he asked.

Datch picked up the tablet in front of him.

"There is something going on under the surface of your planet. We are detecting that the core is becoming unstable."

Kratos looked at Othred and then back at Datch.

"You can detect that?"

"Yes, and it concerns us."

Kratos looked back at Othred. He nodded slowly.

"Your sensors are correct, Ambassador. The planet's core is unstable. Our systems are trying to control it, but we have a few issues."

"Issues?"

"Yes. The fusion drives were designed to dump excess heat into the core to try and keep the inner planet warm during the trip. However, some of our systems have failed during the journey, and the flow control systems are not transferring the heat to the oceans as we planned. The exhaust vent you found is an emergency pressure release system. We are trying to fix things, but most of our people are still in stasis and cannot be brought back as a number of power systems have failed."

Datch looked at the captain.

"Captain, would we be able to help stabilize the core?"

"We could send a team of engineers down and see if we can help, but we would need to understand the systems."

Datch turned back to Kratos.

"Kratos, would you like our help?"

He sighed.

"Ambassador, we would be very happy to have your help, but what would you want in return?"

"We would only want to get to know you as a people. Nothing more. And if you wish to open full diplomatic links afterwards, we can discuss that when the time comes. Captain, can you display the core's current status?"

"Yes. Computer, please display the planet's core below, highlighting any instabilities."

A hologram appeared above the table, showing areas of turbulence. The image was not looking good.

"Oh god!" said Othred.

"Yes, it's worse than we thought." Said Kratos.

"Kratos, how can we help?"

"We need to activate the other control systems to stabilize the core, but we have lost too many power generators to do it."

"Hmm... so you need power. Captain, would it be okay if I took an engineering team to the planet to see if we can help? That is, if it is okay with you, Kratos?"

"After seeing the current status of the core, any help would be welcome."

"Captain?"

"Yes, I shall organize it immediately after this meeting."

"Okay. Kratos, to aid the speed of the operation, please instruct your people to be open with ours. I know you have only just met us, so people are going to be wary of each other. But it could be a very short relationship if they are not. Things could go wrong in a bad way for the planet if we cannot stop the core instability."

"Yes, I understand. I will try my best. Can we get a copy of your data on the core? It may help us convince our people."

"I'm sure we can. We may have to give you a couple of devices for you to display it on, as we need to work out how to connect to your systems in a meaningful way."

"I'll instruct our engineers to give you all the help they can."

"Good. Hopefully, gentlemen, we can save your world. Now that we have come to an arrangement, let us try to relax while the captain's crew sorts out the engineering team and a communication relay."

"Thank you, Ambassador. If you excuse us, we will get straight on it. If you need me, just use the ship's comms." said the captain.

They all stood up and the captain saluted.

"Thank you, Captain. Thank you very much." Said Kratos.

The captain and commander left the room.

"OK, Gentlemen. Let's have something to eat. I'm hoping they have found some ice cream, It's one of my favourites."

"Can I ask something?" Asked Othred.

"Yes, ask away." Replied Datch.

"You are all ambassadors, yet you are all here exploring our planet, why?"

"We're on holiday. We spend a lot of time travelling between stars with our day job. So, exploring a new world, light years from anywhere is a nice relaxing break. Well, it was meant to be."

"I see what you mean. I would imagen being a ambassador over vast distances can take it out of you?"

Datch stopped and looked at hm. He thought being ambassadors was their normal job.

"The ambassador bit is only part time, our main job is making music, we're a galactic rock band. Well, half of it anyway. But we have a habit for saving worlds."

"That's very interesting. How many have you saved?"

"I think it's one president, one King and two entire star systems at the current count. This one will make three."

"Do they normally make rock stars ambassadors in the IPSF?"

"Oh no. That just sort of happened. It was Welly Four that made us ambassadors after was saved their race from the darkness. We have also been made their spiritual leaders as well which can be a bit painful due to all the bowing."

"That's fascinating."

They reached the buffet table. Plark was standing next to it with a scanner.

"Everything is okay to eat, sir," he said to Kratos.

"Thank you, Plark. Datch, what do you recommend?"

"The vol-au-vents are very nice, as well as the Hacks legs in sauce. And for dessert, I can strongly recommend the chocolate ice cream."

"This salad looks very fresh," said Othred.

"It will have been grown on board ship. Ships this size will have their own hydroponic growing area in the centre of the ship. This allows them to have fresh fruit and vegetables in flight. The meat will be replicated, though."

"Replicated?" asked Kratos.

"Yes, it's synthetic. Machine-made, but you can't tell. Even the steaks taste really good."

"That's very interesting," said Othred, taking a bite out of a Hacks leg.

"Plark, what do you make of all this?" asked Tish.

"It's amazing. I've always wanted to go into space. But most of our ships were tiny by comparison, and I never got the chance. Can I ask you what the other worlds you've been to are like?"

Tish smiled at him.

"They're mostly beautiful places, with shining cities and amazing vistas. One of my favourites is Luyten Seven. There's a beach resort there that we sometimes go to. It has a pink sandy beach with palm trees blowing in a soft breeze. The turquoise-coloured sea laps slowly on the shoreline, and above, little white clouds float by. It's also very private, so we can totally relax without the fear of fans turning up and mobbing us."

"I would love to go to a world like that. I don't remember our world being beautiful. By the time I was born, the sun had already started to expand. The forests were starting to die, and the planet's surface was being ravaged by storms. We were living underground in the cities below."

"What's it like down there?"

"It's not good at the moment. Power blackouts and poor air circulation are making living difficult. But until we fix the systems, we have to put up with it."

Tish looked at him for a moment.

"Well, together we'll fix your world," she said.

Othred had been standing behind him, listening to what they were saying.

"Yes, Plark, we'll fix our world and make it beautiful again. But it's going to take time."

Datch and Kratos had taken their plates and walked over to the window. Outside, the world was going by below, with one of its oceans in view. It was still partly covered in ice, but here and there, water could be seen where the surface was starting to melt under the heat from the new sun.

Kratos sighed.

"Datch, do you think we can save our world? That readout didn't look very good."

"Kratos, from what we've seen of your technology, I'm sure with a bit of help, we can get your world going again. We seem to be about five hundred years or so ahead of you technologically, but your Geotech is not far behind ours. I'm sure we can do this, and in the process, I think we can become good friends."

"You know, for a leader of a rock band, you make a very good ambassador."

Datch laughed.

"I suppose the two jobs are not that different. On stage, I make sure the audience have a great time by making music for them, and here, I make sure you have a great time by making good things happen for you."

"That is a very unique way of looking at things, Ambassador Datch."

He laughed.

Just at that point, Othred walked up.

"Ah, Othred. How are you finding the food?" asked Datch.

"It is very nice, Datch. Thank you. Kratos, I've been thinking. We are going to need a person to act as a liaison between our world and the rest of the err, galaxy."

"Hmm, I think you are right, but all of those sorts of people are still in stasis and are not due to be woken up yet. What are you thinking?"

"It may seem a bit strange, but I think Plark would be good. He seems to welcome our new friends and is very excited about being above ground."

"Hmm… I'm not sure Natuk will be happy about losing him, but if you think it would work then I'm happy to try it."

He turned to look across the room.

"Plark, can we have a word, please?"

Plark looked up and then walked across the room to them.

"Yes, sir?"

"We've just been discussing the situation, and if you're willing, we'd like you to be our liaison between our world and the IPSF. It would help things move faster. It will, however, mean that you'll need to spend time above ground."

A smile started to spread across his face.

"Yes, sir."

"It will more than likely mean you'll have to come into space more or even go to other worlds."

The smile was now a very big grin.

"I'm sure I can cope with it, sir."

Kratos looked at him and then at Othred. He just shrugged his shoulders.

"Okay then. You're promoted, but please try not to grin so much."

Plark tried not to grin and totally failed. In fact, the grin just looked worse.

They carried on discussing different worlds and how the IPSF worked for another hour, and then the captain came back.

"Good afternoon again, ladies and gentlemen. I've arranged for a team of engineers to be ready to follow you down to the surface. We've also got a relay system ready with a planetary transceiver array, as well as several communication terminals for the use of the Marduks."

"That's wonderful, Captain. Thank you," said Datch.

"Yes, that's very good news. Thank you," said Kratos.

"Is it possible to have a projector for use in the council chamber so we can show them the issues? It may help convince the rest of the council about the urgency of the matter," asked Othred.

"Yes, I'll have a portable one added to the lead shuttle," said the captain.

"Thank you, Captain. That will help a lot," added Kratos.

"Kratos, it might be an idea if we head to the exhaust vent on the way down. Then our engineers can start work on installing the transceiver array," suggested Datch.

"Hmm, yes. The sooner we can have a permanent line of communication, the quicker we can get the planet back on its feet. Quark, can you go down in the lead shuttle and help them get the transceiver set up?"

"Yes, sir."

"Captain, I take it you can relay all your data through the link?"

"Yes, sir. However, you will need a way to use it, and until we find a way to interface to your systems, it will be limited. The systems we're sending down will display the data as well as being able to analyse it, but we'll have to train your people to use it. I think it would be faster to focus our efforts on getting an interface working."

"Yes, I agree, but I will need to talk to the council about it. Datch, would it be possible for you and your fellow ambassadors to come and meet with the council when we get back to the planet? It may help."

"Yes, Kratos, but can we have dinner first? The buffet was excellent, but I really could do with a full meal beforehand."

"Ambassador, if you wish, you could use our forward lounge if that would help?" said the captain.

"What do you think, guys? I could really go for a steak."

"Can we have a beer?" asked Dapo.

"Well, just one or you're staying on the Raven." Said Tish.

"Forward lounge?" asked Kratos.

"Yes, It's where the crew eat and relax, Councillor," said the captain.

"Would it be okay if we took the delegation with us?" asked Carina.

"Well, yes, but it's getting towards its busy period. It might be a little lively."

"That would be very interesting, Captain. This is a fact-finding meeting after all. Seeing your crew relaxing will give us an insight into your culture or cultures."

"Okay. But I do apologize in advance if anyone causes offence."

"Great. Captain, I take it it's set out similar to the Carpaycus?" asked Datch.

"Yes, Ambassador, but we have three levels. I believe the Carpaycus only has two."

"Yes, Captain. Can I suggest a nice upbeat bar with some lively music and enough tables for all of us?" said Krissy, joining in.

"Hmm, okay. Please follow me."

The captain walked over to the officer at the bar.

"Tell the commander that the delegation is coming to the forward lounge for dinner in an upbeat bar."

"Yes, Sir."

The captain walked to the door.

"This way, please," he said.

The delegation followed him up the corridor to a waiting pod and walked in.

The captain turned to Datch after instructing the pod where to go.

"Ambassador, this is a little unorthodox."

"This whole situation is a bit bizarre, Captain. But lucky for you, The Pack do bizarre a lot."

"I suppose so. Oh, by the way, the President of Welly Four is on his way. He should be here in about two days' time."

Datch looked at him.

"Oh, we'd better hurry up then."

"Why?"

"Let's just say he likes to party. So, the sooner we can get the planet stable, the more likely it is to survive."

"Oh."

"Err, how's he getting here so quickly? It's nearly three thousand light years." asked Hagger, who was sitting next to Datch.

"They have just commissioned their new Destroyer and want to try it out. Apparently, it can reach interspace thirty."

"At that speed, they could be here in an hour."

"I think they are still ironing out the bugs in the systems and also they still need to load supplies."

"Captain, could I ask you a favour?" asked Datch.

"It depends on what it is, Ambassador."

"Could you keep Widfab occupied until things are a little more, err, stable?"

"Occupied?"

"Yes, tell him the planet is unstable and we're fighting to stabilize it, which is not far from the truth. Therefore, it's not safe to go down just yet. Or something along those lines. Hmm... Thinking about it, let me know when he arrives and I'll talk to him. These folks are new to our culture and I don't want them getting the wrong idea about us."

"I see what you mean. Okay, I'll delay him until you're able to talk to him."

"Thank you, Captain."

"Is everything alright?" asked Kratos.

"Yes, Kratos. There is a planetary leader coming to the star system soon and will want to meet with you. We were just discussing when it was likely to be."

"I will look forward to it. Is he or she coming far?"

"About three thousand light years."

"Does that mean it's going to take about two or three weeks for him to get here?"

"No, about two or three days."

"You'll have to excuse me. The speed at which you people travel at is taking some getting used to."

"That's okay, Kratos. I'm sure you'll get the hang of it."

"We should arrange a reception for him?"

"Not at the moment. Let's fix your planet first."

The pod came to a stop and they exited into the corridor. This was a busy part of the ship, and a lot of people were going back and forth. The delegation headed up the corridor and through a set of double doors.

Inside was the forward lounge. In front of them were a large set of stairs leading up to a landing and the first floor. Then another flight of stairs went up from there to the top floor.

The commander came over to them.

"Captain, I have secured a large booth in the chill-out zone. The atmosphere is a bit more relaxed in that area."

"Thank you, Commander. Please lead the way."

The lower level was set out in a similar way to the Carpaycus, with small areas with different styles of music and décor. Each area was separated by a trellis with various plants growing on them, and a forcefield stopping the noise from the adjacent areas. They followed the commander through groups of crew members all enjoying themselves, and arrived at two security officers who stood to the side when they approached.

Behind them was an area with warm lighting and a small bar. The seats had been arranged so that everyone could sit around a central table.

"Councillor Kratos, if you would like to sit here," said the commander.

He went around making sure everyone was seated before saluting and disappearing to attend to other duties.

"So, what now, Ambassador?" asked the captain.

"Kratos, how much do you trust me?" asked Datch, turning to look at him.

"Trust? I'm not sure yet, but I do think you are an honourable man."

"Good enough. Captain Jaxx, steaks and Weega fries all round. Also, a round of Bellatrixian ale if you have it?"

"I believe we can do that." He nodded at an officer who was standing next to him.

"Bellatrixian ale?" asked Othred.

"Yes, it's from my home world and is a popular drink there. It's not a strong ale and shouldn't cause any problems with your bodies."

"How do you know?"

"When you came onboard, the systems automatically carry out a bio scan to make sure you're not carrying biohazards. During the process, it does a genetic scan to make sure nothing on the ship will harm you. I know this may seem a little invasive, but it's for your own safety. It does mean, however, that you can enjoy the steaks that are about to appear shortly, along with the beers, with the knowledge that all you'll get is a hangover if you drink too much ale."

"You have our genetic makeup?"

"Yes, but it will be deleted on your departure. So, do not feel that it is anything more than for your own safety. And please enjoy the steaks."

"Hmm. How do we know your intentions are not covert?"

Datch sat back and looked at them for a moment.

"Okay, I know you're still trying to get your head around things, but put it this way. The IPSF have the power not only to destroy worlds but entire star systems along with their suns. If we felt you were a major threat to the galaxy, you would not be here. A single shot from one of our star destroyers, and that would be it. So do not be threatened by us. We mean you no harm. We are here to help. I just wanted to make that clear."

"Was that a threat?"

"No, no, please don't misunderstand us. We don't do that. It's just a statement."

The steaks started coming out.

"Please, gentlemen, enjoy your steaks," said Datch.

"Datch, you seem to be going out of your way to help us. Why?" asked Kratos.

"It's what I do."

"Kratos, Datch and the rest of us have a soft spot for anyone that needs help. When we can get your language added to the galactic database, you should be able to look up the Pack. Then you will see we are nothing more than what we say." said Carina.

"Your steak will get cold, Kratos. Please eat. This is a bar, not a reception room," said Dapo.

The delegation started eating their steaks, and the Bellatrixian ale was going down well. Soon, everyone was fed and watered.

"Kratos, shall we head back to your planet?" said Datch.

"Yes, the sooner we can fix the core, the better."

"Captain, if you would like to lead the way."

They got up and headed to the landing bay.

The captain led the way back to the Raven. It had been turned around and moved over to a group of four large shuttles. There was a group of officers standing at the back of the Raven.

The delegation walked up to them.

"Kratos, these are our engineering commanders. Leading the task force to help save your world is Commander Sormin. He will be your main point of contact," said the captain.

"Commander," said Kratos. He saluted.

"And this is our power systems team leader, Commander Ripple."

"Pleased to meet you, Commander. We are in dire need of your services."

"I shall try my best for you, sir." He then saluted.

They worked their way along the row of officers until they reached the rear of the Raven.

Kratos turned to face the captain.

"Well, Captain, it has been a very interesting visit. You will have to come and visit us next time."

"Yes, that would be interesting also. I hope we can save your world and form a long-lasting friendship."

"I do too, Captain, or we may be coming to live with you."

Datch turned to face the captain.

"Captain," he said, and saluted.

"Ambassador," said the captain, and saluted back.

"Kratos, if you would follow me." said Datch.

They headed inside the Raven. This time without the honour guard. After everyone was seated, Datch put on his headset.

"Mellardrew, this is Raven, ready for departure," he said.

"Copy that, Raven. Power up your systems and switch to dual band. Four Delta four. That will be your comms channel to the other shuttles," the Mellardrew replied.

"Copy that. Switching to dual band now," Datch said. He pressed a few buttons and brought the engines online. Then the comms burst into life.

"Shuttle Gamma ready for launch," said a voice.

"Shuttle Beta ready for launch," said another voice.

"Shuttle Alpha ready for launch," said a third voice.

"Shuttle Delta ready for launch," said a fourth voice.

"Raven, this is Mellardrew. Lock onto beacon MEL772 and prepare for launch," Mellardrew instructed.

Datch pressed a few buttons.

"Locked on to beacon, Mellardrew. Ready when you are," he said.

Under the Raven, there was a loud clunk as the dock clamps released. The Raven started to move towards the exit. It reached the doors and then accelerated quickly.

Behind it, the other shuttles followed in a V formation towards the planet.

"Beacon will clear in thirty seconds, Raven," the voice on the other end said.

"Copy that," Datch said.

"Raven, this is shuttle Alpha. We are following your lead, sir," said the voice of the pilot of shuttle Alpha.

"Okay, Alpha. Copy that."

"Raven, this is Mellardrew. The Raven is yours."

"Thanks, Mellardrew."

Datch banked the Raven towards the planet. Below them, a frozen ocean glistened in the early evening light. In the upper atmosphere ice crystals created prisms that separated the light from the star into a multitude of colours, causing rainbows across the surface of the planet.

Planet Side

The Raven plunged into the atmosphere, its shields lighting up with fiery plasma as it descended.

Quark's knuckles were turning white as he gripped the seat, waiting for the shaking to start. Plark, on the other hand, was almost out of his seat trying to see out the front windows as the Raven headed down towards the surface.

"You still with us back there, Alpha?" asked Datch.

"Yes, sir. Just enjoying the view," came the response.

Below them, the thruster site came into view. There were also a number of lights around it that were lighting up the area. This didn't matter to Datch as his heads-up display was showing him everything.

"Touchdown in one minute. Looks like someone put the lights on," said Datch.

"Don't you need lights?" asked Quark.

"No, look," said Dapo, pressing a couple of buttons.

The vid screen above them displayed the view from out of the front of the Raven. The image looked like daylight.

The Raven's landing thrusters fired, slowing the Raven almost to a stop. Datch dropped the ship gently onto the surface and he shut down the engines.

"Okay, folks. You're home," he said, getting up.

"Datch?"

"Yes, Kratos?"

"I just wanted to say that no matter what happens, thank you for all your help."

"You're welcome, Kratos. Now let's go save your planet."

Datch got up and they all followed him to the cargo bay.

"I will need to talk to the council before you will be able to start work on the core, but if your engineers want to fit the communications array, I'll instruct my people to help you."

"Sounds good."

"If it's okay with you, I would like you to come to the council meeting. That way if they ask any questions, hopefully you can answer them."

"When do you think it will be?"

"I'll call it as soon as I get back to the main complex. So maybe three hours?"

"Would it be helpful if we are on hand all the time?"

"Yes, indeed, but our living areas are a bit basic at the moment."

"What if we bring our own?"

"Own?"

"Zark, is there somewhere to park the Blackbird near the main complex?"

"Blackbird? Oh, the vehicle. Yes, there is parking near the crater entrance close to the lifts."

"If we bring that inside then we will have our own accommodation. Would that be acceptable?"

"Yes, that would be fine. Would you need some form of communications system?"

"No, the Blackbird has them all onboard. It will connect to the relay when it is up and running. Dapo, could you go and fetch it? I'm sure one of the shuttles will take you."

"Sure."

"Hagger, can you take the main group to get the transceiver running and show them where the beacon is so they can set it up?"

"Yes, Datch."

"Zark, you go with Ambassador Dapo and escort him back. Quark, if you go with Ambassador Hagger and help get the communications up and running." said Kratos.

"Are we ready?"

"Yes."

Datch dropped the ramp down and they walked outside.

Natuk was waiting for them with a group of men and a number of council members.

"Councillor, is everything alright? You have been gone a while." asked Natuk, stepping forward.

"We are fine. It has been an enlightening experience. However, the planet's core is in a worse state than we thought. These people have agreed to help us if we wish it, and I have agreed to let them set up a communications link while I call a council meeting to discuss things."

"Othred, do you agree?" asked Natuk.

"Yes, Commander. I totally agree."

"Commander, I need you to help these people set up communications with their ships in orbit. Quark is going with them, and Zark is going with Ambassador Dapo to fetch their vehicle, so they have somewhere to stay until the planet is safe." said Kratos.

"Yes, sir." said Natuk.

"Are you sure about this, Kratos?" said one of the other councillors.

"Yes, Deimos. If we don't, we're dead. I'll show you what I've seen at the council meeting."

"Commander Natuk, it may be an idea if your senior staff are there too. We need everyone to understand this."

"Yes, sir."

The officer from one of the shuttles now came walking over.

"Ambassador." he saluted.

"Commander. Please could you bring the holographic emitter with the planetary data on and let me have it to take with me, and if possible, one of your men to help set it up. Then if you could please follow Hagger and Dapo. They will inform you of what is happening. Please follow their instructions."

"Yes, sir."

"Thank you."

"Ambassadors, if you would like to follow me." said Kratos, and started to move towards a group of vehicles.

He stopped and looked. There were six shuttle cars and about thirty-five people.

"This may be a squeeze."

"Kratos, how stable is the crater?"

"Err, Natuk?"

"The only unstable bit is the section where the exhaust vent is. The rest is solid rock. Why?"

"Well, it would be easier to fly there and use the entrance we took the Blackbird through last time. Also, we can do the whole trip in about ten minutes instead of the two hours it took last time."

"That sounds like a wonderful idea, Datch. The other council members can see your ship and you to Commander Natuk." said Kratos.

"Err, yes sir." said Natuk, with a slightly frustrated look on his face.

"Fellow councillors, as it is going to be somewhat of a squeeze to get us all in the cars, we have been offered a faster route to the main complex. Our friends are going to give us a ride in their ship." said Kratos loudly.

The other council members looked at him and then at the Raven.

"They are?" asked one of them.

"Yes, and before you ask, it is a very nice ride," Kratos replied.

They looked at the Raven again, with the green flames coming down the wings, which were lit up by the flood lights.

"Really, it is," Othred added, sensing that they needed reassurance.

Just then, the officer from the shuttle came back with another crewman carrying a sphere-shaped device with a flat bottom.

"Ambassador, this is Science Officer Japato. She will be able to set up the system and answer any questions you have about the data contained within it."

"Thank you, Commander. Sorry, but there's been a slight change of plan. We're taking the Raven to the crater as well. It was either that or try and get everyone in the cars over there."

The commander looked at the cars.

"I see what you mean, sir. Is Shuttle Two still taking Ambassador Dapo to Omega Seven?"

"Yes, Commander. All the other shuttles are to follow me. We will be landing in the crater away from the exhaust vent. If you land next to us, you should be good."

"Yes, sir."

"Thanks, get your people ready for liftoff."

The shuttle commander left and headed back to the shuttle.

The other councillors came walking over. As they did, Natuk told a couple of his officers to go and tell command to open the crater service entrance.

"Okay, folks. Let's go," said Datch.

He led the way back to the Raven, and after a short stop in the cargo bay to look at the bikes, they headed up to the cockpit. Datch waited until everyone was seated and had a good look at everything.

"Okay, folks, time to go," he said.

He put on his headset and powered up the systems.

"Raven to shuttles, ready for launch."

"Please standby, Raven. Shuttle Three is lifting off now."

They waited while one of the other shuttles lifted into the air and headed off into the distance.

"Okay, Raven. After you."

"Copy that."

Datch increased power and the Raven lifted off and started to climb in height. Behind them, the other shuttles followed suit.

Natuk was watching everything intently. Carina, who was sitting in the co-pilot's seat, noticed and turned on the vid screen so he could see the view outside.

"There you go, folks. You'll be able to see what Datch can see." she said.

The Raven was in the air for only a few minutes before the crater came into sight. Datch spotted the tracks left by the Blackbird the day before on his heads-up display and brought the Raven in for a landing near where they disappeared into the rockface. The other shuttles came into land behind them.

Datch shut down the systems.

"Okay, folks, we're here."

He got up and waited for everyone to get up before heading to the cargo bay.

They had just walked outside when there was a noise to the left of them. They turned just in time to see a jet of lava come shooting over the edge of the cliff and landing on a mound of rock on the crater floor.

"That's the third time today," said Natuk.

"Third?" asked Datch.

Natuk looked at Kratos.

"Yes, third. The pressure is building up. While we were in deep space, it wasn't an issue as the heat being lost was greater than that being generated. Now the star is supplying heat as well as with the heat dumped from the engines, things are not going as they should. We need to get the core pumps working to heat the oceans. Our scientists calculated that the heat transferred to the oceans would cool the core enough to stabilise it. But unfortunately, seventy-five percent of the pumps are offline and we can't get them back on without power."

Just then, Commander Sormin came walking over.

"Hello, Commander."

"Ambassador. What is that?"

"That, Commander, is an emergency release vent. There are many of them around the planet, releasing heat from the planet's core. From what I understand, the vents should be passing the heat into the oceans, but the pumps are not working."

"Are we good to start operations?" Asked Sormin looking at Datch. He nodded.

"Mission is a go," he said into his comms.

The shuttle reversed over the edge of the gallery and its rear opened, allowing the engineers to exit into the gallery with all their equipment. It was starting to move away from the mountaintop when the mountainside next to the Raven opened up, revealing a tunnel.

Eight shuttle cars appeared in the opening and, one after another, made their way to the back of the Raven.

"Thank you, Datch. This was a lot quicker than the shuttle cars, and to be honest, the two-hour journey in the tunnel was not something I was looking forward to," said Kratos.

"You're welcome, sir."

"Shall we go?" said Natuk, indicating to the shuttle cars.

They all headed across to the little vehicles.

"Commander Sormin, if you and some of your team would like to get in the last car, I'll send them back with a transport car for the rest of your team and your equipment," said Natuk.

"Thank you, Commander Natuk."

The inside of the little vehicles was laid out with three seats at the front and three seats at the back. The driver would sit in the middle seat and control the little craft.

They all got into the little vehicles and they set off into the mountain. This time, instead of branching off and heading to the main tunnel, the shuttle cars headed to a number of what looked like parking bays and stopped. A grill appeared at the back of them and shortly afterwards the bays started moving down.

"Oh, these are lifts," said Carina.

"Yes, they are taking us down to the operations level."

"How far down is that?" she asked.

"About forty levels. It's the same level you were on when you were here last time."

The lift started to slow down and then came to a stop in front of another gate. The gate opened and they drove out and down another tunnel before arriving at a large area.

The trip had only taken ten minutes to complete. Then the little cars pulled into a number of bays at the side of another smaller tunnel. The area was brightly lit and had been painted white at some point in the past, but now the paint was starting to flake off in places.

They got out and waited for the others to come over.

"Okay, Ambassadors. Natuk will look after you. Commander, maybe you can get one of your team to give them a tour of the facility?"

"Yes, I'm sure I can arrange that."

"Datch, if you and Officer Japato could follow me, we can set up the projector in the council chambers. We can get a cup of Poely while the council assembles as well."

"Sounds good, Kratos. Please lead the way."

Datch and Japato went with Kratos down the tunnel.

"Ambassadors, if you would like to follow me," said Natuk.

They followed him through another small tunnel and into an area with three levels.

The inside was like a large shopping mall with restaurants, bars, and a number of shops. The shops were unfortunately shut, apart from one selling fresh water. There were however a few of the Marduk population sitting outside the bars and restaurants who looked at them closely as they went by.

"This is the main area for this facility and is where we all come to relax."

"It's not very big," said Rosey.

"Well, the plan was to keep people in stasis until we start to reclaim the surface of our world. That bit is not going to plan."

They walked over to a bar with seats outside. Two officers jumped up and saluted.

"Ambassadors, this is Commander Talzanken and Commander Ripeples. They will look after you when I'm not about."

The commanders looked at them, not sure what to say.

"Commanders, these are Ambassadors from the IPSF. As you will be aware from the last briefing, things are not going well. They will be helping our world. I know you will make things run as smooth as possible."

They both saluted.

They party carried on with the tour.

When they had gone Commander Talzanken turned to Commander Ripeples.

"What do you think?"

"They look ok and judging by the last lot of readings I've seen; we need all the help we can get."

"Yes, but they are aliens."

"And?"

"Well, you know."

"No, I don't. They have come across space to our world and from what I've heard have been more than open with us. We need their help. Or would you rather die in a magma explosion?"

"Well, when you put it like that."

"Ok then, let's get another beer. Hey, you never know, they may have descent beer up above?"

"Now that would be a miracle."

They knocked back their drinks and went back into the bar to get some more.

On the other side of the complex, Datch and Japato followed Kratos into a large chamber.

They headed to the stage and stood next to the podium.

"If you could set up the projector here so everyone can see it, that would be great," asked Kratos.

"Yes, sir," said Japato.

Datch and Japato set up the system and turned it on. An image of the planet's core appeared in the air above the stage.

"How's that?" asked Japato.

"Very good, officer. Thank you. Datch, if you would like to come here for a moment."

Datch walked up to the podium and stood next to Kratos.

He showed him the controls to let him speak to the chamber and explained how It would light up the questioner with a bright light. Afterwards, they headed to the back of the stage and into a small room with a coffee machine and a few chairs. Kratos made sure Datch and Japato were happy and then went to wait for the council to assemble.

The council chambers soon filled up, and half an hour later, Kratos stepped up to the podium.

"I hereby declare the council is now in session."

He paused for a moment.

"Fellow councillors of Marduk, I have called you here for an emergency session. I am very sorry, but I am a bearer of grave news. As you know, Othred and I have travelled to the aliens' spacecraft. While we were on board, we were given information about our planet's core. I am sure you are all aware of the instabilities and the problems we are having, but from the data we have seen, the situation is much worse. One of their ambassadors is waiting to answer any of our questions, and one of their science officers has kindly come to show you all the data that we have seen. I should like to add that at least some of the data has been verified since our return, and the rest is being processed as we speak. I have proposed a temporary treaty with them to allow their engineers to help fix our world, and then we can decide if we wish to join this IPSF."

He stopped and waited.

A light came on over one of the councillors.

"Kratos, are you that sure we can trust them?"

"Yes, Councillor. They have given me and Othred no reason not to."

Another light came on.

"And they are not after our technology?"

"No, Councillor. Their technology is much more advanced than ours. I doubt they would learn a thing from us. If anything, it will help advance ours."

Another light came on.

"You say they are from another star system?"

"Yes, Councillor. In fact, multiple star systems. While we were on board, we noticed a number of different types of aliens. All were humanoid in shape, and they were working and relaxing together."

The light came on again.

"Relaxing?"

"Yes, the starship is that big it has its own bars and restaurants. It even has its own ecosystem."

Another light came on.

"Kratos, how big was this ship?"

"It was about sixty stories high and a few miles long. Anyway, Councillor, we are detracting from the purpose of this meeting. If you wish to see for yourself, I am sure they would be happy to show you. What you need to do is decide if you wish them to help us fix our world."

He paused. No lights came on.

"Okay, Councillors, please wait while I go and fetch their ambassador and science officer."

Datch was sitting with Japato waiting to be called in.

This wasn't like a gig. Datch knew how to do that, you just went on stage and started singing. This was different. He was going to be standing in front of an alien race trying to be diplomatic. If he said the wrong thing, the planet could end up being destroyed. He let out a sigh.

"Are you okay, Ambassador?" asked Japato.

"Yes, I just have the fate of this planet on my shoulders and I'm hoping I don't mess up."

"You and me both. But as my mum says, 'just do your best and what happens, happens.'"

"Well, that is sound advice."

Datch thought about his dad and tried to work out what he would do.

He was just thinking about the planet's destruction for the third time, which had involved him breaking wind at the wrong time, when the door opened and Kratos walked in.

"Are you ready, Datch?"

Datch looked at Japato, who stood up.

"Yes. I think so."

Kratos walked back across the stage to the podium, followed by Datch and Japato.

"Fellow Councillors, please let me introduce Ambassador Datch."

Datch stepped forward and gave a small bow.

Kratos continued:

"And Science Officer Japato."

Japato saluted.

"Ambassador, if you would like to take the podium."

Datch swapped places with Kratos and placed the translator next to the microphone. He took a deep breath.

"Councillors of Marduk, it is a great honour to be addressing you all. Let me first start by telling you who we are. The Interplanetary Space Federation spans six galaxies and contains over sixty-five million civilizations spread across hundreds of millions of worlds. We all live together in peace and security. Wars and conquests have been stopped for thousands of years, allowing us to develop ourselves in other ways.

Why are we here? We came to your world to explore what we thought was an orphaned planet that had been pulled into another star's gravitational field. We didn't expect to find a world that was inhabited. We did scan your world for life but did not find any on the surface and assumed it was a dead world. Now we see a world that needs our help and we are more than happy to give it. Afterwards, if you wish us to leave, we will. But we do hope that you will want to get to know us and become part of our family. We have a lot to offer you and I'm sure we can learn from you. We hope you feel the same and look forward to becoming good friends."

He stopped and waited.

There were a few murmurs, and then a few people started clapping. When it quietened down, he continued.

"Now, to the matter at hand. We have carried out a number of deep scans of your planet to find out what is happening below our feet. This is Science Officer Japato, who will be taking you through the data we have collected from your planet's core."

Japato stepped forward.

"Councillors of Marduk, thank you for seeing us. Let me activate the holo display and show you what we have..."

He pressed a button and the holo system started displaying an image of the core.

The next thirty minutes went by with Japato explaining about the core and what the IPSF could do to help.

"And there we have it, Councillors. I wish I had better news. But, in about four days, if the core is left unchecked, it will build up enough pressure to breach and you will have a number of very large super volcanoes on your hands. From what we can tell, your facilities are going to be the weak points."

Japato stepped back from the podium and Datch took his place.

"Well, Councillors, there you have it. There is one question that you should be asking yourselves: do you want these aliens to help you save the planet? Yes, we will need to access your systems and to work very closely with you to do so, but we can do it. Now, I will leave it to you to decide. You should know, however, that we have started to evacuate our non-essential personnel from the surface to the science ships. Thank you for hearing us out. Now, do you have any questions?"

A light came on.

"How do we know the data is correct? We have been told your sensors cannot see through the black ore."

"We can see through the rest of the planet's surface, which means our ships' sensors can see all the way to the core. Also, Councillor, I'm sure your working sensors are seeing the same issues."

Another light came on.

"You say you will leave afterwards if we wish it?"

"Yes, Councillor, we will. We would like to stay in contact, though."

Another light came on.

"You say you need to access our systems. Will that be a two-way exchange?"

"You will have access to our systems on the planet. You may even get access to the galactic network depending on how things go. However, you normally need an implant to access that."

Another light came on.

"Implant, Ambassador?"

"Yes, we all have them. They allow our minds to access the knowledge of the universe."

"Do they control you?"

"No. The implant is a tool that we use to record images, get information, and for financial transactions. It also allows our brains to be transferred from one body to another."

"You have more than one body?"

"Not at the same time, but we are allowed five, including the one we are born with. The new body is grown from our DNA and then we are transferred into it."

"If we decide to join the IPSF, will we have to have an implant?"

"No, you don't. Some races do not have them and normally if they visit the other systems, they put a temporary one on their necks for ID and for financial transactions. But the implants can be very handy."

He waited for a short while. No more lights came on.

"Thank you, Councillors. I will now hand back to Kratos and let you debate the matter in question."

Kratos walked up to the podium.

"Thank you, Ambassador Datch. If you would like to go into the room at the back and wait, we will try and come to a decision as soon as possible."

Datch nodded and went with Japato to the room at the back.

"How do you think we did?" Japato asked.

"I don't know. Your bit was very informative and pushed the point home. I hope mine was okay. That was my first time doing the Ambassador thing to an alien race."

"I thought you were ambassadors for the Welly system?"

"We are, but normally we show up, sing a few songs, and then make small talk. We normally let other people do the serious stuff."

"Oh, I see. Well, from my experience, I think you did well."

"Thanks. I think I need a beer, but as we only seem to have coffee here, that will have to do."

They made a coffee each and sat down to wait.

They had just finished their second cup of coffee when there was a ping from Datch's pocket. He fetched out his Vid com and looked at it. It was displaying a message warning him that it had a slow connection speed.

"Well, it looks like the transceiver array is online," Datch said.

"I'll try contacting the Mellardrew then," Japato said, hitting her comms badge.

"Science Officer Japato to Mellardrew. Coms check please?"

"This is Mellardrew, coms are good."

"Thank you, Mellardrew. Japato out."

Just then, the door opened and Othred came in.

"Datch, Officer Japato, please could you follow me."

They followed him out into the council chambers. Kratos was standing at the podium and turned to look at them as they walked over.

"Ambassador Datch, Officer Japato. We have all voted and it is now my duty to formally ask for your help."

"Thank you, Kratos. We will start right away. Officer Japato, would you let the Mellardrew know please?" Datch said.

"Yes, Sir," Officer Japato said.

She pressed her comms badge.

"Mellardrew, this is Science Officer Japato. Please inform the Captain that the mission is a go. I repeat, the mission is a go."

"Copy that, Officer Japato. I will pass on the message. Mellardrew out."

Datch walked up to the podium.

"Councillors of Marduk, thank you for asking for our help. We shall work as fast as we can to save your planet and we will do everything within our power to make sure it is successful. Now, can I suggest we get your engineers to meet with ours and get the ball rolling? We have a lot of work ahead of us and not a lot of time to do it. We have a number of teams on the surface waiting to come down and start work. My fellow ambassadors and I will be on hand until we have fixed your world. We have arranged to have our vehicle brought down here to act as quarters for us. If you have any questions, don't hesitate to come and ask us. Thank you again."

"Thank you, Ambassador Datch. With that in mind, I hereby close this meeting of the council and thank all of my fellow councillors for allowing this to happen."

The lights came on and the councillors started to file out. Japato turned off the holo system and picked it up.

"Datch, Japato. Let's go to Natuk and get your people inside."

"Lead the way," said Datch.

They followed Kratos out of the council chambers and back down the tunnels to find the others. They were chilling in the operations centre, enjoying a coffee. They all stood up when Kratos, Datch, and Japato came walking over.

"Well?" asked Carina, looking at Datch.

"It's a go," said Datch.

"Commander Natuk," said Kratos.

"Yes, sir."

"The council has formally asked the IPSF for their assistance and they have agreed. Please help them get their people and equipment inside and working, please."

"Yes, sir. Right away."

"Commander Natuk, before you go, do you happen to know where the Blackbird is?"

"It entered the thruster about an hour ago, ambassador, so I expect it will be here shortly."

"Thank you. And please call me Datch. The ambassador title is for formal meetings only."

"OK, Datch."

With that, he went off with Japato to start moving people down from the surface.

"Datch, I would offer you all a meal, but I'm afraid our supplies are a little limited. We do have a couple of restaurants and bars, but there are no alcoholic drinks other than a very basic beer and the food is very limited, I'm afraid."

"No problem, we have our own. We brought enough supplies for a couple of months. Maybe yourself, and Commander Natuk could come and have dinner with us? We can discuss the best approach. I'll ask Commander Sormin to join us as well."

"That sounds good. I'll tell my wife I'm working late."

"You can bring her too if you like?"

"Are you sure it will be okay?"

"Yes, she will be more than welcome."

"I must say, she is very curious about you all."

Datch laughed.

"I'm sure the rest of the Pack can entertain her while we talk shop."

Just then, Quark came walking over with a number of IPSF officers.

"Hello, sir. The communications relay is up and running and the interface equipment will be installed when it gets here."

"Thank you, Quark. Please take these officers to Commander Natuk and help get their equipment installed."

"Yes, sir."

He turned to Plark who had been waiting with the Pack.

"Plark, as I'm sure you have just heard, we now have the help of the IPSF and as such your role as an acting ambassador is very important. Please make sure things run smoothly."

"Yes, sir."

"Plark, would you like to come to dinner too?" said Datch.

"Yes, please, Ambassador."

"It's Datch, Plark, Datch and that goes for the rest of us."

"OK, Datch it is."

"Right, let's say you come to the Blackbird in about two hours' time."

"Sounds good. I'll let Natuk know. Now if you will excuse me, I have a few things to sort out." Said Kratos.

"Certainly, Kratos. See you shortly."

Kratos left them with Plark.

"Datch?"

"Yes?"

"Can I ask your advice?"

"Sure, what's up?"

"I'm a little unsure about the ambassador thing."

Datch smiled.

"Don't worry about it. We don't have a clue either. As I said to Japato, we show up, sing a few songs, and then make small talk. That's it."

"I need to learn to sing?"

"No, no, no, just do your thing and make your world look good. The rest just happens."

"It does?"

"Well, sort of. After all this, I think we need to take you to another world."

Plark's eyes lit up and a smile spread across his face.

Datch realized that if they took him to another world, he might not want to come back.

"But you will have to come home afterwards." He added just to make sure he didn't get any ideas.

They carried on chatting for another half an hour, and then a Marduk officer came running over.

"Sir, your vehicle is just pulling into the parking area. If you would like to go to the lifts over there and press level 30, it should be right outside."

"Thank you, officer. Err, just so we can get back, what level are we on?" asked Datch.

"Level 70 sir."

"Thank you."

The officer saluted and left.

"Ok folks, let's go find Dapo, I need a shower and a beer. Plark, I'll see you shortly."

"I look forward to it, Datch."

With that, the Pack headed for the lifts.

Up above them, Dapo brought the Blackbird to a stop. It took up five of the parking bays used for the shuttle cars, and after a bit of manoeuvring, he got it parked sideways. He decided to put the external flood lights on to make the area nice and bright. He shut down the drive systems and got up to go to the door. Zark stood up and started to follow him.

They were just walking down the steps when the rest of the Pack came out of the lifts.

"Hi folks, what's happening?" asked Dapo.

"Hi Dapo, the council have formally asked for our help and we are now working with them to fix the planet."

"Looks like we'll be seeing more of you Zark." Said Dapo.

"I'll look forward to it. I had better go and find the commander and tell him we're here."

"Ok, see you later."

Zark headed off to the lifts.

"So, what now?" asked Dapo.

"We have dinner guests in about an hour, so we need to freshen up."

"Oh, we had better get a move on then, let's go."

They headed into the Blackbird.

"You guys go first, I want to talk to the Mellardrew captain." Said Datch sitting in his driving seat.

"That won't work, will it?"

"Yes, they have the coms link up and running."

"Does that mean we can watch the vid networks?" asked Kissy.

"No. The link is not that quick and I'm sure the Mellardrew would not like us sucking up all the bandwidth to watch a vid." Said Datch.

"Oh, ok."

At this point, there was a sudden exodus in the direction of the bathroom.

Datch turned to the front and located a working coms channel. He wasn't sure what he was going to say, but he felt he needed to update the captain. He put on his headset and pressed the coms button.

"Mellardrew, this is Ambassador Datch requesting a connection to Captain Taper."

There was a short pause.

"Hello Ambassador, please wait, I'll see if he is available."

There was another pause.

"Connecting you now Ambassador."

"Thank you."

"Good evening ambassador, how is it going down there?"

"We are good thank you. We're just about to hold a dinner on the Blackbird for Kratos, Natuk, Plark, and Commander

Sormin. I felt it was important to get us all around the table and work out the best way forward."

"That sounds like a good plan. Ask commander Sormin to contact me afterwards with an update. I know the council has requested our help, but how did the meeting go?"

"It was ok. Officer Japato did a great job of explaining the data, and they questioned me a bit afterwards about the IPSF. I think they just wanted reassuring about our intentions. I believe I put them at ease."

"That sounds good. What were the council like?"

"They seemed to be ok. I got the feeling they were more worried about their planet's core than us. The vote passed easily."

"Good. Sounds like you have things in hand. If there is nothing else, I'll get back to sorting this end out."

"Before you go, Any update for the Welly destroyer?"

"Yes, they are in transit ETA is 11:75 tomorrow."

"Thanks, I'll see if I can get up there after they arrive. It may help err diplomatic relations."

"In what way?"

"Well, Widfab is a bit on the bouncy side."

"Ahh, I see your point."

"Ok Captain, I'll let you get on."

"Thank you, Ambassador. Please keep me informed and enjoy your dinner. Mellardrew out."

The channel closed.

The rest of the evening was spent talking shop and showing the Marduks some of the images from the Bellatrix and other worlds that the Pack had visited.

Datch found out that because of the link to the transceiver, a gap had opened in the shield and the Blackbird was now able to talk to the systems on the Raven, which was sitting in the crater above them. This meant that they had a connection to the interspace relay that the IPSF had put in orbit. Krissy was very happy as she could now watch Star Warrior.

Time to save the World.

Datch woke up and clambered out of his bunk. Carina, Krissy, and Tish were already sitting eating breakfast. He pulled his trousers on and headed across to them.

"Morning," he said, sitting down at the big table.

"Morning. Do you want a Jeader roll?" Carina asked.

"Sure."

"So, what's the plan?" Krissy asked.

"Hmm, we just go and make sure there are no problems between the IPSF and the Marduks I guess."

"And if we find one?" Tish asked.

"We tell them to stop being morons and to get on with saving the planet."

"And that will help?" Carina asked, placing two rolls in front of him.

"Hmm... Maybe we don't call them morons." He said and took a bite out of one of the rolls.

"Safety wise and hypothetically speaking, if lava comes rushing into a tunnel, what do we do?" Krissy asked.

"Err, run like a rampant Jaxx."

"OK. That's pretty clear."

The others slowly appeared and came over for breakfast. Krissy thought it was important to tell them about the new safety protocol involving a Jaxx.

After everyone was finished eating, Datch finished his second coffee and stood up.

"Ok folks, let's head to the command centre and find out what is going on."

The Pack got up and headed to the lifts. Five minutes later they entered the main control room.

The room was a scene of organised chaos. There was a large console in the centre which had the markings of the IPSF on it and was being manned by three officers. Around the walls were a number of other consoles, most of which had red flashing lights on them and were being manned by the Marduks. People were running about shouting things across the room and the translation boxes were working overtime.

Commander Sormin came running past.

"Commander?" Datch said.

He stopped and turned to Datch.

"Morning Ambassador. Sorry, we're a little busy."

"What's happening?"

"We found out this morning that the Marduks are only getting 25% of the energy they need as three out of the four power systems have failed."

"Oh. So, what's happening now?"

"The Mellardrew and Canthar are sending down power units that have been configured to the Marduks' power grid. They should bring the power systems back up to a workable level. The pressure is building in the core and at the moment we can't control it."

"Can we do anything?"

"Unless you know how to fix the core, I suggest you get ready for evacuation. Things here could go from bad to really bad very quickly."

"Hmm, ok. We'll go and find Kratos and prep the Raven. I have faith in you."

"Thank you, ambassador. Now if you will excuse me."

"Certainly Commander. Good luck."

Datch turned to the others.

"Let's find Kratos."

They left the command centre and headed towards the council chambers, hoping to find Kratos or Othred. They ran down the tunnels to the doors.

Inside, half the council was there with Kratos, looking at the holoprojector.

The Pack came running through the doors.

"Ambassadors?" Kratos said.

"Morning," Datch said. "We understand things are not going well?"

"Yes, we lost another power system last night and the core is out of control. Your people are trying to get power back, but I fear they are fighting a losing battle."

"We understand they are bringing systems down to try and sort it."

"Yes, but looking at our data and yours, we have about five hours before it breaches our tunnels. Can I suggest you get on your ship and get ready to depart?"

"We are the Pack and we don't give up that easily."

"Well, unless we can release the pressure, we are doomed."

Datch stood there for a moment, thinking.

"Datch?" Carina asked.

He was still looking into space, but then a grin started to appear.

"Ambassador, are you okay?"

He turned to Kratos with a big grin.

"Get your people out of the tunnels under the ocean and seal the tunnels."

"Why?"

"I'm going to release the pressure into the ocean."

"Are you mad? It would take a huge amount of power to cause a core breach under the ocean. We don't have time or the power to do it."

"No, you don't, but I do! Trust me and seal the tunnels."

"Datch?" Krissy asked.

"Widfab," he said, still grinning.

"Oh my god," Krissy said, realizing what Datch was thinking.

"What's going on?" Kratos asked.

"I think Datch is planning to shoot your planet," Dapo said.

"What!"

Datch's grin got bigger.

"Trust me, Kratos. The planetary president who is coming is in a planetary destroyer. They're normally used to stop stars from going nova and destroying populated star systems next to them. If we get it to fire at the ocean floor, it's more than capable of making a big hole and releasing the pressure."

"You're mad."

"And you're dead in five hours if we don't."

"Ambassador, you're asking a lot."

"We have people on the surface. I don't want them to die. This may sound crazy, but it will work, I promise."

Kratos looked at him for a moment.

"I'll give the order to seal the tunnels, but once they're gone, the only way to the facilities will be above ground."

"Don't worry about that. We can sort that out for you."

"Datch, if I do this, can I request that you evacuate everyone you can before you fire?"

"Yes, start getting your people to the surface. I'll talk to the captain of the Mellardrew."

"Okay. I'll seal the tunnels."

"Come on, folks, we have to fix this," Datch said, heading for the door.

"You're really going to let them blow a hole in the planet?" Othred asked.

"What choice do we have? Anyway, if it goes wrong, the survivors will have some decent steaks."

The Pack arrived back at the main control centre and Datch walked over to Commander Sormin.

"Commander, I need to talk to you."

"Sorry, Ambassador, I'm a little busy."

Datch looked at him for a moment, then took a deep breath.

"I'm going to shoot the planet."

Sormin carried on for a moment, then what Datch had said sank in and he turned to look at him.

"You're going to what?"

"I'm going to ask the Welly destroyer to release the core into the ocean."

Sormin looked at him.

"You're going to release the pressure into the ocean?"

"Yes. Will it work?"

"Err, maybe. Their systems are screwed. We can't control it. But it will flood the complexes."

"Kratos is going to seal the deep tunnels. That should keep the complexes safe."

"You're mad, you know that."

"Yes, but it will work, won't it?"

"Err, it should stop the planet exploding, but I wouldn't want to have any beachfront property."

"I don't think there is any," Krissy added.

"Good point."

"Can you put me through to Captain Taper? It might be an idea if you were with me when I talk to him."

"Sure, I wouldn't want to miss this for the galaxy."

They walked over to the comms unit and Sormin opened a channel to the Mellardrew. After asking to be put through to the captain, his face appeared on the monitor.

"Ambassador?"

"Hello Captain, I know you're very busy, but I have a way to save the planet."

"You do?"

Datch explained the plan to the captain, and when the captain had put his eyebrows back down, he looked at Datch.

"So, I'm meant to tell the Welly destroyer that you want them to put a big hole in the planet that we're trying to save?"

"Err, no. I'll do that. Widfab will just say yes to me."

"Commander Sormin, what do you think?"

"It should work sir, at the very least it will give us some breathing space."

The captain sat back in his chair, thinking for a moment.

"Hmm, OK. I'll start evacuating our people near the coastlines. The Welly destroyer will be here in four hours."

"Kratos has asked if we can evacuate his non-essential people as well. They are being told to head to the surface."

"I'll get the Canthar to start sending shuttles down to the Raven's location."

"Thank you, Captain Taper."

"Don't thank me. This is on your head. I hope it works."

"So do I, captain."

"I'll be heading to the Welly destroyer in the Raven."

"May I suggest you take Kratos and Othred with you?"

"Yes sir, I'll see if they will come."

"Ok, get to it ambassador. Mellardrew out."

Datch turned to Sormin.

"Sormin, you make sure the generators get up and running. We're going to need all the power we can get after the pressure drops as their power system may fail."

"I'll try and make sure we get at least one of them working, Sir."

"Ok, I'll go and find Kratos."

Datch turned to the rest of the Pack.

"Guys, you had better head up to the Raven and wait there."

"I want to stay with you," Carina said.

"Me too," Krissy added.

Datch looked at them. They knew it was risky and wanted to be by his side.

"OK, but if I say run, we run!"

They both nodded.

"Dapo, I need you in the Raven. Make sure all the systems are in standby so we can leave in a hurry if we need to."

"No problem. I'll go through the power-up checks as soon as we get there."

"Ok, let's move."

Dapo, Hagger, Tish, and Rosey went back to the Blackbird to get their stuff on their way to the Raven. Datch, Carina, and Krissy headed off to the council chambers in search of Kratos.

When they arrived, Natuk was standing talking to Kratos and Othred. A couple of other council members were standing listening to them.

"Ah, ambassadors," Natuk said as they walked up.

"Hello Commander."

"Please tell me you're not going to blow a hole in our planet."

"Err, I'm not. My aim's not that good. The Welly star destroyer will carry out a precision strike to the ocean's bed, releasing the pressure and warming the water up at the same time."

"You do know how big a hole you need, don't you?" Natuk said, looking very worried.

Datch was glad he had a link to his implant and, after a moment, said, "Yes, about a kilometre wide should do the trick."

"It could destroy our remaining power systems."

"Sormin is going to make sure that at least one of our power generators is up and running beforehand. Hopefully all three."

"I take it they will be leaving before you shoot us."

"No. They will be staying to make sure your world survives."

He looked at Datch and then at the girls.

"They are doing that?"

"Yes, all of our engineering teams are staying on the planet. We are only evacuating the coastal bases and ordering everyone else into the protective domes. The shields they have will be able to cope with any fallout from the pressure release."

"You really think this will work, don't you?"

"Yes, we do. Your systems cannot be brought back online fast enough to stop the planet's surface breaking up. This is like lancing a boil. Trust me. It will work."

Natuk stood thinking about it for a moment and then came to a decision.

"OK, I'll get my people to blow the sub-ocean tunnels. I hope you're right."

"Thank you, Commander," said Kratos.

"Now, if you will excuse me, I need to go and tell my teams that we've gone mad."

"Before you go, Commander, the Canthar is sending shuttles down to evacuate your non-essential people. They will be coming to the crater. If you have people down at the thruster, it might be faster for them to head to the base south of it. There is a road to it, and they should be able to get there within an hour."

"Thank you, Ambassador."

With that, he left in a hurry.

Datch turned to Kratos.

"We have room on the Raven for all of you and your wives. The Welly destroyer is due in about three hours, so I suggest we leave shortly before that."

"But I wish to stay," said Kratos.

"Yes, but your planet can't risk losing you. You're too important. Also, we'll be able to display the live planetary data for you so you can assess it."

"He's right, Kratos. If things do go wrong, we'll need you to lead our people wherever we end up." said Othred.

The other councillors were nodding.

"OK, I will come."

"Good. The Raven can take about twenty extra, and we'll meet you all in the command centre in about two hours, OK?"

"OK. I'll tell my wife."

"We're going to go to the command centre now and see if we can help with anything."

"We'll see you there, Ambassador."

With that, they headed back to the command centre.

The next two hours were spent watching screens for Sorin and shouting when things did things they weren't meant to. They managed to get two generators online and had put a shield up around the Marduks repository where the population were being stored.

Natuk came running in just as Kratos arrived.

"We're ready to seal the tunnels, sir," said Natuk.

Kratos looked at Datch, and he nodded.

"Do it, commander."

Natuk turned and pressed a button on one of the consoles.

There was a rumbling and slight shaking from below them, and then another rumble shortly after.

Natuk looked at the displays.

"The tunnels are sealed, sir."

"Good. Now let's pray this works!"

The rest of the councillors who had been outside the chambers started to come in with their partners. The explosions deep down seemed to have got them to hurry up a bit. There were about twenty-three of them in total with wives and children.

"Councillors, I think it's time to go. Sorin, is your team okay?"

"Yes, we're good."

"Well, if it gets dicey, the Blackbird has shields. It won't stop a complete collapse, but it will stop rocks hitting your heads. I'll leave the door unlocked."

"Thank you, Ambassador."

"Kratos, is everyone here?"

He looked around.

"Yes, I think so."

"OK folks, let's head to the Raven. Good luck both of you."

They headed to the lifts carrying bags with precious belongings inside. They reached the parking area and got in a fleet of shuttle cars for the short trip to the entrance. The Raven was sitting with its ramp down. When they emerged from the tunnel, the cars pulled up behind it.

They all started to get out of the cars and one of the young children shouted,

"Is that a spaceship?"

Carina went over to him.

"Yes, it is and you're going inside it." She said reassuringly.

"Oh cool! Come on mum." He said and started to pull his mum towards it.

Datch led the way up the ramp and into the Raven.

"Carina, if you and Krissy can help to get folks settled, I'll take Kratos, Othred and their wives to the cockpit."

"We're on it." Said Carina.

"OK, ladies and gentlemen, if you would like to follow me."

Datch headed up the stairs and into the cockpit.

Dapo was sitting in the co-pilot's seat, listening to the coms chatter on the cockpit sound system. Plark was sitting behind him, chatting to Tish.

"Hi folks," said Datch.

"Hey Datch. How many we got?"

"Twenty-three with a couple of kids. What's happening on the comms?"

"It's very busy. It sounds like they've got the camps on the ocean seaboard just about cleared. The last few shuttles have just landed for pick up."

"Good. I'll contact Mellardrew and find out where the destroyer is."

"OK, the Raven's ready to go when you are."

Datch put on his headset and sat down.

"Mellardrew, this is the Raven. We have a number of council members with us and are preparing to launch. Can you update me on the Welly Destroyer?"

"The Carina will be entering the system in 3 minutes."

"The Carina? Well, my wife will be pleased about that. OK, tell Captain Taper, we'll be heading straight to the Carina. Can you ask him to request that they power up their forward energy cannon and tell them I'll explain when I get there."

"I shall pass the message on. The sky is quite busy as you know, so please wait until cleared to launch."

"Copy that. We're still getting people settled, so we'll be about five or ten minutes yet."

Rosey and Hagger came walking down from the rec room, looking very happy with themselves.

"What's up with you two?" Said Datch, looking up.

"We've made these for the Marduks," said Rosey, holding out her hand.

In it were a number of tiny earpieces.

"They do the translation thing, so we won't need the boxes or big earpieces anymore," said Hagger, grinning.

"Good thinking. Give one to Kratos."

She did and he put it on.

"Can you understand me?" Datch asked.

"Yes, very clearly."

"Cool. Plark, your next."

Plark smiled and turned his head, showing his ear. He already had one.

"He was the guinea pig," said Rosey, smiling.

"It's very good, Datch. I've been chatting to Tish for a while using it."

"Awesome job, guys. Hand them out to everyone."

Rosey and Hagger started handing them out and soon everyone had one. Carina and Krissy helped convince the kids to put them on after a bit of bribery involving chocolate.

Soon everyone was sorted and settled, ready to go.

Datch turned to the front.

"Mellardrew, this is the Raven, ready to launch en-route to the Carina."

"Copy that, Raven. Two minutes, then head on vector 223.98,122.57."

"Copy that. Raven standing by."

Carina stuck her head around Datch's seat.

"The Carina?"

"Yes, it's the name of the Welly Destroyer."

"They named a starship after me?"

"Apparently so."

"Raven, you're cleared for launch. The Carina is expecting you. After clearing orbit, head on vector 234.56, 715.02 and switch to channel Beta 9872."

"Copy that. Lifting off."

Datch increased power to the engines, and the Raven took to the air. They headed up through the atmosphere pushing the clouds out of their way in the process. Then the stars came out. There were a few intakes of breath from the Marduks as the view outside took their breaths away.

Datch banked the Raven away from the planet and onto the new vector. He switched bands and opened a channel.

"Carina, this is the Raven en-route. Requesting landing instructions."

"Good afternoon, Raven. Please lock on to Beacon CAR99721 for automated landing."

Datch hit a few buttons.

"Carina, Raven locked on to beacon."

"Thank you, Raven. The Minister Prime will be waiting for you on arrival music warriors, and the forward weapon is being powered up as per your request."

"Thank you, Carina. Raven out."

Datch released the controls. In the distance appeared a ship. It was a very long ship, five or six times the size of the Mellardrew. It was much larger than the other Welly Destroyer, that was for sure. The front had a huge cannon with lightning flashing across its power couplings. Datch realized he had seen its like before at Arcaneus when the destroyers had fired on the Plantar battleships, totally obliterating them. And here he was about to fire this monstrous weapon at the planet. A shiver ran down his spine as he remembered the explosions.

The Raven flew alongside the massive vessel. Datch looked at it. It wasn't pure white like the rest of the IPSF fleet. It had a light blue hue and bright green flames running along the sides. Datch shrugged his shoulders.

"Nice paint job," said Tish.

"I like the green," added Carina.

"Raven, docking in 1 minute," came a voice over the comms.

"Copy that, Carina."

The Raven started to move away from the hull and then turned towards it. In front of them was a large landing bay. There were a number of ships inside sitting on their pads, but the bay had a lot less ships than the Mellardrew. The Raven entered the bay and headed over to pad 1. It then dropped down onto the pad, and there was a clunk as the clamps engaged.

Widfab was standing outside with a large group of officers all in dress uniform.

"Raven, this is Carina. Please shut down your engines and open your power ports."

"Copy that, Carina. Shutting down."

Datch shut down the engines.

"A second royal welcome," said Kratos.

"Yes, but I think this one is for us," said Carina.

"Kratos, this may be a little weird for a while. We are the spiritual leaders of Welly, and this is one of their ships. They have a habit of bowing a lot, and also have a few odd ideas about partying a lot."

"Oh..."

"I wonder how they ended up like that," said Othred.

"Right, let's go release some pressure," said Datch, getting up before people started pointing fingers at him.

They headed to the cargo bay, collecting people as they went. Datch opened the door and lowered the ramp.

They walked down the ramp to the small party at the bottom. Widfab was standing at the front and took a deep bow when Datch reached him. All the other officers also bowed. Datch and the Pack bowed back.

"Music Warriors, it's great to see you again," said Widfab.

"Thank you, Minister Prime. I trust you and your wife are well?"

"Yes, thank you."

"Please let me introduce you to our new friends. This is Kratos, leader of the Marduk Council."

Datch went around and introduced everyone, and afterwards he turned to Widfab.

"I'm sorry we don't have time for any more talking, but we need to make a hole in the planet below."

"You want us to blow up the planet?"

"No, not all of it. We need you to make a hole in the bottom of the big ocean to release the pressure from its core. Or the planet will blow up by itself."

"When?"

"In about three or four hours. The systems below the surface have lost control of it."

"Oh, I see. That's what the Mellardrew was on about. Captain, I think we need to go to the bridge."

"Yes, Sir."

"Could we put the kids somewhere on route?"

"Oh yes, maybe their mums would like to take them to the soft play centre."

"You have a soft play centre?"

"Oh yes, and seven nightclubs, three party zones, and a number of very good restaurants. We were going to install a water park too, but the IPSF said that was going a little bit too far."

"Sir, if I may." Said the captain.

"Yes, Captain."

"Lieutenant, if you would like to take the children and the mums to the soft play centre while we err, do the business."

"Yes sir. Ladies, if you would like to follow me."

He led half the party down the corridor and disappeared into a pod.

The rest of them headed to another pod to take them to the bridge.

"Your Holiness, the Mellardrew has said you have worked all this out?" said the captain, looking at Datch.

Datch sighed.

"Yes, Captain. I know it may be hard for you, but please just call me Datch. We prefer our names to our official titles. The plan is to release the excess pressure into the ocean that is currently still semi-frozen. The systems on the planet were meant to do this over time, but they have failed, and we don't have time to get them back online before... well, boom. So, we need to blow a hole one point one five of a kilometre wide right down to the core itself. The ocean should then take the heat and pressure, melting in the process."

"You know this is a precision strike. The ocean will also flood all of the coastal areas, and it is going to cause earthquakes travelling through the whole planet."

"Yes, we have moved everyone from the coastal areas and have shielded sensitive installations underground. We should be good."

"Okay, Your Holiness... sorry, Datch."

He pressed his comms badge.

"Command, tell the Mellardrew and Canthar to clear all flight paths and to make sure everything is secure down on the planet. We are moving into position above the deepest point of the ocean. Bring the weapons stabilisers online. I'll be on the bridge shortly."

"Eye sir."

"Okay, it should only take a few minutes to get in position."

"Can we get a comms link to Sorin on the planet?" asked Carina.

"Yes, Carina. I'll arrange it when we get to the bridge."

"Thank you, Captain."

The pod slowed down and then came to a stop. They left the pod and headed up the corridor. There were two security guards standing either side of a very large door.

They saluted and then bowed.

The Pack bowed back.

The doors opened and they walked onto the bridge.

It was a huge room with consoles all around the edge. It had a massive viewscreen in the centre showing the view from the front of the ship. The planet was slowly moving into view.

As the Pack walked in, people started bowing. Datch sighed again and bowed back.

"They really like the ambassadors, don't they?" said Othred in Kratos's ear.

"Yes, they do." He whispered back.

"Fire control, I want a one point one five kilometre hole in the centre of the ocean, deep enough to breach the core."

Status lights started to flash red as the ocean came into view. Then a red target sight appeared on the screen over the centre of the ocean. Then, after a few moments, the planet stopped moving as the ship came into synchronous orbit.

"Target locked, sir. Energy level set at nineteen point five percent." said the fire control officer.

"Open a channel to the surface, please. Music Warriors?"

The captain looked at Datch and nodded.

"Sorin, are you there?"

"Yes, sir."

"We're powering up the cannon now, get people ready for the blast."

"We're ready, sir. Commander Natuk and his men are here, and we've put an extra shield up over the command centre."

"Good. Hold on tight."

"Yes, sir."

Datch looked at the captain.

"I think we're ready when you are."

"Comms, tell the Mellardrew and Canthar we're about to fire, and put out a ship-wide broadcast: 'Brace for firing'. Commander Thackery, battle music please."

"Battle music?"

"Yes, it makes us feel better." said Widfab.

"Oh."

Supernova started to blast out of the bridge's speakers, and the lights flashed blue.

"Music Warrior, weapons are at your command." said the captain.

Datch suddenly had a feeling of dread. He was about to blow a hole in a planet. Shivers ran down his spine, and he felt sick inside. Carina grabbed his hand and smiled at him.

"FIRE!" he said.

Massive arcs of energy appeared over the length of the ship's superstructure, and then started to compress towards the front of the cannon. Then the ship shuddered as a plasma beam shot out the front of the ship, heading towards the planet.

It hit the ocean, and the ice turned to superheated steam as the plasma went through it, sending clouds into the atmosphere. Huge waves of boiling water started to melt through the ice. The plasma then hit the bedrock of the ocean floor, and fire erupted as the rock was vaporized by the huge amount of energy. Smoke and fire could be seen from orbit as the weapon melted its way to the core.

Finally, it reached the core. The combination of the plasma and the highly pressurized core created temperatures close to that of a star. The core came rushing up the hole to the surface. It had found a release at last. The bottom of the ocean exploded as millions of tonnes of liquid rock erupted through the hole. The boiling water was now trying to rush back in after the plasma bolt, and hit the core as it came rushing out. There was a massive explosion as fire and water mixed. Steam and molten rock erupted high into the atmosphere, showering the planet with a fiery rain. Then the shock waves started to spread out across the planet, rippling its surface as they went. The magma filled up the bottom of the ocean, and the waters now came rushing back in, carrying ice as they came.

The ice was being consumed by the boiling waters and molten rock. The sea level increased rapidly in height, carrying huge waves inland. The Pack could see a massive shock wave sweeping across the planet's surface. Mountains were trembling as seismic wave after seismic wave hit them. Finally, they started to subside, and the ocean waters rushed back to the centre, solidifying the magma from the core into a new land mass.

"Sorin, are you still with us down there?" asked Datch.

There were a few nervous moments until the reply came.

"Yes, we're still here. I think they may need to do a spot of redecorating though."

"How are the systems looking?"

"Natuk is just checking them now."

After a few moments, Natuk's voice came over the comms.

"Ambassador, is Kratos with you?" he asked.

"Yes, I'm here, Commander. How's it looking?"

"It looks like there were a few minor tunnel collapses, but most of the complex is intact. The power generator is still running, but its output has dropped. As far as people go, it looks like, other than a few minor injuries, they're okay."

"Thank the gods. What about the core?"

"It looks like the pressure has dropped to normal levels, maybe even slightly lower. I'm still trying to contact the facility on the far side of the ocean. The blast must have taken out the communication lines, but the tunnel seal seems to be holding."

"That's good news, Commander."

"How's it looking up there?"

"The ocean is all water again, and we seem to have a new island in the middle of it."

"It looks like it worked then."

"Yes, Commander. We'll be coming back down shortly."

"Sir, as a safety precaution, please wait until I give you the all-clear. There could still be structural issues."

"Kratos, we'll need to wait for the atmosphere to settle down before we can fly to the surface anyway." added Datch.

"Okay, Datch. Commander, please keep us informed. We're on board the Carina with the leader of Welly Four."

Datch looked at Carina, who was grinning.

"What's up with you?"

"I got a ship named after me." she said.

Datch suddenly felt like he was missing out.

"Don't worry, I'm sure they will name something after you at some point." she said quietly.

"Captain, I think that was a good weapons test. I think we can shut the battle music off now." said Widfab.

"Yes, sir."

"Councillors, Music Warriors, shall we go for some refreshments? We have some Bellatrixian Ale on board."

"Oh, cool. Sounds like a plan."

"Okay, Captain. We'll be heading to the Datch Inn. Please can you let the others in the soft play area know where we are going."

"Yes, sir."

They walked off the bridge and down to the pod.

"You named a bar after me?"

"Yes, all the areas are named after the members of the Music Warriors. For instance, we have the Timbo Gym."

"And you called the ship Carina?"

"Err yes, well, it was only fair. We renamed the main spaceport on Welly to The Datch Complex."

"Cool, I have a complex." Said Datch, grinning.

"Yes, we know that." Said Dapo, sarcastically.

Carina and Krissy burst out laughing.

Datch looked at them, then realized what he had said. He grinned.

"So, Kratos. What can us Welly folk do for you?" Asked Widfab.

Kratos smiled.

"Well, I think stopping our entire civilisation being wiped out was a good start. Thank you very much for that."

"You're very welcome. How many of you are there?"

"We have just over three hundred and sixty-eight million in storage and about forty thousand currently awake."

"In storage?" Asked Widfab.

"Yes, we digitised ourselves and placed ourselves in a digital storage vault. Then, just before the planet reached the new star, the systems started reviving us."

"That is very interesting, did it hurt?"

"No. We just went to sleep and then woke up in our new bodies."

"Well, the galaxy has changed a lot in the last hundred thousand years or so."

"Yes, Datch and his friends have been telling us about some of the other worlds."

The pod came to a stop and they stepped out into a very large and busy corridor. As they made their way to Datch's bar, people would stop and bow to them, and the Pack felt obliged to bow back.

Finally, they arrived at the bar. In fact, it was the Barber's Inn, or at least a very good copy of it. The only difference was that the sign above the door said "The Datch Inn."

The Pack looked at the bar for a moment before going inside. It was a strange feeling to find it there.

"Widfab, it's the Barber's!" said Rosey.

"Yes," said Widfab. "We tried to make it as close to the original as possible. We even have bands playing here twice a week."

They walked up to the bar and, after another round of bowing, ordered their drinks.

"Do you happen to have a big table upstairs?" asked Tish.

"Of course," said Widfab. "It's just like the one in the Barber's Inn."

"Did you send a man around with a tape measure?" asked Dapo.

"We did scan the original to make sure we got it right," said Widfab.

"I can't wait to tell Jim about this place," said Datch. "It's going to blow his mind."

They headed upstairs to a very new-looking big table and sat down on some very comfortable chairs. Soon after, the others came in from Rosey's soft play area.

The next three hours were spent drinking beer and eating wings and pizzas. The kids thought the pizzas were fantastic.

Two thousand light-years away, Tank, Fred, and Clax were relaxing in the hotel bar while Peebop had gone off to have a sauna. They had been having a fun time on their bikes in the mountains and were now recovering. The bar had the news channel on, and the galactic news came on just as Fred was taking a drink.

Datch's face appeared on the vid screen with the headline "The Pack does it again." Tank got sprayed with beer.

"Sorry," said Fred, handing him a napkin. The newsreader went on to read the report from the new planet.

"Looks like Datch is having fun," said Clax.

The vid screen showed the Welly destroyer Carina firing on the planet and releasing the core.

"We can't let them out of our sight for two minutes," said Fred.

"Yeah, and Carina's going to be full of herself now she has a ship named after her," said Clax.

"I wonder how Datch took that," said Tank.

"Knowing Datch, he's likely to be busy partying," said Fred.

The channel moved on to the next news story.

"So, what are the odds that he's going to bring an alien back with him?" asked Tank.

"I'd say two to one, odds on," added Clax.

Just then, Peebop came walking back from the sauna.

"What did I miss?" he asked seeing the look on their faces.

On the Carina, the Pack and friends were just finishing their fourth round of drinks. Datch had introduced Kratos and Othred to non-alcoholic beer, while Hagger and Rosey had found out that the bar had Old Man's Boots.

An officer came walking through the doors and headed up the stairs to the big table. She bowed.

"Sorry to disturb you all, but we have just had another report from the surface."

"Go ahead," said Kratos.

"Commander Natuk has carried out a full survey of the facilities and they are all secure. There have been forty-seven injuries, two of which are quite serious, most of which were caused by falling rocks. They have moved the serious ones to the IPSF medical facilities on the planet. He has asked us to let you know that it is now safe for you to go back down and he will give you a full report on your arrival, sir."

"Thank you, officer. Has the atmosphere cleared yet?"

"It is clearing slowly and we have now started flight operations in support of the Mellardrew. However, the ride down is a bumpy one, sir, as there is still a lot of dust and volcanic ash in the atmosphere."

"Thank you again, officer."

"You're welcome, sir."

She bowed again and left the table.

Datch noticed that Plark was sitting with a puzzled look on his face.

"Plark, what's up?"

"Err, I've noticed that you are all talking different languages, but all understand each other. Is that the implants?"

"Yes, it translates straight into our minds. To us, we hear our own languages."

"Hmm, I think I'll need one, Kratos, if you want me to be an ambassador permanently."

"You would do that, Plark?"

"Yes, sir. I feel it would be very handy to have."

Kratos looked at Othred.

"What do you think?"

"Why not if he wishes to do it. He's been helping out a lot and it will be interesting to see him with it."

Kratos turned back to Plark.

"If you want to get one then please do it and let us know how it feels."

Widfab, who was sitting listening to them, spoke up.

"If you wish it, we can do it here. The med bay is set up for making them, in case we have, err, offspring when in deep space."

"You mean I could have one now if I wanted?"

"Yes. It takes about an hour to prepare them."

"Could I have one please?"

"Are you sure Plark?"

"Yes, sir, I am."

"I'll arrange it." Widfab said, getting out his vid com.

Five minutes later a medical officer came in and scanned Plark so they could configure the implant for his biology.

It was decided that they would wait to go back to the surface until after Plark had been given his implant. That way Kratos and Othred could see how it was done.

They ordered another round of drinks and some crisps for the children.

Soon it was time for Plark to go to the medical bay. Datch, Krissy, Kratos, Othred, and Widfab all went with him. The others were introduced to Solar Ball by Tish, Rosey, and Carina. The children loved it.

Plark arrived at the medical bay with his entourage and was taken over to a bed to lie down. A small box was sitting next to it. The medical officer turned to him.

"I just need to scan you to check the calibration is correct for your physiology."

A beam of energy passed over his head.

"There we go. The implant has the standard Welly boot up. Pleasure moon, temple, and the capital. Minister Prime, we're ready when you are."

Datch stepped forward.

"You're going to love this bit."

Widfab nodded and the medical officer pressed the top of the box.

The box started to hum and then Plark's mind was blown.

"He's coming around," said the medical officer.

"Err, wow," he said, opening his eyes.

"Are you okay?" asked Kratos.

"Err, yes sir. Just a little shaky, that's all."

He turned to Widfab.

"Is that place real?"

"Yes, it's all real."

"I want to go there."

"I'm sure we can arrange it."

"What place?" asked Kratos.

"The implant comes with startup memories, normally from our parents, but in this case, he has just seen Welly Four in his mind as it started up. It's like he was standing there." Said Datch.

"It's amazing, sir," said Plark, sitting up and then wishing he had done it slower.

"Take it easy. Wait until the yellow dot stops flashing."

"What yellow dot?" he asked.

"It's in the corner of your eye. When the implant is ready, it will flash green and then disappear. Just stay there until then," said the officer.

He sat on the bed until it flashed green.

"It's stopped. Now what?"

"Take your earpiece out," said Datch.

He took the earpiece off.

"Okay."

"I take it you can understand me?"

"Yes, but you're talking Mardukian."

"No, I'm not, I'm talking Bellatrixian, you are just hearing it as Mardukian. The implant is using your own language matrix to do the conversion."

"Oh wow, Minister Prime. Please say something?"

"Err, welcome to the club."

"This is amazing. Can I get up now?"

"Yes, you're good. Just take it slowly for a bit."

He got up and then spotted a sign on the opposite wall.

"Please observe clinical hygiene at all times." He said quietly and then turn to Kratos

"I can read signs as well."

"Are you sure you're okay?" asked Othred.

"Yes sir, I'm fine. I'm seeing and hearing everything in Mardukian. The implant is translating everything."

"Yes, but do you feel like yourself?" asked Kratos.

"Yes sir, I'm still me."

"Right, let's head back to my place to let you recover." said Datch.

"Your place?" asked Widfab.

"Yes, my place, the bar!"

"Oh, I see."

They started to head back to the bar, taking their time so Plark didn't overdo it. They came out of the pod and Plark stopped, rooted to the spot.

"Oh my gods!"

"Are you okay?" asked Othred, looking concerned.

"I can read it," he said, standing and looking around.

"Read it?"

"Yes, all the signs and notices. This is incredible."

"Err, let's get you to the bar before you go into meltdown."

"Meltdown?" asked Othred.

"Yes, sometimes when people get the implants installed, the brain overloads and shuts down."

"You mean die?"

"No, no, they black out," corrected Datch. "When I had mine, I blacked out and slept for five hours. Krissy on the other hand just felt a little shaky for a bit. The beer helps to keep you relaxed and stops the black out. Though he may sleep well tonight."

"Oh, I see. In that case, Plark, stop reading things and head to the bar. That's an order."

"Yes, sir," said Plark, and started moving again.

This time, however, he had a permanent grin on his face as he looked around, trying to covertly read things as he went past.

They finally got him to the bar and back up the stairs to the others.

Datch put a beer down in front of him and told him to drink it. After he had drunk it, Datch looked into his eyes.

"How are you feeling now?" he asked.

"Good, thanks. This implant is pretty amazing."

"Yes, they are very handy. Your language matrix will also act as an update for our matrix."

"You said they can give you knowledge as well?"

"Yes, ask it something in your head," said Krissy helpfully.

"What, just think it?"

"Yes," said Datch.

He looked into space and stared grinning.

"Well?" asked Kratos.

"It's talking to me. I asked it about Datch's home world and it's telling me about it and showing me pictures."

"Where do you live on the planet, Datch?"

"Near Yuland city."

He looked into space again.

"Wow, I love the desert and the glass towers. Oh, there's a spaceport."

"Yes, here, have another beer," said Widfab, handing him a glass.

"Are you feeling well enough to go back to the planet?" asked Kratos.

"Yes, I think so, sir."

"Let's finish these and head down to the surface."

"Would it be okay if I came down with a team of engineers?" asked Widfab.

"Yes, I have a feeling that any extra help would be welcome, but be warned that the facilities are a bit messy."

"That's okay, you should see my office on Welly." Said Widfab smiling.

He contacted the captain and told him the plan. Afterwards, they carried on chatting for a while. After they finished off their drinks, they headed back to the Raven.

When they arrived in the landing bay, the Raven was looking very clean, considering it was covered in dust when they arrived.

"Widfab, what happened to the Raven?"

"We've cleaned it, serviced it, refuelled it, and restocked your beer supplies."

Datch looked at him.

"Thanks, but why?"

"You are the Music Warriors."

"Oh, okay, thanks."

There was no point saying anything else. At least he knew where to get a free service from now on.

The captain was there and thanked them for coming. Widfab whispered in Datch's ear.

"Captain, we will bring Widfab back in a bit and if you wish, we will carry out a short blessing for the ship. Oh, and we may do a couple of songs. But we are missing our backing singers and our instruments."

The captain's eyes lit up.

"That would be a great honour, thank you, your holiness."

He gave a bow.

"Okay, folks, let's get moving."

They all headed on board. This time, of course, Plark could read everything and made every effort to do so. He was told a number of times to stop it by Othred.

Finally, they sat down ready for launch.

Datch powered on the systems and put on his headset.

"Carina, this is the Raven ready for launch."

"Copy that Raven, automated launch in one minute."

The clamps were released and the Raven lifted off the pad.

"Raven, we have two engineering shuttles and a squadron of fighter jets to follow you down."

"Copy that."

The Raven started to move and headed out of the hangar. Outside, two large shuttles were hanging in space waiting for them, along with ten fighter jets.

"What are they?" asked Plark.

"It's a squadron of fighter jets. That's our honour guard."

The Raven turned towards the planet and started to accelerate. The other ships followed and the fighter jets spread out to the side of them.

"Sorin, do you copy?" asked Datch.

"Yes, Ambassador."

"We're on our way down and we will be landing in the crater in about fifteen minutes."

"I'll tell commander Natuk."

"We are bringing more help down as well."

"Thank you. We could use it."

He pressed the comms button to switch to quad band.

"Mellardrew, this is The Raven and escort on approach to the planet."

"Copy that Raven, your airspace has been cleared to the surface. Please note the air is still a bit unpredictable so it could be a bit turbulent on the way down."

"Copy that, Mellardrew."

The Raven headed through the clouds to a rainy and wet surface below.

"Engineering shuttle teams, land as close to us as possible. There is a pressure vent near the centre of the crater and we don't want you to get melted."

"Copy that Music Warriors, we'll come into land right next to you."

The crater came into view in the distance and Datch started to slow down. He landed the Raven close to where they had taken off from. The other two shuttles came down on either side of him.

"Fighter wing, thank you for the escort."

"It was an honour sir. Heading back to the Carina."

"Carina, we're down safe and sound. I'm shutting down the systems."

"Copy that. Raven. Carina out."

Datch shut down the Raven and they all headed outside.

Natuk was waiting with a number of shuttle cars and transports for equipment.

"Hello Commander, is everything ok."

"Yes sir. We have got another generator up and running. The power grid is now at ninety-five percent and thanks to the IPSF beacons we have managed to connect to the facilities on the other side of the ocean. They are a little shaken up but okay."

"That's good news commander. These people are from the Welly star system and are also aiding us. This is their Minister Prime, Widfab, who has come to see what they can do to help."

"Minister Prime," said Natuk, saluting. "This way please."

They went inside and down to the lower levels. The tunnels were a lot brighter now. The walls were glowing with energy. There were still a few piles of dust and rubble that had come down when the core was released, but they had been pushed to the side while more important things were carried out.

When they arrived at the control centre, all the flashing red lights on the control panels had now turned off or changed to yellow. Sorin was talking to a group of engineers when they came in.

"Commander Sorin."

"Good afternoon, ladies and gentlemen."

"This here is the Minister Prime of Welly."

He saluted.

"Pleased to meet you, sir."

"I have come to see what help we can give."

"Well, sir, we are supplying power from our systems at the moment and are currently trying to get their systems back online. So, any assistance with that would be a great help. Also, Commander Natuk wishes to start waking more of the population to help get the planet on its feet again, but we think we are going to be short of living areas as the ones on the surface have been destroyed during the course of their journey."

"I see. I shall ask for temporary quarters to be shipped into the system."

The walls started to shake for a few moments and then stopped again. Small bits of dust drifted down from the ceiling. They all looked around nervously. Then Datch's implant made a loud ringing noise in his head and he grabbed the side of his head along with the rest of them with implants.

"What was that?"

"It's okay, folks. Just a small aftershock. They are getting less and less now as the core settles down. We get them every couple of hours, but now that power has been restored, we can monitor the core more closely. It is still 'coughing' a bit as it calms down." said Natuk.

"What happened to my implant? It just screamed in my head?" asked Datch, shaking his head. The rest of the pack, Widfab, and Plark had also put their hands to their ears and were shaking their heads.

"It's an energy pulse from the core. It seems to unsettle the implants interface. We've done a few checks and it doesn't seem to cause any damage, and it should stop when the core settles down." said Sorin.

"Oh, okay. But is there anyway of warning us next time?"

"Sorry sir, but no. it's a sudden pulse of energy."

"Oh, OK"

"Commander Natuk, is it okay if I give the Minister Prime a quick tour around?" asked Kratos.

"Yes, sir, just don't use any of the side tunnels. Some of them are still unchecked."

"Thank you."

"Commander Sorin, these are two of our engineering crews. Please make use of them." said Widfab.

"Yes, sir."

"Kratos, if it's okay with you, we'll head to the Blackbird to freshen up a bit while you show the Minister Prime around."

"Okay, Ambassador. Thank you again for your help."

"Minister Prime, please let me show you around. I'm sure you will find it interesting."

They went over to one of the consoles and Kratos started explaining where they were going.

The Pack turned and headed back to the Blackbird. When they arrived, Datch sat down at the big table and opened a beer. The others did the same.

"Well, we've saved another world. What are we going to do now?" asked Tish.

"Well, they won't want us digging up their cities now, and I think we found out what's under the black ore," said Rosey.

"We have to bless the Carina," said Carina, grinning.

Datch raised an eyebrow.

"Yes, I suppose we could go back and meet up with the others," said Dapo.

"Or we could take the Blackbird back and drive it across the desert for fun," added Datch.

"You really like driving it, don't you?" asked Krissy.

"Yes, it's fun."

"It's a long way home without the cargo bay though," said Hagger.

"Yeah, it is."

They all sat looking into space for a moment. Because of everything that had been going on, they had forgotten they were two thousand light years away from home. Then Datch had an idea.

"I'll ask if Widfab can drop it off on the way back," he said.

"Yeah, he might do it. He normally does what we ask," said Carina.

They took it in turns to have a shower and then had another drink before heading off to find Widfab.

They found him in the Marduk equivalent of the shopping mall. He was sitting outside of a restaurant with Plark and a number of council members, having coffee.

"Music Warriors, we were just talking about you. Come and sit down."

"You were?" asked Datch, pulling up a chair.

"Yes, I was just telling them how you saved our world."

Datch looked a little pink.

"Widfab, we were just talking and wondered if you could drop the Blackbird off at Bellatrix on your way back."

"Of course. We will be here for a week though helping these people get everything working. Then heading back to Welly to collect supplies and the Carina will then bring them back. If you like we could drop you off as well, we can probably do it in two hours if you like?"

"We would like a beer on the way back."

"Hmm, maybe four hours then?"

"That sounds good. I like my bar."

"So do you need a lift back to the Carina?" asked Dapo.

"No, we have a number of shuttles coming down. One of them will be taking me back. I'm just making sure I have a full list of what they need before I head up. I've told the IPSF senate that I'll send them a full report. I will of course be telling them about your exceptional work in helping the Marduks."

"That sounds like it's going to take some writing." said Carina.

"Well, yes it will be, I'm due in Olympus in two weeks time for a senate meeting and they will likely want to go through it with me."

"It is nice there though."

"You don't want to come with me, do you? You do know these people better than anyone. The Senate would love your input."

"You're asking us to come and stand in front of the senate?" said Rosey, looking a bit alarmed.

"Well, err, only if you wish it." He was looking slightly nervous.

Datch sat back in his chair and looked at Widfab. He had not seen him nervous before.

"Hmm..." he said.

"Datch?" said Carina, looking at him and not liking the view. She knew what he was about to say and the telepathy wasn't currently working.

"We haven't been there for a while and Krissy hasn't been there at all."

"Yes, but we were gigging last time."

"Maybe we can take Plark with us. He could answer any questions they have." Added Widfab hoping that would sway them.

"Me?" said Plark.

"Yes, you did say you wanted to see space and this would be a great opportunity."

"I'll have to ask Kratos first."

"Of course."

They all sat in silence for a moment, thinking about the offer. It was a big decision, but it was also a great opportunity. The rest of the Pack looked at Datch. He hadn't grinned yet, but they knew it was coming.

Finally, Datch spoke.

"So, what do you think, folks? Quick trip to Olympus Prime before heading home?" Now the grin appeared.

He looked at the others. When they thought about it, the prospect of going back to Olympus and meeting the senate was quite exciting.

"That sounds awesome," said Krissy, grinning too.

The others just sighed and nodded.

"We'll do it," he said. "We'll come with you to Olympus."

"Thank you," said Widfab. "I'm sure it will be a great experience for all of us."

There was a look of relief on Widfab's face.

"Could we have a look at the report before we arrive?"

"Yes, certainly. We're stopping at Welly on the way. Do you want to go to the desert complex for a few days while I sort things out?"

"Sure, sounds like a plan."

They sat back and some beers magically appeared, along with an emergency kebab machine that was put into immediate operation.

The next week went by with the Pack helping out around the complex as much as possible. They also had a number of meetings with the Marduk Council and three more volunteers came forward and had implants fitted so that they could work better with the IPSF. Plark was also given permission to go with them to Olympus Prime.

Another two IPSF starships came into the system with supplies and housing structures for the planet's population. It was decided that the crater above the complex would become a temporary town for the expanding population. The emergency vent was no longer active and as the crater was almost flat, that meant it was an ideal spot for it until the cities could be rebuilt.

The core settled down and became stable once more. Slowly, the control systems for the core were fixed and put back into operation.

It was decided that the Carina would be blessed while they were at Welly as the press could be involved and they could make a big thing out of it. The Pack were also asked for an interview by the galactic press who were now starting to turn up in ships above the planet.

By the end of the week, the IPSF had, with the permission of the Marduks, created a temporary flight control centre for the planet and set up a virtual beacon network. This allowed for automated flights that increased the flow of people and equipment between the ships in orbit and the surface. Slowly, the scientists and archaeologists were replaced by engineers and construction teams.

Welly Time

The end of the week arrived and it was time to go.

The Blackbird was loaded onto a cargo shuttle and taken to the Carina, as it would be easier to store on board and would allow the Raven to be used on Welly Four without having to squeeze past it every time they wanted to get in or out.

Plark was given final instructions on what to do while he was out among the stars.

The area outside the crater doors was now a landing area, with a town appearing behind it. The weather was warmer now as the heat generated in the core release had boosted the planets temperature.

As the Pack came out of the tunnel, a shuttle came into land on the newly constructed landing pads.

"Datch, thank you for all you have done for us. We hope to see you again in the not-too-distant future," said Kratos.

"I'm sure we'll be back. Maybe you could come and visit us," said Datch.

"That would be an interesting experience. I may take you up on that offer."

He turned to Plark.

"Plark, please make sure you follow your instructions out there."

"I will, sir."

The Pack boarded the Raven with Plark and sat down in the cockpit.

"Are you ready for this, Plark?"

"Yes, I'm looking forward to it," he said, grinning.

Datch put on his headset and powered up the systems.

"Marduk control, this is the Raven, ready for launch on route to the Carina."

"Raven, please lock on to Beacon 77312, automated launch is available."

"Requesting auto and locking on to beacon."

"Copy that, Raven. Beacon confirmed, launch in thirty seconds."

The Raven's engines started to increase power, and it lifted off into the sky.

Plark watched as they headed into space. This time, the sky was not clear. There were ships of all shapes and sizes bringing supplies and people to help the Marduks get their planet going again.

"Raven, this is Marduk control. We are transferring you to the Carina. Please standby."

"Thanks, Marduk control. Raven out."

There was a short pause.

"Raven, this is Carina. Please lock on to beacon CAR11895 for automated approach."

Datch locked onto the beacon.

"Carina, you have the Raven."

"Thank you, Raven. Please enjoy the ride music warriors."

Datch leaned back and watched as they approached the Carina. It had moved further out from the planet now and was facing towards deep space.

The Raven slowed and entered the rear landing bay.

Widfab was waiting for them with a couple of other officers as they walked down the ramp.

"Welcome, Music Warriors," he said, bowing.

"Widfab, it's us. Let's just drop the other bit for now, please."

He looked at them for a moment.

"Okay, if you would like to follow me, we thought Plark might like to see the departure from the bridge."

"Thank you. That sounds really interesting." Said Plark.

They followed Widfab to a pod. As they entered, the lights started flashing green.

"Err, what's that mean?" asked Plark.

"It means we are ready for departure, Ambassador," said one of the officers.

"Oh, Thank you."

The pod soon arrived at the bridge and they filed inside. After a round of bowing, the captain turned to Datch.

"Music Warrior, would you like to give the command?" he asked.

"Thank you. I would be very honored."

He cleared his throat.

"Helm, set course for home. Interspace twenty-three."

"Course laid in, your holiness," came a voice from the helm's pod.

Datch raised an eyebrow.

"Engage."

The lights on the bridge flashed yellow three times, and then Plark's stomach did a backwards summersault. The stars outside disappeared, and then started to streak past.

"Wow. What was that?" Plark asked.

"That was interspace twenty-three," said the captain.

"Captain, why are the stars not flickering?" asked Carina.

"The screen has an anti-flicker filter on it so it only updates when we're in normal space."

"Oh, cool."

"How fast are we going?" asked Plark.

"We are doing approximately eight hundred and six light years per hour," said the captain.

"Wow, thank you, Captain."

"Right, let's go have a drink. If we are lucky, we might get two in before we get there," said Widfab.

"Let's go to my place," said Datch, grinning.

"Can I come back to see our arrival?"

"Certainly, Ambassador. I'll send an officer for you just before we are due to arrive."

They headed off to the bar in search of a Bellatrixian Ale.

Three hours later, they were back on the bridge watching as the Carina came into high orbit above Welly Four.

"Wow, an alien world," said Plark under his breath.

"Yes, it is, but just remember you are the alien on this world," whispered Carina in his ear.

"Oh, yes... I am," he said as he realised what Carina had said.

It was a very impressive sight. As the Carina slowed, they passed the pleasure moon with a multitude of ships coming and going from it. They came to a stop and entered a high orbit above a blue and green world.

"Ambassadors, we have informed The Oasis Spa complex you are on your way, and a gentleman called Dag said he would have the beers waiting for you when you get there," said the captain.

"Sounds good, thank you, Captain. Widfab, are you going to send the report to us when it's complete?" asked Datch.

"Yes, I will do."

"Thanks."

"Ambassador Plark, we have arranged for you to meet our government and give you a bit of a tour. I have put you in a hotel in the capital. Afterwards, if you wish, we can transfer you to the Music Warriors hotel?" said Widfab.

"I would like that. Thank you."

"Right, I'll just escort the Music Warriors to their ship, and then we can take a shuttle to the capital. If you would just like to follow me, dudes and dudets."

The Pack turned and thanked the captain for the lift. They then bowed to the captain and crew.

Ten minutes later, the Raven left the Carina and headed for the resort. As usual, they had a fighter escort. Datch had a big smile on his face.

"What's up with you?" Dapo asked.

"I was just thinking. We've travelled over five thousand light-years in less than three weeks."

"Wow, we have, haven't we?"

They all started to smile, and then the not-so-little town with the Gem came into view.

"Quaki control, this is the Raven. We are on approach to Oasis Spa Complex. Requesting landing instructions."

"Welcome back, Music Warriors. Airspace is clear, please land on pad one."

"Thank you, Quaki control. On final."

Datch brought the Raven in over the landing field and gently dropped her down on pad one.

"Thanks for the escort, dudes."

"You're welcome, your holiness."

The fighters turned and flew back across the desert.

"Quaki control, Raven has landed. May our blessings be with you."

"Thank you, Music Warriors. Control out."

Datch shut down the systems and got up.

"Last one to the cargo bay buys the beers," he said, and made a run for the stairs.

There was a rush to the cargo bay, with a fair amount of cheating. The result was a pile of bodies in the cargo bay as everyone fell through the door and ended up in a pile on the floor.

They picked themselves up, laughing about it, and collected their bags from a pile in the corner. Datch opened the door. Dag was standing at the bottom of the ramp with a couple of porters.

"You lot look happy," Dag said as they walked down the ramp.

"Yes, it's good to be here. I take it you have the beer ready?" Datch said, handing one of the porters his bag.

"Of course. This is a somewhat unexpected visit?"

"Yes, it is a bit. Widfab asked if we could go with him to senate on Olympus. We said we would if he gave us a lift home. It took us a week of continuous flight to get to the Marduks' home world, but on the Carina, it took just under four hours to get here."

"Wow, that's a bit of a difference. I can see why you agreed."

They reached the hotel bar and went to their usual table. As they sat down, a waiter came out carrying a tray of ice-cold beers.

Dag sat down with them.

"So, what are the Marduks like?" Dag asked.

"Like us really. You'll meet one soon anyway. Plark is coming here later in the week. He's meeting the government in the capital first."

"He is? Err, do we need any special food for him?"

"No, he's cool with our normal stuff."

"Taking of normal stuff, what are your plans while you're here?"

We're blessing the Carina in a couple of days time, followed by an interview with the galactic press. After all that, we're chilling until next week when we go to Olympus."

"Hmm... well at least you get a bit of a break between jobs."

"We're meant to be on vacation." Rosey said.

"Oh. I did wonder where the bikers were."

"They're on Bellatrix in a mountain resort chilling in the bar I expect." Datch said.

"Can we move to the pool?" Tish asked.

"Yes, sounds good." Rosey said.

"I was hoping to see the Gem." Krissy said.

"Don't worry about that. It knows we're here and you won't miss it at night." Carina said.

"It knows?"

"Yes, it can tell when we're close by. Didn't you see the green flash as we came into land?" Tish asked.

"I thought that was the sun reflecting off of something."

"No, that was the Gem. It gets all excited when we turn up." Datch added.

"Anyway, let's go to our rooms and get changed." Carina said.

"Dag, Krissy is with me and Carina, so she's in our room."

"Do you need another bed?"

"No, the one in there will be just fine thanks."

Dag looked at Rosey, she smiled at him and gave a little nod.

They got up and headed to their rooms to change into swimwear.

Over the next couple of days, The Pack went to the monastery to see the monks and the Gem, much to Krissy's excitement. She was also given an honorary gem of her own at a small ceremony where The Pack performed a couple of songs for the Gem. The Gem in turn gave them a light show. This of course made The Pack glow, and Datch and Carina got their telepathic link back.

Then it was time for the blessing. Father Jamby decided to come with some of his fellow monks as it was a religious event.

The Carina sent down a shuttlecraft to collect them. The Pack were dressed up in their ceremonial robes and each of them had their own monk scattering flower petals as they went.

They were taken to the ship's meeting room, which turned out to be about the size of a hangar. The crew were waiting along with a number of members of the press. The Pack walked slowly up the centre aisle towards a stage at the far end. The monks threw their petals in front of them as they went.

The eyes of the galaxy were watching them. Vid bots circled above their heads as they reached a small stage at the far end of the room.

Widfab, Father Jamby, the captain of the Carina and his senior officers were all standing at the back of the stage waiting for them. As The Pack stepped onto the stage, they all took a deep bow. The Pack bowed back.

On the wall was a set of curtains with a pull cord next to them, and a small gem was sitting on an ornamental post in front of them. Just in front of it all was a small podium. Datch stepped up to it and cleared his throat.

"Ladies and gentlemen and other beings. We have come here today to give our blessing to this ship. Since we brought Welly Four out of the darkness, it has become a vibrant and wonderful world. This beautiful and powerful ship is a testament to the people of the world below us. It has already saved one world from destruction and helped the people of that world to survive. The ship is also named after a Music Warrior, Carina my wife. We are all very honored that you have done this. Now, before we get this party started, time for the blessing."

The Pack moved to stand around the Gem on the post and Father Jamby stepped forward with a small bowl of water.

Datch put his hand in the water and then flicked it at the Gem at the same time he said,

"We hereby bless this vessel and all that travel in her. May she help to keep the galaxy a safe place for us all to live in and may she have a long life amongst the stars."

The rest of The Pack did the same with the water, and as they flicked it on the Gem, they each said, "I bless you."

Afterwards, Datch stepped up to the curtains and pulled the cord, revealing a golden plaque behind them that stated that The Carina had been blessed by the Music Warriors and the date.

"Thank you, Music Warriors. We are all very honored and thankful for your blessing." said the Captain, and he bowed again along with his officers.

Datch and The Pack turned to the front. There were a number of officers standing at the side of the stage.

"Our weapons, please." said Datch.

The officers stepped forward and handed them their instruments.

"Let's get this party started!"

They started to play, and their gems energized, turning them into columns of light. Then the Gem on the post energized, bathing the crew in green light.

On the planet below, the main Gem increased in brightness and started to release rings of energy.

They played four songs before they left the stage in search of the buffet they had been promised.

The bikers were sitting outside the restaurant at the top of one of the mountains, having a drink after heading up it on their bikes. It was Fred who noticed it first.

"Tank, your shirt is glowing green."

"It is?" he asked.

"Yes, it is." said Clax.

Tank looked down and opened his shirt. He had his gem on, and it was glowing bright green. Clax unzipped his jacket, and his was glowing too.

"Mine is doing it as well."

"Hmm... Why do I get the feeling the rest of the guys are going to be on the news feed later." said Fred.

"I wonder what they're doing?" asked Peebop.

"I hate to think." said Fred.

"Well, I'm getting a feeling they're having a good time." Said Tank.

"Me too." Said Clax.

"I'm not sure that Datch having a good time is necessary good thing for the rest of the universe." Said Fred.

"I'm sure we will find out later." Said Peebop.

On the Carina, the Pack headed to the forward lounge for the buffet. It was a very nice spread. They were thanked again by the captain and Widfab. Plark was also there and seemed to be really enjoying being away from Marduk.

They chilled out for an hour before heading to Datch's place, as he was calling it, where they had arranged to give the galactic press an interview at the big table.

They walked in and headed upstairs to the big table, where a presenter and a vid crew were waiting for them.

"Hello, I'm Jadzia. I'll be conducting your interview."

"Hello, Jadzia. Let us just get comfortable and then we can start. We also have a surprise for you shortly."

"Oh, you do?"

"Yes, but you'll have to wait for it." Krissy said, sitting down.

A waiter came up the stairs with a tray of drinks and handed them out to the Pack.

"Okay, Jadzia. We're ready when you are."

She sat down just to the side of them and put her vid com on the table.

"Okay, let's start." She said, looking at the vid operator.

The two little vid bots took to the air just above the table. She looked straight at the vid bot.

"I'm here with the Pack, who are the spiritual leaders of the Welly star system and IPSF ambassadors. Firstly welcome. So, Datch, how are you guys doing?"

"We're doing great, Jadzia. It's been a busy few days, and now that Carina's blessing is complete, we're going to chill for a bit on Welly before going to Olympus Prime."

"Yes, Welly has named a star destroyer after you. How does that feel, Carina?" She said, turning to her.

"I am very honored. It is a beautiful ship, and it has already saved one world. I hope it goes on to do more good in the universe."

"Yes, I understand it was instrumental in helping you save another world."

"Yes, the Marduks' world was tearing itself apart when Datch came up with the plan to use it to release the pressure. It saved the planet and the population."

"You guys have had more contact with the Marduks than anyone else. The whole galaxy wants to know what they are like?"

"Well, Jadzia, we have a scoop for you." Datch said, standing up.

He turned around and shouted over the balcony.

"Plark, come on up."

Jadzia looked a bit confused.

"Who is Plark?"

"He is Ambassador Plark from Marduk. We know none of the press have seen them yet, and we thought it would be nice to introduce them to the universe." Rosey said.

"Oh wow. Thank you." Jadzia said.

Plark came walking up the stairs. Datch waved at him to come and sit next to him. The vid bots turned to look at him as he came over and sat down.

"Jadzia, this is Ambassador Plark from the planet Marduk."

"I'm very honored to meet you, Ambassador," she said.

"Thank you. I'm very pleased to be here."

Jadzia looked a bit like a rabbit in the headlights.

"Ambassador Plark, Jadzia was just asking us what you were like as people."

"Yes, sorry. Meeting you just threw me for a moment."

"That's okay, Jadzia. Datch said you might be a little surprised to meet me."

"Plark, maybe you could tell them a bit about your people?" suggested Krissy.

"Yes, I would love to. Well, Jadzia, we were a very planet-oriented race, and our people focused on making our planet a garden paradise. Then we found our sun was going to go supernova, and to save the planet, we decided to move it..."

He carried on explaining about the journey and how the entire population had been in storage. He then explained about how first contact was made.

"So, you waved at Tish and Dapo, and they waved back?"

"Yes, pretty much. They seemed nice enough, and I thought it would be nice to meet them."

"We were very nervous, though," said Dapo.

"Yes, but we went with our instincts, and the rest is history," said Tish.

"I believe you're heading to Olympus now to meet with the senate?"

"Yes, the Minister Prime of Welly asked us if we could go with him. We decided it would be good to bring Ambassador Plark with us to help us answer any questions the senate has about his world." said Datch.

"I can see by the sparkles around his head that Ambassador Plark has been introduced to your style of music?"

"Yes, I quite enjoyed it."

"Ambassador, these people around this table are some of the most highly thought of in the galaxy, and I hope you have seen how good it is to be part of it."

"Yes, Marduk owes them and the IPSF a great debt for saving us. Thank you all."

"Well, I'm afraid that's all I have time for, but it's been great chatting with you all and absolutely amazing to meet you, Ambassador Plark."

She turned back to the vid bot.

"This is Jadzia Tatwell for the Galactic Press, signing off."

The vid bots landed on the table.

"Thank you all for the interview, and thank you Ambassador Plark for coming to meet us."

"You're welcome."

With that, she got up and left with the vid crew.

The Pack had another drink before heading back to the surface with Plark this time to chill at the resort.

The bikers had just gotten back from the mountain and were sitting in the hotel bar when the galactic news came on. The main headline was "The Pack Do It Again" and had an image of the younger half of the Pack sitting around a table glowing, along with another man who was sparkling.

"Guys, look!" said Clax.

After the other headlines, it switched back to the interview with The Pack and Ambassador Plark.

"Guys, does that look like the Barbers to you?" asked Peebop.

They all looked closer at the screen.

"Yes, but why didn't Datch tell us they were back?" said Clax.

"I'll call Jim," said Fred and got out his vid com.

The news report carried on.

"Fred, the news reader just said they're on Welly," said Tank just as Fred connected to Jim.

Fred told Jim to put the news on and hung up.

"Wow, that's a pretty good copy of the Barbers," said Clax.

"It sure is," added Fred.

"So that's what the Marduks look like," said Clax.

"I think they need to get a bit more colour, they're very pale," said Peebop.

They all turned to look at him. Peebop was normally a light brown colour, but as he had been sitting in the sun too long, he was currently a bright pink.

"Like you?" asked Clax sarcastically.

Peebop looked at him and then at his arms that were radiating quite a lot of heat.

"Err, no, maybe not as much as me."

"Well, they have been underground for a quarter of a million years. I'd turn white too," said Fred.

The news report finished and the bikers got another round in.

The Senate

The Raven approached the Carina and landed in the main bay. The trip to Olympus would only take eight hours, but the Carina was a very large ship and had to come in slowly to the IPSF marshalling area.

After the meet and greet, they headed to Datch's place for a drink and something to eat. Widfab had arranged for hotel rooms for all of them in the capital, and the Pack were going to be looking after Plark while they were there. Widfab had also transferred some credits to Plark for expenses, as he was there on official business for Welly.

Eight hours later, they were back in the landing bay, sitting in the Raven's cockpit. Datch powered up the systems and put on his headset.

"Carina, this is the Raven, ready for departure."

"Raven, please lock on to beacon 101.OP717.023 on exit from the bay. Olympus control will take over the flight automation."

"Thanks, Carina. Beacon locked on and ready for launch."

"Launching in 5, 4, 3, 2, 1."

The Raven lifted off and left the cargo bay. The sight outside was incredible. There were two IPSF carrier ships with their support ships, and a number of other clusters of IPSF ships.

"Olympus control, this is the Starship Raven from the IPSF Carina, heading to Olympus Prime, Private landing area seven on beacon 101.OP717.023."

"Raven, this is Olympus control, lock confirmed. Please enjoy the ride."

"Will do, Olympus control. Raven out."

Plark was transfixed by the sight outside. There were a huge number of ships coming and going from the planet, space stations, and larger ships. The space was full of just about every type of ship you could imagine. Everywhere you looked, there were ships.

"Wow, that's a lot of ships. Where do they all come from?" he asked.

"All over the galaxy," said Hagger. "This is the seat of power for it. There are a lot of deals done here, and also the trans galactic ships leave from here."

"Trans galactic?"

"Yes, they go to the Andromeda galaxy from here," added Dapo.

"Andromeda! How long does it take them to get there?"

"About six months. You won't see them this close to the planet though. Their mass is about that of a small planet and would destroy the world we're going to. Therefore, they are kept further out in the system."

The Raven joined a line of ships heading towards the planet, and Olympus came into view.

"I wish I could show Quark and Zark."

"You can," said Krissy helpfully. "Your implant can record it, and then you can play it back on a vid com."

"I can?"

"Yes, just think 'remember' and a green dot should appear in the corner of your eye telling you it's recording. When you want to stop, just think 'stop'."

"Oh wow, it does. So, I just need a vid com?"

"We'll go shopping tomorrow and get you one. We're not due in the senate for three days, so you have a bit of time to do some sightseeing with us."

"Thank you. They will love seeing all this."

"No problem. We did sort of drag you along, so it's the least we can do."

The Raven turned into another line of ships and started to head down towards the surface. Then Olympus Prime came into view, with the late afternoon sun glistening on its glass towers and making them light up with rainbows.

"Oh, it's so beautiful. Our world used to look like this before the sun started to expand."

"Raven, this is Olympus Control. Landing area in 1 minute."

"Copy that, control."

The Raven flew over the towers before starting to descend to a landing area full of ships.

"Raven, please get ready for manual."

Datch placed his hands on the controls and waited.

"Ready when you are, control."

"5, 4, 3, 2, 1. You have control, Raven."

Datch manoeuvred the Raven over to its allotted landing pad and gently put her down on the pad.

"Control, Raven has landed."

"Copy that, Raven. Enjoy your stay."

"Thanks, control. Raven out."

Datch shut down the engines and got up.

They left the Raven and took a shuttle to the hotel.

The hotel was called The Artemis. It was a very nice hotel, but not quite as grand as The Grand Palace that they had stayed in last time they were on Olympus. Plark thought it was the height of luxury and had never seen anything like it.

They spent the next two days looking at the sights of the city, and brought Plark his vid com.

Then it was time for the senate. The last time they went into it, the senate was not in session, and they had gone around as part of a tour group. This time, they were going to be standing in front of the leaders of the galaxy.

The Pack were nervous, which was strange for them. They could stand in front of a hundred thousand people and play music without any problem. There were thirty thousand expected in the senate today.

They headed over to the Welly embassy to meet Widfab, who was going to take them in with him.

"Hello, Music Warriors, and Ambassador Plark," he said as they walked in.

"Hi, Widfab. How's it going?"

"Okay, thanks. Are you folks ready for this?"

"No, but it's never stopped us before," said Carina.

"We have a shuttle waiting outside to take us to the senate. We go in through a secure entrance at the back."

"Well, let's get moving. If we stand around too much, we'll get all jumpy," said Rosey, who already was.

"Okay, let me grab my bag and we'll go."

He walked over to the desk and was handed a small bag.

They then followed him out of the back of the embassy to one of Carina's shuttles that was sitting waiting for them.

They went on board and sat down. The pilot waited for clearance, and then the shuttle took off and started weaving its way through the city's structures.

The flight was quite short, and then the Senate came into view. It was a huge building built of white marble and edged with gold and silver. It was ringed with large white towers capped with gold, and two massive particle cannons sat on either side of the building. The sky above it was very busy with shuttles landing and taking off.

The shuttle slowed down and after a few moments started to descend. At the rear of the Senate, out of sight, was a large landing area with a covered walkways running to the back of the building. The shuttle came into land with military precision. They got up and followed Widfab out of the door.

"You'll all be sitting with me at Welly's table. I have asked for the correct number of chairs. I understand there is seventy-five percent attendance, so you have pulled quite a crowd."

"Wow," said Hagger.

"And that's meant to make us feel better?" asked Krissy, who was more nervous than the others.

"I think it's cool," said Dapo, who had started waving at people for no reason anyone could think of.

They arrived at a security checkpoint and were scanned before being allowed inside.

They followed Widfab down the corridor. Near the end of it, Datch spotted Coola and Tinfa. As they got closer, Coola put his hand up and waved for them to come over.

"Hello, Widfab," said Coola as they approached.

"Hi, Coola, Tinfa."

"Hi, guys. I would ask how you're doing, but it's been all over the news networks." Coola laughed.

"Yes, we've been a bit busy, as you can see. Coola, Tinfa, let me introduce you to our new friend, Ambassador Plark of Marduk. Plark, this is the President of our home world, Coola, and this is the head of the ruling council of Arcaneus, Tinfa." said Datch.

"It's an honour to meet you, Ambassador," said Coola.

"Yes, a great honour. Any friend of the Pack is a friend of mine," added Tinfa.

"Thank you. It is an honour to meet you both, and it's wonderful to be here."

"You'll have to come and visit us at some point," said Coola.

"I believe I'll be visiting Bellatrix soon. Datch has offered to take me for a beer when we call in on the way back to Marduk. Widfab has offered to drop Datch and the guys off on route for all their help."

"Well, that should be interesting," said Coola, looking carefully at Datch.

Datch just smiled back.

"So, are you ready to come and see how we do things at the top?" asked Tinfa.

"Yep, I think so," said Datch and grinned.

"Shall we go in?" said Widfab, who wanted to get it over with.

"Yes, let's go in. Are you going straight back after the session?" asked Coola, starting to head for the door.

"Yes, Well, almost, tomorrow. I have a few meetings to go to later to organize Marduk's aid if it all gets approved."

"I'm sure it will, the people I've spoken to are quite keen to help them."

"That's good news. Okay, gentlemen, we'll see you after?"

"Yes, let's have a beer. I always feel I need one after these sessions."

"Okay. We'll wait on the plaza out the front."

"Sounds good."

They reached the doors and split up. The Pack and Plark followed Widfab to their seats.

The inside of the senate was a very large amphitheatre which was set out in sections, some of which had clear enclosures with different atmospheres inside. The room was very crowded, and some beings could be seen in the enclosures breathing their own atmospheres. In the centre was a platform with screens all around it, which were displaying pictures of Marduk and the words "Welcome - Please take your seats." in the centre of the images.

The Pack sat looking around. There was a buzz to the place, and people would look across at them. They were, for a change, wearing suits. Carina had said that if they were about to address the galaxy, jeans would not look the part, and everyone had reluctantly agreed.

The senate soon filled up, and when it was full, a beeper sounded. Everyone settled down, and a hush fell over the room.

A man in a white and blue robe walked up to the podium in the centre of the stage area.

"Good morning, fellow leaders of the federation. We have come together today to discuss the level of aid we should give the planet Marduk. To that end, the Minister Prime of Welly has produced a report about their needs, tech level, and society profile. We also have their ambassador with us, as well as the Welly ambassadors known as the Pack."

There was a bit of murmuring from the room. The screens switched to the Welly insignia.

"Please can everyone take note of the report and keep any questions until the Minister Prime has finished going through it. Copies are on the system for you to read through as we go."

There was a rustling in the room as the other leaders fished out their vid coms and found their copies.

"Okay, let's get started. Minister Prime, please take the podium."

Widfab stood up.

"You folks wait here. I'll call you up after I've gone through the report." He said and headed for the stage.

The next hour was very boring, with Widfab going through the report page by page. There were images and vid recordings to go with it, showing the planet and the state of the infrastructure. The report was very detailed, with lists of what was needed to help Marduk get back on its feet.

Finally, he finished and paused for a moment.

"I know you have many questions, as would I, so please put them into the system as normal. There will now be a short pause for you to do so."

Widfab looked down at the Pack and nodded at them.

The rustling in the room quietened down again.

"Fellow leaders, before I start, I would like to introduce you to both the Welly ambassadors who made first contact and the Marduk ambassador."

He beckoned to the Pack.

"Looks like we're up, folks," said Datch, standing up.

The others, including Plark, got up and followed him onto the platform.

"First, let me introduce the Welly ambassadors, Datch, Carina, Krissy, Dapo, Tish, Hagger, and Rosey."

As he went along the row, they all gave a little nod.

"And last but not least, the Marduk ambassador, Plark."

Plark gave a small bow, and there was a round of applause.

"Okay, let us see what we have," said Widfab, looking at the vid on the podium.

He pressed a button on the screen, and one of the other leaders stood up.

"President Cloks of Sirius?"

"Good morning, ambassadors. Datch, I know the Minister Prime has covered this in the report, but I just wanted your take on what the Marduks are like?"

"They are a pleasant race, and we have found them very easy to get along with. While planet-side, they have always treated us with the utmost courtesy, and we have become good friends with a number of them. Carina, would you say the same from a female standpoint?"

"Yes, the girls and I felt comfortable with them, and there were no signs of any form of prejudice towards us. Their race seems very enlightened."

The others nodded.

"Thank you." He sat down.

Widfab pressed another button, and the Prime Minister of Regulus Five stood up.

"Ambassador Plark, we are about to agree a very large aid package for Marduk, and a number of us were wondering if you are thinking of joining the Federation after you are back on your feet?"

"Prime Minister, we have been talking about it in the council. It is very likely; however, it is early days yet, and I believe we need to get to know each other better before we make a formal application. After all, we have only known each other existed for the last four weeks. It would not be wise to rush into anything as binding as that at this stage. Would you agree?"

"That is very wise thinking, ambassador, and was just the answer I was looking for. Thank you."

He sat down.

Widfab pressed another button, and another leader stood up. This process continued for the next hour and a half. They asked questions about the planet, the level of infrastructure required to get it working again, how their government worked, and how many people were on Marduk.

After the last question had been answered, the leader of the senate came back on the stage and walked up to the podium. Widfab indicated for them to go back and sit down.

"Thank you, Minister Prime and ambassadors. Your input has been very enlightening."

There was a round of applause. The leader waited until it had died down.

"Fellow leaders, it is time to vote on the package."

The screens changed to show two numbers: green for in favour and red for against.

"Please vote now."

The numbers on the screens started to increase, displaying the percentages. The process took four minutes, with the numbers going up and down on both sides. Finally, the green number climbed up and finally stopped at 77% to 33% in favour of the aid. The screens then flashed to show that the vote was over.

"Thank you all. I hereby announce that the initial five trillion credit aid package has been agreed. I shall instruct the fleet to start full support of planet Marduk."

Plark put his hand up and waved at the leader.

"Yes, Ambassador Plark."

He stood up.

"On behalf of my people, I would like to thank you all for this very generous help. We will be eternally grateful to all of you. Thank you."

There was another round of applause, and Plark sat back down.

"Now that the vote is complete, I call an end to this session of the senate. Tomorrow we will be discussing the Arachnoid outbreak in quadrant 2. Please download details of the events from the reports section. The outbreak has been dealt with, but we need to decide if further action needs to be taken against their home world. Thank you all for your attendance. Now I believe lunch is in order."

The screens switched back to tranquil scenes from around the planet.

The leaders started to get up and leave. Some came over on their way out and said it was nice to meet a Marduk in the flesh, so to speak.

They waited until the rush was over and then headed outside into the sunshine.

"That was quite intense," said Tish.

"Yeah, just a bit," said Krissy.

"I thought it went very well," said Widfab.

"I enjoyed the experience," said Plark.

Just then, Tinfa and Coola came walking over.

"Hi folks. Nice presentation," said Coola.

"Hi guys. Thank you," said Widfab.

"Widfab, fancy heading to the Gold Bazar for lunch?" asked Tinfa.

"Yes, I can do."

They set off across the plaza towards the city centre.

"Widfab, Tinfa and I were just talking. Would you have room for two more on board that nice new ship of yours?"

"Sure, why?"

"Well, Tinfa has been wanting to visit Bellatrix for a while now, and it would also save me tying up one of the IPSF ships to get home," said Coola.

"Yes, and if it's okay with you, I'll tag along to Marduk to have a look for myself. Then I'll just head back with you to Welly and get a ship home from there," added Tinfa.

Widfab thought about it for a moment.

"Yes, I'm sure that would be okay, dudes. We're leaving in the morning."

"Cool. I'll contact the Hermes and let them know I have a lift and have my things transferred to the Carina."

"Yes?" said Carina, who hadn't been paying attention.

"No, not you. The Carina."

"Oh, sorry."

"Yes, Coola. I'll let the captain know you and Tinfa are coming."

They arrived at the restaurant and went in for lunch.

Homeward Bound

The next morning, the Pack checked out of the hotel along with Plark and headed to the Raven.

The flight back to the Carina was very entertaining for Plark, who was amazed by the multitude of ships outside. Datch wondered if at some point he would stick his nose to the window to get a better look.

They landed and headed to the bar for a drink while waiting for Widfab, Coola, and Tinfa to show up. Datch had sent the bikers a message a couple of days ago to tell them they would be in the Barbers later on for a drink and if they wanted to meet a Marduk to make sure they were there. He also decided to message his mum.

The trip home was only going to be a short one, as the Carina wanted to try out interspace twenty-five. This meant that it would only take about thirty-five minutes once they cleared the system. However, the system clearance would take another twenty minutes.

The Carina's crew set about putting the Blackbird in the Raven's cargo bay ready for their return to Bellatrix.

Plark had been offered to be taken down with Coola, Widfab, and Tinfa in a shuttle, but he had decided that a bike ride into the city on the back of Datch's flying bike sounded like a lot more fun, even if it meant squeezing past the Blackbird to get in the Raven.

They had just ordered a second round of coffees when an officer came over to them and bowed.

"Music Warriors, Ambassador. The Minister Prime has just landed. We will be leaving Olympus shortly. The captain has asked if you wish to come to the bridge to watch the flight?"

Datch looked at his coffee and then at the others.

"Yes, we would love to." Said Datch and turned to the others.

"They are giving us a lift after all," he said.

"Yeah. We're going to the Barbers later anyway," said Carina.

They got up and headed to the bridge.

Five minutes later, they were standing on the bridge watching as the Carina navigated the traffic in the system. They were rewarded as a Trans Galactic ship had just arrived and was just coming to a stop. Plark's face was a picture of amazement as he realized how big it was. He stood there with his mouth open, looking at it as they went by.

"That was huge!" he said after they had gone by.

"Yes, they are the biggest ships in existence," said the captain.

"Five minutes to clear space, sir," said the helm.

"Standby, for interspace twenty-five."

"Wow, Qwots would be so jealous," said Datch quietly.

"Yeah, just a bit," said Hagger.

They watched as the ship reached the edge of the system.

"Entering clear space, sir."

"Set course for Bellatrix interspace twenty-five."

"Course laid in, sir."

"Helm, engage."

The light flashed yellow three times then Hagger burped.

"Did you have to?" said Rosey.

"Sorry."

The stars outside started to streak past very quickly.

"Cruising at interspace twenty-five, sir. All systems are normal."

Just at that point, Widfab, Coola, and Tinfa arrived on the bridge.

"You've just missed all the fun," said Hagger after everyone had said hi.

"Looks like we're really moving," said Coola.

"Yes, it's amazing. I used to dream of being able to fly to our moon, and here I am going at... err, how fast are we going?" said Plark.

"We are currently at Interspace twenty-five, that is approximately three thousand four hundred and fifty-six light years per hour," said the captain.

"Wow! And our people thought you couldn't go faster than light."

"Technically, we're not. We just warp space and then make a hole in it and fly through the gap. The ship itself is traveling quite slowly. It's the space outside that is being bent around us at quite some speed."

"How amazing."

They stood watching the stars shoot past. There was no point going to the bar, as by the time they got there, it would be time to leave again.

"Captain, one minute to Bellatrix space, sir," said the helm.

"Thank you, helm. Slow to interspace four on entry to the system. Coms, contact Bellatrix control and inform them of our arrival."

"Yes, sir."

They watched as the stars started to slow down and then came to a virtual stop. Up ahead came the familiar image of Bellatrix Five.

The Carina slowed and came to a stop in a high orbit above the shining world below.

"Captain, what's the local time?"

"Ops?"

"The local time is 12:42 PM, sir."

"Thank you. Okay, folks, that means, if we hurry, we can get lunch in the Barbers."

"Lunch? That sounds good," said Dapo.

"We haven't long had breakfast," said Krissy, who was feeling a bit bloated.

"It was two hours ago, and it's going to be at least another hour before we get to the Barbers," said Datch.

He turned to Widfab, Coola, and Tinfa.

"Guys, we'll see you in the Barbers in about an hour?"

"It might be two. I need to drop my things off at the palace and pick up a security detail," said Coola.

"Okay, we'll see you there. Captain, we would like to thank you and your crew for the trip. May our blessings be with you and your crew."

"Thank you, Music Warriors. I will pass them on," he said, then bowed.

The Pack bowed back.

"Come on, Plark, let's go."

With that, the Pack headed to the Raven. They carefully squeezed past the Blackbird and made their way to the cockpit. Datch sat down and started powering up the systems, and Dapo started going through the pre-flight checks.

"Okay, folks, let's go home," said Datch, putting on his headset.

"Carina, this is the Raven, ready for departure."

"Raven, automated launch will be in thirty seconds."

"Copy that, Carina."

The Raven's engines started to increase power, and then the clamps released. The Raven headed across the landing bay and out into space.

"Raven, you are clear to navigate. Please contact Bellatrix control. Have a safe trip, Music Warriors."

"Thank you, Carina. Raven out."

Datch pressed a couple of virtual buttons.

"Bellatrix control, this is the Raven, heading to landing area YUL2759. Requesting automated approach."

"Good afternoon, Raven. Welcome home. Your manifest and IDs have already been transferred to us by the Carina. Please lock on to beacon 13282 for automated approach and contact Yuland control for final. Traffic is currently heavy."

"Copy that, Bellatrix control. Locking on to beacon 13282."

The Raven started to dive down towards the planet, its shield lighting up with plasma as it entered the outer atmosphere. Soon, they were in the high cloud, following a freighter on its way to the spaceport. Below them, the desert came into view. Plark was again staring out of the window, watching everything he could.

"Yuland Control, this is Raven on approach to landing area YUL2759, requesting instructions."

"Good afternoon, Raven. Beacon will disengage in 1 minute. Please bank to the left away from the main flow of traffic on release. When clear, navigation will be at your discretion."

"Thank you, Yuland Control."

The Raven dropped closer to the sand, and Datch rested his hands on the controls.

"The Raven is yours in 5, 4, 3, 2, 1."

Datch took the controls and banked to the left away from the freighter. Up ahead, they could see the edge of the desert and then a ranch came into view, with a landing pad and a flashing beacon. He slowed the Raven down and came in for a soft landing on the pad.

"Yuland Control, Raven has landed."

"Have a good day, Raven, Control out."

Datch shut down the systems and got up.

"Err, it may be an idea to back the Blackbird out first. Then we can get the bikes out." He said.

They got up and headed to the cargo bay. Outside, Dechow and Tansya came walking over. The ramp dropped down, and then Dapo came walking out on his own.

"Err, where is Datch?" asked Tansya.

"He's just coming. Please stand back."

There was the sound of turbines starting up in the Raven, and then the Blackbird started to edge down the ramp. Bit by bit, it left the Raven's bay, and then Datch parked it next to the Raven on the pad and shut the systems down.

The door opened, and Datch came walking out, looking pleased with himself. At the same time, the rest of the Pack came walking down the ramp with Plark.

"Hi Mum, Hi Dad," said Datch, walking over.

"Hi Datch," said Tansya, giving Datch a hug.

"Hi Datch, err, where are you going to put that?" said Dechow, staring at the Blackbird.

"I thought it could go near our house."

"Oh." Dechow said, as images of more remodelling started going through his head.

"It's open, so feel free to have a play with it. It's a lot of fun to drive."

At that point, Krissy and Carina arrived and also got a hug each. The others all said hi, and then Datch turned to Plark.

"Plark, I would like you to meet my mum and dad. Mum, Dad, this is Ambassador Plark of Marduk."

"It's a very great honour to meet you both," said Plark.

"The honour is ours, Ambassador." Said Tansya.

"It's just Plark, please. I'm not officially here."

"Okay, Plark. How long are you here for?"

"Just a few hours. I wanted to see Datch's home world for myself. He is taking me to the Barbers Inn, where Coola, Widfab, and Tinfa are meeting us for a drink."

"Now that's a surprise," said Dechow sarcastically, while looking at Datch.

"We just have time to dump our gear and then we're heading into the city."

"Well, you had better get a move on, you don't want to keep the President waiting."

"Oh, he's got to pick up a security detail from the capital on route. So, he's going to be another hour and a half yet." Said Datch.

"Yes, I need a drink," said Hagger.

Datch, Carina, and Krissy took their bags to their house and gave Plark a quick look around before joining the others who had fetched their bikes from the barn. Krissy now had her own bike and fetched it from outside the house. Soon they were ready to head into the city. Plark got on the back of Datch's bike, and then the Pack took to the air.

Plark spent the whole trip going "wow.", "look at that." or "what's that over there?"

They arrived at the Barbers Inn, and the bikers' bikes were outside. Datch landed next to them, followed by the rest of the Pack.

There was a banner stuck to the inside of the window next to the door saying "Welcome Ambassador." Datch looked at it for a moment.

"I see the bikers told Jim we were coming," he said.

"Well, at least he didn't put it on the outside," said Tish.

They opened the door and went in.

Jim was standing at the end of the bar talking to the bikers. He looked up when the door opened.

"Talk of the devils, here they come now," he said.

The bikers turned around.

The younger members of the Pack came walking over to them.

"Hi guys," said Datch, walking up.

"Hey Datch, how was your holiday?" said Fred, smiling.

"It's been busy."

"Yes, we saw it on the news channel," said Clax.

"We let you out of our sight for five minutes and you blow a hole in the side of a planet," said Tank, grinning.

"We did save the planet," said Rosey.

"Talking of which, let me introduce you to Ambassador Plark," said Datch, before they got into the whole story thing.

"Plark, this is Fred, Clax, Tank, and Peebop."

"Hello, gentlemen. I'm very pleased to meet you. These folks have told me all about you."

"All good I hope, Ambassador?" said Fred, looking at Datch in case snow had come into the comments at any point.

"Yes, it sounds like you have some great adventures together. And please, just call me Plark."

"Plark, this here is Jim, the owner of the Barbers Inn and one of our close friends."

"Hello. Welcome to the Barbers Inn, Plark."

"Thank you."

"Err, Jim, not to put you in a panic, but Coola, Widfab, and Tinfa are coming in about thirty minutes, so there might be an influx of security officers shortly." said Datch.

"Oh crap, you could have let me know?"

"We were on Olympus at the time, and if we had sent a message, you wouldn't have got it until tomorrow."

"Oh... Ok, let me make a couple of calls. I take it you're going up to your table?"

"Yes."

"Plark, I know what these guys want, but what would you like to drink?"

He looked at the bar for a moment.

"Please, may I have a large Bellatrixian ale?"

"Certainly, I'll bring them up shortly."

"Come on Plark, follow us." Said Datch.

They headed off up the stairs to their table.

Jim fetched out his vid com and called in a couple of extra staff while he was pulling the beers.

Forty minutes later, a number of security officers turned up and after a quick check inside the building, went and stood next to the door so they could check everyone coming in.

Five minutes later, a shuttle landed in the street outside. The door opened and the three leaders and Coola's wife and daughter came walking out. They came in and Jim came over to meet them. After a few moments, they headed up the stairs, and Jim went and fetched some more drinks.

The next four hours were spent telling the story of the Marduks and also how the Pack came together, during which

Widfab talked them into doing a few impromptu songs for them after they had eaten. To that end, Timbo was called and came down bringing his partner with him.

"Hello, Mr. President, Widfab, Tinfa, and Err," said Timbo, noticing Plark.

"Hi Timbo, Hi Marsala. This is Plark." Said Datch.

"Hello Plark."

"Hello."

"Did you guys have a nice time on vacation?"

"Yes, Datch shot a hole in a planet." said Dapo butting in.

Timbo looked at Datch.

"Why?" he asked.

"Err, to save it. Haven't you been watching the news?"

"No, we don't watch the news unless we're on it."

"Oh, well, we saved another planet."

This didn't faze Timbo at all.

"Good. I've picked up the gear on the way here. Do you want me to set it up?"

"Yes, please, Timbo."

"I'll come give you a hand," said Tank.

The rest of the bar noticed Tank and Timbo bringing the gear in, and a number of them started messaging their friends. Shortly after, the bar suddenly started to fill up.

"Looks like the word got out," said Hagger, looking over the balcony.

"Hmm, I hope they don't want a full gig. I'm still getting over the trip, and I'm feeling stuffed from all the food," said Krissy, rubbing her belly.

"Me too." Said Carina.

"We'll just do one set. Does that sound okay?" said Datch.

"Yeah, sounds okay," said Carina, who was feeling the same as Krissy.

"Okay, let's do our normal first set, but finish with Star Lovers."

Timbo and Tank came walking back up the stairs to sit down.

"We'll give it another half hour to let our food go down a bit more, and then we'll go and do it," said Datch.

They had another round of drinks and then headed down to the stage. The bar had filled up and was almost at capacity. The security detail was doing a very good job as bouncers and restricting access to the bar.

Instead of running on stage from the dressing room, The Pack just stepped onto the stage and, after putting their hands in for the one, two, three, let's party bit, Datch picked up his mic.

"Ladies, gentlemen, and planetary leaders. This is a bit of an impromptu gig, as we've just got back from Olympus. Therefore, there will only be one set, as to be honest, we're all knackered."

There was cheering from the crowd.

"So, let's get this party started!"

Tish hit the drums, and Hot City Nights blasted out, and The Pack went into party mode. Their gems energized, and they turned into columns of light. Carina's and Krissy's auras were brighter than Datch's for a change, but soon the three of them merged into one huge column surrounding them.

Song after song blasted out, and then finally, Star Lovers came on, and Datch, Carina, and Krissy came together for the kiss, and the bar exploded with green energy.

After Star Lovers, the bar was cheering for them, and Coola's daughter had managed to get on the dance floor and was cheering at the front. Datch turned to the others.

"Supernova?"

They nodded.

"Okay, folks, this is the last one. Supernova."

The bar screamed as the song blasted out.

At the end, The Pack took a large bow before leaving the stage, running behind the bar and up the stairs to the big table. Luckily, it was still early, so even though the bar was full, it wasn't rammed like a normal gig.

The Pack arrived back at the table and downed their drinks.

"Wow, that was something else," said Plark.

"Yes, they put on a really good show."

"Oh, look, I'm sparkling," said Plark.

"That should be interesting when you get back to Marduk. They last for a couple of weeks," said Rosey, smiling at him.

Timbo came walking up the stairs with another round of drinks.

"We'll have one more round and then we'd better be making a move, or the Captain may get a bit annoyed with me," said Widfab.

"We'll make a move as well. We need to have a good meal."

They sat talking for the next hour, and then Coola called in a shuttle to pick them up.

Widfab turned to Datch.

"Okay, it's been great being back here. And congratulations, by the way, to the three of you."

"Err, thank you, and you're welcome anytime."

They got up and left, taking Plark with them.

"Well, folks, I think I need an early night," said Datch.

There was a general agreement that sleep would be good, that was apart from the bikers, who decided to stay for a few more beers with Timbo and Marsala.

The next morning, Datch woke up to the sound of someone being sick in the toilet. He got up and went into the lounge and waited.

Carina and Krissy came out of the bathroom, Carina was carrying a hand scanner.

"Is everything okay?" he asked, looking worried.

"Err, sort of. We just found something out."

"You did?"

"Yes, you know the energy surge on Marduk?"

"The one that made our implants scream at us?"

"Yes, it also reset our implants' settings."

"And?"

"Err, well, it turned off our inhibitors, and you're going to be a daddy."

"What, which one of you is pregnant?"

There was a pause, and Carina sighed.

"Both of us."

Datch look first at Krissy and then at Carina. They both nodded.

"Oh wow, that's awesome." He said.

He went over and gave them both a big hug.

The End

Datch – The Great Adventure.

The Datch Pack.

The Mystical Gem

Arcaneus.

The Quest for Earthly Delights.

Hunting Jackars.